Praise for Amparo Ortiz's

BLAZEWRATH GAMES

"The best way to get nerds like me invested in sports is to add dragons, and that is something *Blazewrath Games* does beautifully. Featuring a heart-pounding, inventive competition and a compelling, global conspiracy, Ortiz knocks it out of the park with this debut."

— Rachel Strolle, Teen Services Coordinator, Glenside Illinois Public Library District

"*Blazewrath Games* lingered behind my eyelids in cinematic flashes: Witches and wizards! Dragons! Life and death stakes! Ortiz delivers it all with dazzling imagery and a heroine who wins the gold cup for personality and voice. This is an incredible debut and marks Amparo Ortiz as an author to watch in the YA arena."

— Karuna Riazi, author of *The Gauntlet* and *The Battle*

"Rich in magic, history, and ride-or-die friendships, Ortiz's debut blazes into dragon canon bringing with it complex identities, a love for Puerto Rico, and fiery Sol de Noche dragons! I'm excited to see what Ortiz does next!"

— Mia García, author of *The Resolutions*

Last Sunrise in Eterna

Last Sunrise in Eterna

Amparo Ortiz

PAGE STREET YA

PAGE STREET YA

Copyright © 2023 Amparo Ortiz

First published in 2023 by
Page Street Publishing Co.
27 Congress Street, Suite 1511
Salem, MA 01970
www.pagestreetpublishing.com

Distributed by Macmillan, sales in Canada by The Canadian Manda Group.

27   26   25   24   23   1   2   3   4   5

ISBN-13: 978-1-64567-614-0
ISBN-10: 1-64567-614-5
Library of Congress Control Number: 2022946784

Cover and book design by Rosie Stewart for Page Street Publishing Co.
Front cover illustration © Nicole Medina

Printed and bound in the United States

To the Iron Keys,
Karuna Riazi & Natasha M. Heck
for your magical friendship, feedback, and
Studio Ghibli movie nights

CONTENT WARNING

This book contains references to blood, cancer, violence, death, suicide, hanging, grief, panic attacks, electrocution, dismemberment, mental health, and vomiting.

Congratulations!

You Are Cordially Invited
To Attend
A Most Magical Retreat . . .

Date: May 7th
Where: The Island of Eterna

Sincerely,

Your Royal Hosts:

*Prince Feyn Herrera &
Prince Aro Herrera*

of the
Iron Staff clan

*Please present this invitation
before boarding.*

*Only those with an official invitation
may enter the island.*

No exceptions.

ONE

THERE'S AN ART TO CHASING AN elf.

It would be easier if they were the ones in fantasy books. Those with flowing robes that sweep the grass, waist-long hair covered in leaves and flower petals, skin as light as porcelain. Creatures that shoot arrows from great distances and still find a heart to pierce. Their names are either in Gaelic, Old High German, or an invented language straight from a storyteller's mind.

They can be mischievous yet resourceful. Sometimes they're even trustworthy.

Then there's Prince Aro.

He's been inside Krispy Kreme for fifteen minutes. Whoever introduced him to donuts cursed him with constant cravings. His ensemble tonight reminds me of banal spy movies—black vest over a white shirt, black pants, and combat boots. Aro wears one black velvet glove, and it's always on his left hand. An ivory ring glimmers on his right hand's middle finger. It has the royal sigil engraved at the center: an iron staff beneath the sun.

The youngest prince talks to himself—probably about glazed donuts—then uses American Sign Language to communicate with Raff, his best friend and director of security. He's also the prince's chauffeur for the evening. I remember how enrollment for ASL classes skyrocketed among teen girls three years ago. Instead of valuing its purpose in their daily lives, they learned it to impress the only deaf elf in Eterna—someone whose taste in romantic partners doesn't even include humans.

I'd never admit it out loud, but Aro and Raff *are* handsome. They could easily pass as high school seniors. Aro would be the vivacious charmer cutting class and sharing self-made memes in all his group chats; Raff would simultaneously be the straight-A bookworm *and* the most decorated athlete. They'd fit in anywhere. However, those elongated ears, their black clothes, and the fact that they don't cast shadows divulge their true nature.

Raff signs to the rest of their royal security detail. That's an additional *five* elves protecting the prince. They keep a close watch on the perimeter.

I blast Andy Black's "They Don't Need To Understand" on my headphones. The couch I've claimed inside the Mall of San Juan helps me pretend I'm studying. Instead, I draw skulls with intricate flower crowns—red roses, mostly—erasing and starting over multiple times. Writing the next scene in my short story would be too much hassle; I can't write in public for the life of me. I draw almost everywhere, though. Even if it's *terrible*.

A little girl's eyes widen as she walks past me. She inches closer to the lady holding her hand. I read her lips: "¿Esa nena es una vampiresa?"

I smile. She's probably never seen anyone with black lipstick and heavy eyeliner.

Little girl, even if I were a vampire, elves are the ones to fear.

I steal a quick glance at the store. Raff points at the donuts with loopy frosting designs, vibrant colors, and creamier fillings. Aro focuses on the glazed ones. I wouldn't be shocked to discover he has a secret Pinterest board dedicated to them.

The golden glow outlining their bodies is more noticeable. Before the elves of Eterna came out of hiding in 1942, scholars would refer to this ability as glamour. But ten years ago, Aro's parents shared its true name with the world: ensueño. Thank God for Doctor Ramírez's elixir. Two drops on each eye and the ensueño has no effect on me.

Elves wear ensueños when one thing is certain—they're ready for a battle tonight.

And I'm snatching a corpse.

Bring me an Iron Staff, Sevim. No Iron Staff, no payment.

For the past eight months, I've abducted elf bodies and collected a cool grand upon delivery to Doctor Ramírez. While the royal family *swears* their kind respects humans, there are elves hiding in the mainland to kill us. The rebelling elves that Aro's parents banished stood against the royals' decision to reveal their island and create the annual Exchange, which begins again tomorrow morning.

I heave a sigh. I despise the concept of a magical retreat in my enemy's homeland, but the rest of the world *loves* the Exchange. Three teenagers may spend seven days in Eterna, a secluded stretch of land floating off Puerto Rico's eastern coast, right between Culebra and Vieques.

For seven days, these unlucky teens—also known as ticket

winners—will temporarily borrow the elves' magic. All they have to do is give up their dreams. Once elves figured out how to extract dreams from people to infuse their ensueños, their illusions became even more powerful. And since dreams are impossible to steal or acquire through force, they offer their powers to entice humans into cooperating. It's worked thus far, but how could I trust those who murder my kind?

Those who've already taken someone from me?

Prince Aro approaches with three boxes of donuts.

I mute Andy Black on my phone. Aro laughs at something Raff is signing to him. His laugh is just as deep as his speaking voice, which is a stark contrast to his lean build. A bodyguard offers to take the boxes, but Aro swiftly moves away, scowling like a scorned child.

He walks right in front of me.

I look down and play the music louder. I can't afford to raise suspicions. After ten long seconds, I check the glass doors.

The Iron Staff clan walks to the parking lot.

I shove my belongings into my Maleficent backpack. I don't have to follow them too closely. The elixir lets me see the golden rays that trail behind ensueños, especially when they're speeding through the streets. It's a shimmering dragon's tail in the dead of night.

I make my way to Mami's 2012 Elantra. Aro loads the boxes in his town car's trunk. As I slip my keys into the driver's side door, he nosedives into his car's backseat like it's a ball pit.

For a royal prince, he doesn't act like one.

Raff is the only one laughing. He closes Aro's door while I settle into Mami's car. I turn on the ignition, letting the A/C and my Within Temptation album blast to their full capacities. All the elves hop into their vehicles at the same time, as if they're trained to move as one.

Nobody drives away.

I retouch my black lipstick. The Iron Staff clan rarely sits in place. It's currently 8:00 p.m.—the rebels should've found their most hated prince by now.

Once I'm done with my makeup, I tuck my lipstick into the backpack. I really need to start buying leather miniskirts with actual pockets. I check the town cars again.

They're gone.

"What the hell?" I whisper. Their engines didn't make a peep. Even with their ensueños, I'm still supposed to hear their tires scraping cement.

Something bumps the car from behind.

Before I can even turn, another car materializes in front of me. Raff's hazel eyes are fixed on mine. He waves hello with a grin.

Fuck.

There's a knock on my window.

"Room for one more?"

Prince Aro leans against the driver's side door. The bodyguards stand behind him.

My breaths are almost as fast as my beating heart. They'll want to know how I can see them. What if they take me as their prisoner? What if they kill me here? Mami has already lost her job, her husband . . . and now her daughter.

"Oh, come on. No one gets lost with me in the passenger seat."

Prince Aro's brown eyes don't have that feline, otherworldly appearance elves have in literature and film. Still, they root me to the spot with fiery focus. He presses his gloved hand on the glass, and it instantly fogs up. The prince traces a figure. When he's finished, he waves at his masterpiece—a rose. He taps the glass once.

The window shimmers in golden light.

A *real* rose falls on my lap.

"I hope you like roses. They would look lovely in your hair." Aro points at my short bob, then at his windswept waves. "Black as a crow's feathers like mine, so I might be biased."

I've never received flowers from a boy. This one isn't even human. He's only trying to lower my defenses before he attacks me.

Play along. He might let you live.

"What do you want?" I say.

"How about we start with your name?"

"Sevim."

"Lovely. Are you Turkish?"

"No."

Aro cocks an eyebrow. "Interesting. Why the Turkish name?"

"My parents met in Istanbul. They wanted a name that would remind them of their trip."

I shouldn't be surprised I have to explain this again. Growing up, my classmates would jokingly call me Seven, and it's what most coffee shop employees write down on my receipts.

"That's wonderful." Aro nods with a wide, warm smile, as if he's a sucker for sentimental anecdotes. "It's a pleasure to meet you, Sevim. My name is—"

"The whole world knows who you are."

"Sure it does." He pushes away from the door, folding his arms. "Now that introductions are complete, let's get to the good stuff. What have you done with the bodies?"

Even though my skin is brown like his, I'm quite certain I've gone pale. This isn't about me being able to see them through ensueños—they know why I'm following them. When have I been sloppy during the past eight months? Have they been secretly monitoring their battlegrounds after a fight? They've fooled me into thinking I was alone. But if they've seen me snatching corpses, why haven't they intervened? What were they waiting for?

Unless . . . this visit to the mall isn't really for donuts . . .

They've laid a trap for me.

"You've got the wrong girl. I was just studying in there and—"

"So there's another beautiful Goth running around San Juan and stealing dead elves?"

I hate that I *almost* smile when he says I'm beautiful. "Yes."

"And she looks exactly like the beautiful Goth in front of me? Does she also have stars on her fishnets, a passion for leather miniskirts, and a Maleficent backpack?"

This is useless. Denying it could anger him more.

But Aro simply laughs again. "It's best we move this interrogation to a more comfortable environment. I'm getting in the passenger seat now, and you're going to follow my directions. The faster you cooperate, the faster you can go home to your parents."

"It's just my mom . . ." My voice cracks.

I don't even know why I say it. I grip the steering wheel, steadying my breath. I refuse to show him any sort of emotion, least of all the rage that's bubbled up within for so, so long.

He doesn't deserve to hear the story of a twelve-year-old girl who pressed a hand against her father's chest and felt his heart stop beating. How she thought his cancer would kill him instead of the elf he begged for a cure. How she grew up hunting that elf down.

Eight months ago, I found that elf's body in a dark alleyway. There wasn't an ensueño around him—someone left him there for the world to see. I screamed at the moon and stars; I couldn't avenge Papi's murder. But my enemy had other uses. I clung to his blood-soaked shoulders, dragged him into the trunk of Mami's car, and sold him to my local highest bidder. Each transaction feels like the closest thing to justice I can achieve. These creatures dispose of us as if we're nothing. I'm simply returning the favor.

"Please. I'm all she has." I speak louder, clearer.

"Don't worry. I'll personally escort you home," Aro says, "after we finish."

"Why should I believe you? You kill your own kind. You kill mine, too."

Aro frowns. "*I* don't. Those murderers don't represent me."

I pick up the rose. "Was this your attempt at manipulation? It's not working, *Your Highness*. So what if I've been stealing corpses? Why do you care what happens to them?"

"Aha! She finally comes clean!" Aro claps.

"Whatever. If you really cared about the dead, you wouldn't kill them in the first place."

CRACK!

A bodyguard hits the floor.

Behind him, an elf stands with a staff gripped tight—the same weapon used to fatally strike the bodyguard in the head. The dead bodyguard bleeds from his ears as more elves tear through the parking lot on golden motorcycles. The metal contraptions wrapped around their heads resemble gilded cages.

Rubies and spikes cover most of their faces, but I can still see their sun-kissed skin, their dark eyes burning with hate . . .

The rebels are here.

TWO

"**D**RIVE!" Prince Aro signs at Raff.

As his best friend backs up, Aro leaps over my car.

Then he's sitting next to me. He's *way* too fast.

"Sevim, how calm are you in stressful situations? Because I need you to stay very, very calm while you get us out of here."

Spying on him should've prepared me for this. I could've been caught in the crossfire ages ago. But sitting next to the spokesperson for elf-human peace puts me at greater risk. At least Aro is selfish enough to protect us both. He needs a getaway car *and* he wants to arrest me.

"Sevim! Why aren't you driving?"

I need that corpse three feet from my door.

"You should definitely be driving!" Aro's voice rises in pitch, which makes him sound slightly hysterical. Raff and his bodyguards have conjured their staffs and are firing gold lightning bolts. They keep missing, though. Rebel bikers keep closing in. The parking lot glows bright with bolts scraping the spell's barriers.

I press a finger to my lips. "Don't speak to me while I'm thinking."

"What do you have to think about? There are elves trying to kill us."

A lightning bolt hits my rear window. It blows into shards of glass.

I duck and cover my head. Then I glare at the elf sitting next to me. "They're ruining my mom's car because of *you*, Aro! Don't be such a coward! Get the hell out and fight them!"

"So you can escape while I'm distracted? Hmm. Let me think about it." Aro rolls down the window. "Estos cabrones . . ." Smoke swirls around his gloved hand. Then the smoke fades, revealing his iron staff clutched tight in his grasp. A series of *pops*! blasts from where he sits. He's launching spells at the bikers over the car's roof.

"Be careful!" I yell at him.

"Don't worry! They'll never get me!"

"No, I mean be careful with *my mom's car*!"

Aro mumbles something, but it's lost in the cacophony of detonations.

One by one, his bodyguards drop.

That's five thousand dollars I can make in a single night.

I can't fit all five bodies into the car. And I definitely can't grab them with the prince breathing down my neck. What if the bodies are gone when I come back? Will the rebels steal them as proof of their victory? They're usually the ones who lose battles—taking a royal guard's corpse would definitely earn them more respect among their group.

"We need to go *now*!" Aro's panicked cry is almost as loud as the ringing shots. He shows no signs of a broken heart, solely focused on the rearview mirror. It's like he's on combat autopilot; there will be another time to mourn his losses.

I crush my boot against the gas pedal.

The path out of the Mall of San Juan is short yet uncomfortable. There's an armored truck taking up most of the space between the sidewalk and the parking spots. I'm swerving past *even more* patrons with Krispy Kreme boxes.

Raff honks at me. He's almost bumper-to-bumper.

The rebel bikes are at either side of his car, but he swerves it at them in swift pivots, forcing them against walls and other vehicles. His enemies retreat just before collision.

I turn right and blend into the steady stream of cars leaving San Juan. The slightly less hectic roads to the town of Carolina stretch out before me, with three lanes that morph into two. The first stoplight in my path glows bright red.

Aro bangs his fist against the car's roof.

Golden rays explode from his hand. They shoot into every inch of my mother's Elantra, fading only a second later. He's cast an ensueño around us.

"You can cut across lanes. The ensueño will protect you as long as you're close to me."

He speaks softly, carefully, as if he's trying to remain calm with each word. He looks at me like he's waiting for a response. Once I nod, he pulls his upper body out the window and shoots more spells at the bikers. I hear tires grinding to a halt, then metal and glass slamming against the pavement. One of the rebels has been shot. He's pinned underneath his trashed motorcycle.

The stoplight is telling me not to advance. There are four cars in front of me.

I shrink in my seat as I grind my teeth.

Please don't let me die tonight.

When I drive my mother's Elantra into the cars ahead, it's no longer a tangible, solid object. Aro's spell makes it move through everything like a ghost. My body is also temporarily phantasmagorical—I can't feel the strangers or their belongings. A surge of adrenaline rushes from my fingertips to my toes. I'm drowning in waves of searing-hot energy, as if a dragon has spat me out in a fireball. Sweat pours out of me and dries up twice as fast.

I wish I had time to freak out. But when lightning and gold flames keep flying past my windows, I cut through traffic like a knife out for blood. I don't even know where I'm supposed to go. My house is in Carolina, but that's the last place I'll ever take Aro. Heading back to San Juan would be the safest choice . . . unless more rebels are waiting for him.

"Where am I going?" I ask Aro.

"There's a Costco up ahead. I need some caramel popcorn."

"Aro, I'm being serious!"

I don't know if this is his way of coping with tonight's losses. Maybe his ill-timed humor started after his parents and oldest brother were murdered, but something tells me the youngest prince of Eterna has always been unbearable. At least he's shooting at the biker chasing Raff. The rebel elf leaps into the air. He's abandoned his motorcycle in favor of the town car's roof. He smashes Raff's window with his staff, then seizes his neck, squeezing with all his might.

Raff tries punching him off, but he misses.

"¡Déjalo quieto!" Aro pulls himself onto the Elantra's roof.

I don't know if the ensueño is distorting my senses, but his pounding footsteps are louder than a thunderclap. He jumps onto his best friend's car, landing in the smoothest crouch I've ever seen.

I cut off oncoming traffic and check the rearview mirror. The rebel is now focused on Aro, aiming his staff at his chest. One blow and Aro's heart will fail forever.

The prince is quick to duck. When he rises again, his weapon clashes with the enemy's. Never mind what I said about Aro's footsteps—these staffs are much louder. Without casting ensueños, every town in Puerto Rico would know the elves are dueling. Zeus himself must've picked his most potent lightning rods, shaped them into seven-foot-tall sticks, and gifted them to Eterna's inhabitants.

Raff pulls up next to me. We're speeding forty miles over the limit. He points at the curve to my right—the road that leads closer to home.

If I make a U-turn instead, I'll return to the Mall of San Juan.

There's a slight chance Raff will chase me. There's an even greater chance he'll prioritize Aro's safety and defeating that rebel. *The ensueño will protect you as long as you're close to me*, Aro had said. His spell will no longer work once I abandon him.

For a swift, unbearable second, my chest tightens.

He'll be fine. Besides, he's trying to arrest you!

Raff jabs a finger at the curve.

Aro and the rebel are still splitting the heavens with their staffs' thunderous roars.

When the curve comes up, I turn along with Raff.

Then I hit the brakes.

The rolling heat waves intensify as I speed off in reverse. The faster I flee from Aro's magic, the brighter it burns me. Still,

I race out of their proximity as if the fate of the world depends on how quickly I can make it back to the dead bodyguard. Once I swerve into the lanes in the opposite direction, I'm no longer on fire. The heat pulls away like a tide rolling farther from shore. Sweat sticks to my clothes and stays for good. Wide-eyed drivers are staring at me like I've just dropped from the sky—Aro's magic is gone.

"SEVIM!"

I hear my name in the distance. It's a brief, anguished cry.

I carry onward, forcing myself not to search for him.

THREE

I DON'T GO BACK TO THE MALL.

Elves don't scare me. I can't be afraid of something I don't respect.

But I have no intention of bumping into Aro again. Or worse, more royal bodyguards sent as backup. They could be waiting for me right now. I'm not trained in combat, let alone do I possess any magic to retaliate in case of an ambush. Aro knows I'll want to pick up as many bodies as I can. That I could take a long, long time grabbing corpses all by myself. Long enough for him to return and capture me. Especially after abandoning him in the middle of a fight.

Thank God my employer isn't on campus tonight. As much as I'm dying to enroll at the University of Puerto Rico's Río Piedras campus, I'm not in the mood to have anything stolen because the

Elantra's missing the rear window.

I enter the gated neighborhood in Carolina where my employer lives. These houses remind me of matchboxes; they're pale yellow cuboids that have been copied and pasted—hideous doesn't begin to cover it. I pull up and park in the doctor's driveway with the rose still on my lap. It's not a corpse, but an elf prince created it. This should be worth something, shouldn't it?

On drop-off nights, Doctor Ramírez has an open door policy. I walk into his house, the rose gripped in my clammy hand. I ignore the Sprite cans all around the living room; this man runs on caffeinated drinks that look like hair gel. Yellowed pages are piled high on his couch and dining table. I catch glimpses of sketched body parts, illegible scribbles, and question marks.

The doctor sits in his favorite brown recliner. A local channel is running a special on the two teenagers chosen for the Exchange so far: Kang Ryujin, a sixteen-year-old gymnast from Gwangju, South Korea; and Jason Baxter, a Black trans high school senior from Atlanta.

"How are you feeling about the Exchange tomorrow?" an off-camera reporter asks.

Jason presses his hands against his chest. "I literally have no words. This is what I've wanted for ten years. It's . . . I have no words!"

Ticket winners always act like being forced to complete a series of magical challenges is a blessing. As if taking one physical test after another, prepping your psyche for the wildest dreams possible, then being enchanted to fall asleep in front of watchful, invasive elves, is the definition of paradise. Only the chosen teens know just how strenuous these missions really are. While there have been a few social media posts and interviews here and there, the simple act of accepting their tickets magically forbids humans from sharing too much. They can discuss the island's amenities, how they spent their leisure time, what using their borrowed powers felt like, a brief glimpse into what each mission entails . . . and nothing else. That doesn't scream "normal and totally ethical retreat" to me, especially when you could get kicked off the island for failing challenges.

I roll my eyes. Every media outlet has reported about Jason and Ryujin for the past three weeks. Prince Feyn—Aro's older brother—personally handed them their invitations for the Exchange. Only one teenager is left, and the globe desperately awaits their announcement.

It waits for another young person to lose their dreams and privacy forever.

Human scientists aren't the only ones who believe adolescence is a prime period for lucid dreaming. We spend more hours sleeping, which makes us similar to newborns, but our dreams have greater depth thanks to cognitive development, social interactions, and, most importantly, heightened emotions during puberty. And that's exactly what the elves require—dreams fueled by the most potent feelings. Love, hate, rage, sorrow all build a strong fictional landscape in the dreamer's mind. The stronger the dream, the stronger the elves' magic will be.

"You don't expect to see an elf prince waiting for you outside of gym class," says Jason. "My initial thought was, 'Oh, now he can sign my copies of *The Island of Eterna: A History.*'"

"How many copies do you own?" the reporter asks.

"Four. I collect every edition."

"Daebak," says Ryujin. I don't speak Korean, but she's smiling like she's impressed. "You admire them a lot. You'll have fun at the retreat, then."

Jason offers her a high five. "*We* will have fun."

She nods, even though her smile is smaller. "We will." She high-fives him.

This is so pathetic.

I clear my throat. "Good evening, Doctor."

He kicks down the recliner's footrest extension. Then he flies out of the seat and towers over my five-foot-four body. A book falls onto the carpet—another self-help bestseller on grief. To the public, Alberto Ramírez is a forty-something nerd who gives talks on DNA forensics. I know him as my father's introverted childhood friend from Vieques.

And the man with dead elves in his lab's secret freezer.

"Sevim. Thank God you're here," he says hoarsely.

That deep rasp makes me cringe, especially over the phone. When I stole my first corpse, I considered posting on a dark web forum to sell elf body parts, but I called him instead. He's the only adult I could trust with something as disturbing as a dead elf. The doctor wouldn't scold me like a parent or judge me like the rest of society. I'd never be ashamed to bring him what I'd taken.

His line of work helps, too. As part of the Natural Sciences department, Doctor Ramírez studies different life-forms, but after Papi's murder, he dove into elf biology and magic. He spoke about it nonstop at my father's wake. The doctor wanted to break our enemy as much as I did—find their weaknesses and exploit them. Without hesitation, he bought my first corpse and hasn't stopped since. I never thought a college professor would be interested in illegal endeavors.

Maybe I shouldn't put higher education instructors on a pedestal. They have shit to deal with, too. But I do love working with Doctor Ramírez. It makes me feel one step closer to belonging in the halls of Río Piedras. La IUPI, as everyone here calls it, is my dream school. If it weren't for my horrible grades, my low scores on the College Board Entrance Exam, and giving Mami every dime I make, I'd learn about Victorian poetry in an actual classroom. Some teachers in private and public schools branch out of their curriculum, but we're primarily taught English as a Second Language—twelve years stuck with grammar and pronunciation rules.

Perks of being a U.S. colony . . .

"Where is it?" he asks.

"I . . . I'm so sorry. I couldn't catch one tonight, but . . ." I glance down at the rose. "I brought you this instead. Aro conjured it, and since he's an Iron Staff, I figured you—"

He snatches the rose, examining its every inch. "This is Aro's magic?"

"Yes."

"There's no blood on the thorns."

"No, he didn't—"

"Where did you find it?"

I sigh. "He gave it to me."

Doctor Ramírez's widened gaze flies to mine. "You *blew your cover*?"

"He, uh . . . well, he laid a trap for me . . ." Admitting defeat is definitely a skill I need to practice harder. "I don't know how long they've known, but Aro made it sound like they've *allowed* me to steal corpses. They must've hung around the crime scenes and spied on me. Maybe they've been watching me this whole time."

"Did he mention me?" the doctor says.

"No. Aro wanted to know what I've done with the bodies. He didn't even care that I could see and hear him. It's like his mission was to recover those corpses." I slowly scratch the back of my ear. "But why let me take them in the first place? They're *elves.* They can take me down. Why wouldn't they catch me red-handed or follow me? What were they waiting for?"

Doctor Ramírez circles me. His eyes are locked on the dusty floor. "You didn't get an Iron Staff and the prince knows about your missions."

"Yes, but I got away! They were in the middle of a battle when I bolted."

My chest tightens yet again. I wonder if it's over . . . if the annoying, donut-obsessed prince and his best friend are still alive or if they've been dumped in a ditch somewhere, hidden within their invisible, magical shields.

I shouldn't care about their well-being. They wouldn't care about mine.

"I needed another body tonight. The ones you've brought me are proving rather difficult for further studies." Doctor Ramírez fetches his remote control but still hangs on to the rose. He clicks while aiming it at the TV. Jason and Ryujin are replaced with surveillance camera footage.

His walk-in freezer is three times the size of his living room. Thankfully, it's also much cleaner. Small, beeping machines record changes in temperature. Operating tables fill up the white chamber. There's a test subject strapped to them by their cold, pale wrists—five rebel elves lay dead next to each other. The previous eight I'd delivered must've been disposed of.

The doctor slowly runs a finger down the middle of the

screen. "Countless clinical studies have yielded the same results. Humans and elves share connective, nervous, muscle, and epithelial tissue. They look, move, think, and feel like us. But they're born without the ability to dream. I haven't been able to find anything in their biological constitution that explains this." He's as delighted as a starving wolf. "I need more for comparison."

"And I'll get you more. I swear. Let me just—"

"They'll be expecting you. They might be searching right now." He walks toward me, raising the rose high. "How much are you willing to bet this is a tracking device?"

I should've tossed it the second I escaped. I've never heard of magical trackers disguised as flowers, but those with power will always seek to expand it.

"You've brought this into my home, Sevim. You have not only put us in great danger but also risked any chance we had of avenging your dad."

"That's not true. We still have a chance. We can't—"

"Your father believed he knew better than me, too. How many times did I tell him not to go to them? Striking a deal with those devils . . ." The doctor lowers the rose. "He never said what they made him do. We only saw the consequences. We saw exactly what we feared and we couldn't stop it."

The doctor turns off the television. He doesn't face me again.

I don't expect to understand his pain. I've never lost a childhood friend to a bad deal with the elves. A deal that was supposed to cure Papi's cancer. Mami and I had no idea he'd snuck out to meet with them. Even after he started disappearing for long hours, we never suspected the real reason. What would an algebra teacher have to offer such magical beings anyway? But they liked whatever he promised. They liked it enough to promise him good health in return.

The royals could've stepped in a long time ago. And not just for my father.

They once lived in Vieques, too—elves were its first inhabitants.

When the United States Navy arrived in 1942, the elves living in secret on Vieques finally revealed themselves, created a separate island, and fled. Reasons for this exodus haven't been confirmed; it remains one of the most baffling parts of Puerto Rican history.

These elf assholes will never care about other Viequenses. Vieques still doesn't have a hospital. Its supermarket runs low on stock every week. The ferry that takes Viequenses to the mainland—the *one* vessel that transports limited food and medicine—is often breaking down. If they'd stayed, people like my father wouldn't have needed them more than ever. He wouldn't have risked his life in order to save it in the first place.

Doctor Ramírez is mourning the same man I am.

He's acting like he's the only one suffering. It's one thing to know your friend didn't heed your warnings. What about *not* knowing your father was embroiled in elf-related shit and watching him get killed? To wake up in a house without the man who cooked you breakfast every morning and called you the most gorgeous girl in the world? To have spent months sobbing when you looked in the mirror because you're his spitting image?

Grief is never a competition, but there are always people who want first place.

I still have to help Mami. This can't be over.

"Give me one more chance, Doctor. *Please*. My mom's last unemployment check comes in this week. I can't afford to lose this job. I can get you an Iron Staff."

He offers me the rose. "Goodbye, Sevim. Take care of yourself."

"No, I—"

"Get out of my house," he snarls.

This is the first time Doctor Ramírez has given me attitude. For someone who swears he loved my dad, treating his daughter in piss-poor fashion speaks volumes about his loyalty.

He's letting me down, but *I'm* letting my mother down. The realization is like pouring salt into a gaping machete wound. She's not aware of how I earn money. Even though the shame is only mine, my failure will take root in both of our lives. I've just condemned us to far greater uncertainty than we already face.

I don't know when Doctor Ramírez opened the front door. I hate how easily my doomed thoughts can sweep me away from my surroundings. The doctor remains silent as I walk past him. As I slide into Mami's car, he slams the door shut. All the lights inside are turned off.

I picture him stuffing a suitcase with his clothes and illegible scribbles, slipping out of the neighborhood in the dead of night, constantly looking over his shoulder.

Ten miles away from his house, I toss the rose out the window.

I picture myself fleeing town, too.

The tears come fast.

FOUR

MY ALARM BLARES AT 5:00 A.M. sharp.

I slam a hand on the clock. Then I rise with the stamina of a newborn giraffe.

Tiptoeing around my books on the floor is a fine art, especially with one eye open. I almost step on *Wuthering Heights* and *Mexican Gothic*. When you can only pirate novels and poetry collections, physical copies become that much more precious. All I need are the wrought iron bookshelves waiting in my digital shopping cart to keep them safe.

By the time I reach my closet, the sound of sizzling bacon wafts down the hall.

Mami is awake.

And I have to tell her about the damaged car in her garage.

The last time Mami received terrible news, she ran out of the restaurant where we'd just had dinner and found me clinging to Papi's lifeless body in the parking lot. The elf that killed him had already fled. People started to gather around me, but I can't remember what they said.

My strongest memory is Mami picking me up and setting me aside like a discarded doll. Then she pinned my father's body and sobbed into his shirt. I also remember how she'd tearfully hum songs, telling me they were my father's favorite. She changed the pronouns in Oscar Wilde's "Requiescat" and recited it in choked whispers.

"He was such a realist," she'd say. "Facts and numbers moved Eduardo Burgos. An algebra teacher through and through. Only God knows how he swayed a dreamer like me."

And only God knows how I'll get through today.

"¡Sevim! ¿Quieres revoltillo, mi vida?" Mami yells excitedly. She must've heard my alarm. One would think she's overjoyed to be cooking me scrambled eggs.

"¡Sí!" I put on the first Within Temptation shirt and black shorts I can find, then head to the living room. I'll change into my school uniform once breakfast is over . . . *if* I'm still alive.

There are daisies in my mother's frizzy hair. She also has dirt on her yellow dress. While we can't afford to keep a garden thriving in our home, Mami helps an old coworker with hers in Caguas, and she always forgets to wash her clothes afterward. She'll spend hours in someone else's natural haven and pretend it belongs to her. Then she tells me how she loves moth orchids the most, and how she hopes to own a whole forest filled with them one day.

All we have in our living room is a sad, lonely aloe. Smoke trails toward the skylight from the lavender incense right next to the tangerine pot.

"How do you get more beautiful every day?" Mami dances as she plants a quick kiss on my forehead. "People say black clothing looks great on everyone, but that's a lie. *You* pull it off." She sets my breakfast on the dining table—a cup of hot café con leche and the promised revoltillo. "How was the coffee shop last night? What time did you get back? I didn't hear you."

One of the few things that makes it easier to lie to my mother is the fact that she doesn't use computers. She doesn't even have a smartphone. Googling her daughter's nonexistent Etsy shop and trusting that she spends her nights editing art to sell online? Never in a million years. The way she so easily believes my untalented ass is successful enough to pay our bills with skull prints and noir filters . . . I wish everyone had mothers like her.

"Um . . ." I fidget, avoiding her brown eyes. "The coffee shop was okay. I didn't get to write, but I sketched a little."

"Oh, good! What did you sketch?"

"Skulls with flower crowns."

Mami nods. "Are those featured in that short story you're working on, too?"

In addition to encouraging my so-called talent for drawing, my mother always wants me to finish what I'm writing. She'll read a scene or two, then beg me for more. She even thinks I'm capable of completing a full-length novel someday. Having an only child who shares her love of literature must feel like a dream come true. Like she did something right.

"Not really," I say. "They're just things I draw for fun. And I still don't understand what this story is even about. I don't know who the main character is or what they want. I don't know who's standing in their way. The beginning keeps changing all the time."

"Maybe if you actually *told* me about it, I could help you untangle its threads."

I force a smile. "There would have to be threads in the first place."

"So it's only . . . what do you call it? Vibes?"

"Yeah. It's just vibes for now."

She gently tucks my hair behind my ears. "Remember your promise?" she says.

"Of course. I'm naming a supporting character after you." I'm the one who sighs now. "And she's an evil queen living in a haunted garden."

"Even if there aren't any fantasy or horror elements in your story."

"Sí, Mami."

"Así me gusta, mi amor. Give me a really expensive wardrobe, too."

"Anything else?"

"A Lamborghini."

"Why would you need a Lamborghini if you live in a garden? How big is this place?"

"That is for *you* to figure out." She taps my nose, then points to my breakfast. "Tu comida se está enfriando. Eat."

I wish I cared about my food getting cold. I wish letting Mami talk about her fictional self would make breaking bad news more bearable. At least agreeing with whatever she wants in my story has kept her in a great mood. Hopefully, she won't be too irritated now.

"Actually, I have something to show you, but you have to promise me not to freak out. I swear it's worse than it looks."

I'm used to saying that last sentence. The first time I cut my own bangs, when I bleached my split ends because I was bored, that one night I got food poisoning from reheated meat lovers pizza that left me vomiting for hours. Mami should get paid just for having to deal with my messes. But I've never broken anything that belongs to her, especially something that will cost a lot of money to fix, given that her basic insurance plan doesn't include collision coverage resulting from elf violence. Not even from normal *human* violence.

"Well, that's never a good sign," Mami says. "What is it? Did something happen to you at the coffee shop? Am I getting in someone's face today?"

"Natalia Ruiz getting in someone's face? Sounds unlikely."

"Will you let me act out my revenge fantasy, please? What's going on?"

"Just . . ." I sigh helplessly. "Come with me."

I don't look at her as I walk to the garage. Her echoing footsteps are the only evidence I have that she's nearby. My fingers are slow to grab the keys and unlock the door that leads to the last place I wish to visit. I swing it open without sparing a glance at the Elantra or at my mother.

"What am I looking at? Other than the car, I mean." Mami almost sounds bored.

The window has been repaired. It gleams spotlessly under the garage lights.

There's something cradled between the wiper and the windshield.

A red rose.

FIVE

"**O**H! IS THIS WHAT YOU WANTED me to see?" Mami flocks to the rose and caresses the petals. "Why would this freak me out? This is such a thoughtful gift! I haven't held a rose in so long!"

"I . . ."

"Ugh, it smells amazing, too." Mami softly presses the petals against her cheek, smiling like a princess in the garden of her dreams. Flowers have always held a special place in her heart, especially after she was fired from her call center job three years ago. When she's not working in her old coworker's garden in Caguas, she's collecting flowers into bouquets to decorate our home. This rose, however, could never be anything other than an undeniable threat—Prince Aro is still alive.

And he's found my house.

I try steadying my breath in vain. Is an ambush on the way?

Are they already staking out the property and waiting for me to come outside? Will they take Mami in for questioning, too? How am I supposed to protect her from the Iron Staff clan? I'd have to strike a deal just like my father so they leave my mother out of this. That's like spitting on Papi's grave—I don't want to betray my promise to avenge him, least of all resort to the elves' manipulation tactics. They can lock me up all they wish, and I'll endure whatever they throw at me, but Mami is off-limits.

Or we can just run.

The elves will catch us if we stay. I don't know where I'd spend the night, or the nights after that, but I should call Doctor Ramírez. Even if he wants nothing to do with me, even if he's spitting on Papi's memory by cutting ties with me, we're still facing the same enemy. Sticking together might be the only way out.

I rush to my mother and snatch the flower. "Don't put this against your skin. We don't know where it's been and you can't—"

"What are you talking about? Didn't you leave this here for me?"

"I . . . I did, but it's been sitting out here for a while. And, um, you could get a rash?" I wave to the car. From my vantage point, nothing looks tampered with inside, but I'll have to check the seats and under the hood just in case. I'm not driving without proper inspection. "Why don't we go to the beach? Or to El Jardín Botánico? That sounds like fun, yeah?"

I can't think of a more perfect cover than the University of Puerto Rico's botanical garden. Two hundred eighty-nine acres with a varied selection of our nation's flora is my mother's idea of paradise. It will give me ample time to brainstorm our next move while she loses herself among the palm trees and patches of grass.

"But you have school," says Mami.

"I never miss class, so it's not a big deal if it happens once, right? I can call in sick. We'll have a girls' day out." Hopefully, my grin isn't too tight to seem believable.

Whatever is running through my mother's mind is taking too long to settle. She's looking from me to the rose to the car. She sighs longingly.

"It *has* been a while since we had a girls' day out," she says.

"Yes. And spending it al El Jardín Botánico would be perfect, wouldn't it? We can read our favorite poems out loud and even act them out like we used to before—"

I almost say Papi.

She offers me a wide smile anyway, as if she's trying her hardest not to crack in front of me. "Sounds delightful. We should shower and change."

"You go ahead. I'll put the rose in water for you."

Mami kisses my forehead, then she's off to the kitchen again.

I leave the rose in a cup of water. Mami will want to know I kept my word, even if this is a tracking device or a cursed object. Then I fetch my phone and call the doctor. Endless ringing accompanies me while I peek through the living room windows. My neighborhood is usually quiet at this time, but today's silence is absolute. All the roosters have chosen to slumber through dawn; every human clings to bedsheets and intoxicating dreams.

The doctor isn't answering.

Come on. I can't do this alone.

A speck of light glimmers down the street.

No. It's more like a thick, golden thread, flickering on and off.

It's coming from the narrow alleyway at the end of my street, which is littered with broken glass and empty potato chip bags.

The alleyway leads straight into an abandoned Burger King by the main road. A no-man's-land covered in graffiti, cobwebs, and mold. The longer I stare at the golden thread, the faster I see it for what it is—an ensueño's trail.

"Fuck."

Aro must be waiting at that Burger King. The rose was left behind to announce his arrival, but he needs me to walk into *his* battlefield, where more armed guards are surely at his side.

I hope this means they're only interested in me. I can't let them hurt Mami. And I can't run away. They're too close by. I'll have to surrender and beg for my mother's freedom.

But why is the ensueño flickering? It's not supposed to look like someone is playing with a light switch. Could a less experienced elf have cast it? Aro might be too tired or even injured after yesterday's battle.

I can't decide whether or not I'm relieved that Aro's probably still alive. Did I want the rebels to murder him? No. But the last thing—or creature—that would grant me any peace is the youngest elf prince. It's his fault I'll be separated from my mother. He's responsible for whichever terrible fate clouds my skies after today.

I call the doctor again.

It rings only once.

"What do you want?" he says.

"Oh, thank God you answered! Listen. They found me."

With a breathless laugh, Doctor Ramírez speaks louder. "Who found you exactly?"

"Prince Aro. I haven't seen him yet, but he left me a rose at my house. He's *here*. The ensueño's trail is flickering, though, so I'm wondering if something is wrong. Maybe an elf has been injured? I mean, I know I have to run, but——"

"Bring me the prince."

My eyebrows knit into a single thread. Taking *a member of the royal family* is suicidal. Whichever fate Aro had planned will be much tamer in comparison. What if he has double the amount of bodyguards today? They won't let me breathe in his direction before they strike.

"What if it's a trap? What if no one's hurt at all?" I ask.

"It's a risk worth taking."

Easy for you to say from wherever you're hiding!

"Doctor, if the prince *is* hurt, the moment his brother notices Aro hasn't returned, he'll come over to the mainland and I could—"

"Prince Feyn will never find him. He won't know our involvement, either. I promise you, Sevim, this won't lead back to us."

"But he's—"

"Last night, you upset me, but you also made me rethink many things. I have a plan now. I know how we can get them off our scent. And if you bring him to me," he pauses to catch his breath, as if he's been pacing around, "I'll pay you five grand."

This is the exact amount I would've made last night. It could change Mami's life for the next few weeks. Our water and electric bills would be paid while we wait to hear from the telemarketing companies she's interviewing with. Besides, the doctor has a plan. He's the most meticulous person I know, and he's only in danger because I screwed up.

He's still human, Sevim. His mind is no match for the ones who dwell in Eterna.

"Can you hear me?" the doctor says. "Hello?"

"I can hear you. I just . . . Are you home?"

"Yes. If the prince is really injured, bring him here and I'll explain everything. I'd rather talk about this in person."

"Okay. I'll be there soon."

I hang up.

I drive to the Burger King before Mami catches me leaving. She'll freak out and wonder where I am, no doubt picturing the worst for her teenaged daughter, but if this keeps her safe, I can't turn back now. The path is a familiar comfort despite its heinousness. Through the open window, I smell spilled soda, cigarette smoke, and vomit; they mingle into a single stench bomb.

I drive faster, the ensueño turning on and off with greater speed.

What's wrong with your magic, Your Highness?

Farther ahead, the darkened fast food restaurant sits under a beaming sun. Its windows and doors have been removed; illegible phrases blend together across the graffiti-covered walls. Half of the playground's slide rests on the floor, surrounded by cracked, grimy tiles. I can almost hear the fluttering of cockroach wings just by looking at that ransacked home of the Whopper.

Raff's town car sits in the parking lot, the engine still running. Its driver-side door is open.

Someone's leg dangles outside.

"What in God's name . . . ?" I get out of Mami's car, but I don't know how to approach. There are no signs of wreckage, but why would Raff stay in a place like this? Unless he's hurt?

This could be another trap.

I move slowly toward the open door. When I'm close enough, I clear my throat. "Raff?" I peek at the driver's seat, my fists prepared to connect with flesh.

"Stay back . . ."

Raff isn't here.

There's a hole right through Aro's chest.

Blood pools down his shirt, staining the white fabric with an ungodly amount of red. His lips have been stained, too, and he coughs up crimson onto the shoulder he rests his head on.

"Stay back!" Aro repeats, reaching out for me in the slowest motion.

Reaching for the speechless girl who's staring at him blankly, piecing together that he's really lying on that driver's seat, bleeding out.

Dying.

"Aro . . ."

His hand drops. His eyes are pressed tightly shut.

He's not breathing.

SIX

NO ONE SHOULD BE BEAUTIFUL WHEN they're dead.

But death and beauty have always been two clasped hands. I stare at that blooming red stain, hoping for renewed life, but it only offers eternal rest.

It's not until the teardrop lands on my shoe that I notice I'm crying. Aro means nothing to me. Just a mythical creature determined to ruin my life. But he was once breathing and I watched him stop. I've always approached elf bodies after the light in their eyes has already faded. I never thought I'd have a front row seat to the actual fading someday, least of all from Aro. I heard him plead for me to retreat instead of asking me to save him. Did he not want me to see him die? Was he seriously thinking about my mental health instead of focusing on the more pressing matter?

I don't know why that makes me cry more. How could I ever

be touched by my enemy's empathy toward me? It's like I want to just . . . hold him . . . even though he's already dead.

I shake my head. There's no need to be sentimental over a stranger, let alone an elf who tried to arrest me.

Golden light still flickers around the car—the ensueño remains active. Aro must've cast a powerful spell right before the battle. He knew he wouldn't make it out of this parking lot.

I should call Doctor Ramírez. Tell him the prince really is dead.

Saying it will make it final. It will be true.

It will also mean another human will know what I know. When the media catches wind of this, they'll be merciless in searching for answers, hunting down anything that can help them piece together the tragic passing of Eterna's youngest royal. Then again, I doubt the Iron Staff clan will be fully transparent. We still don't have details on King Arón, Queen Relynn, and Prince Lexen's deaths. The two remaining princes blamed the rebels, but wouldn't they have conquered Eterna by now? Why focus on killing humans when you've stolen the thrones?

Then again, this is Raff's car, and he's not here. Neither are the prince's bodyguards. If they're all dead, the rebels must be even more powerful than I thought.

So will be their retaliation.

The media might never know I was here, but the elves will. Could Aro have told his older brother about my crimes? Are they aware he'd planned to ambush me yesterday?

Am I in even greater danger than I feared?

Mami must still be choosing her outfit or blow-drying her hair; she's not one to rush. I'll text her that I've left something at the coffee shop and need to pick it up ASAP.

I park with the trunk facing him. Usually, I drag my catches by their legs, but I can't stand to see Aro's pained face. I suddenly have the urge to caress his cheek, as if his skin is somehow . . . calling to me . . . I softly pull on his left arm instead. Once he's sliding out of the seat, I hook my arms under his, then move him as quickly as possible without battering him further.

"You're stronger than I thought."

I freeze.

Aro is *awake*.

Gold light wraps around my wrists.

I let go of the elf and back away, but the shimmering rays still cling to me. Then they morph into chains. The iron squeezes me like a snake coiled around its meal.

Aro smiles through bloodstained teeth.

SEVEN

"**L**OVELY TO SEE YOU AGAIN. I miss the fishnets, though."

Aro shuts the door and rests against it. The hole in his chest closes up like a portal made of flesh and fabric. Even the blood on his shirt, his mouth . . . it all disappears.

"You *tricked* me." I can't move—his magic binds me.

"I did what was necessary. And that was only the beginning."

Daggers pierce through my heart at his cold, vengeful promise. I don't know how he's planning to unleash his rage. He could've easily ambushed me at home. There must be a reason why I'm chained up at an abandoned Burger King. Does he want to discuss something in private? Is he waiting for someone? This *is* Raff's car.

"You said you'd let me go home. I just needed to answer your questions."

"That was before you left me to die."

A lump forms in my throat. He's going to make me pay, and he's going to enjoy it.

I should trick him, too. Make him think I'm sorry. It might lessen the punishment.

"I'd like to apologize, Your Highness. What I did was inexcusable and—"

"Funny how we regret our wrongdoings when justice comes knocking."

Aro licks his teeth. His narrowed eyes travel around my face, as if he's trying to choose a spot to bite into. He hasn't looked at me like this before. Is he trying to unsettle me? Make me cower?

Don't let him.

"My regret is genuine. I'm sorry."

"Save it." Aro runs his gloved hand through his hair. It messes up his waves even more. "Royal guards are stationed at your house. They're taking your mother to Eterna."

His words are hammers against my chest. They're splitting it open, revealing the barely beating heart underneath, and smashing it into crimson dust. "She has nothing to do with this," I whisper. If I speak louder, I'll start crying, and I refuse to give Aro that satisfaction. "*Please.*"

"Nothing will happen to her if you do exactly what I command."

"Okay! Whatever it is, I'm in. Just don't hurt my mom. She has nothing to—"

Aro raises his bare hand. An ivory ring glints in the sunlight.

"I'm choosing you as the Exchange's final winner. I'll drive you to the marina so you can hop on our boat and depart at once. You must successfully complete each challenge and participate in our dream study sessions. You have until your last sunrise in Eterna to save your mother. If you fail our lessons or refuse to hand over your dreams, she dies. Are the rules clear?"

He wants to strike *a deal*?

I've never heard of an arrangement like this. Humans are the ones who ask something from these assholes. Riches, beauty, good health, getting an ex-lover back . . . The internet is rife with claims of delusional people who've sought help. Papi's lung cancer had progressed to the point of certain death. Desperation led him to the worst mistake he ever made.

But the prince has come to *me* for a favor instead.

"Um . . . what?" is all I can say.

Aro repeats his instructions. Once he's done, he says, "Are the rules clear, Sevim?"

My mother has seven days to live.

I have to spend seven days on the last place on Earth I want to be in.

Aro might not be sticking me inside a prison cell, but making me take part in his poor excuse for a peaceful retreat between species is just as torturous. From what little I've heard about them, the challenges should be fine. Past winners have uploaded footage on social media and provided interviews about their experiences. Combat drills involve properly holding and swinging a staff. Nobody actually fights. Strength exercises are all about carrying trees and splitting them in half. Mastering stealth is an elaborate hide-and-seek game. And ensueño lessons are like assembling Legos straight from one's imagination.

It's the dream extraction that worries me. Powering the elves' ensueños is bad enough. Does Aro think getting a front row seat to my subconscious will reveal my employer's identity? Maybe the red rose I gave Doctor Ramírez wasn't a tracking device. He's still in danger, though, and it's still my fault.

But I would never choose him over Mami.

I've already lost a parent to these creatures. I won't lose another.

"This is the last time I'm asking you," says Aro. "Are the rules clear?"

Fuck you.

"Yes, Your Highness. Take me to Eterna."

EIGHT

BY THE TIME WE ARRIVE TO Ceiba, the eastern town where the elves dock their boat, it's already ten minutes past departure.

An ivory flag whips in the wind farther ahead. It sits at the top of a golden mast.

Prince Feyn hasn't left yet.

"We have arrived at your final destination." Aro imitates the robotic voice that comes out of a GPS. He parks far from the marina's entrance, where reporters and eager bystanders are waiting for the last Exchange winner. "Happy travels."

"You're not coming?"

"There's something I need to take care of first, but don't worry. You won't miss me for too long." He grins like a crossroads demon collecting mortal souls.

It doesn't offer me any solace for what the Exchange has in store.

"Will I see her?" The question barely leaves the tip of my tongue. I don't want to anger him, but how am I supposed to sleep without proof that Mami is unharmed? If he's expecting me to take him at his word, this will indeed be the longest fucking week of my life.

"On your last sunrise in Eterna," says Aro, "if you obey."

"I will."

"Smart choice. Now let me get those off you. We can't have you showing up in shackles."

The golden chains disappear.

"And take this. Feyn will want to see it."

He hands me a golden slip of paper—my invitation to Eterna.

The passenger side door flies open.

I don't speak to the prince again as I exit his best friend's car. Once I slam the door behind me, I'm off to the media circus that lies in wait. Camera crews. Vloggers. Regular people recording on their smartphones. I'm flying past the gathered crowd, ignoring their shouted questions and requests to share my name for the people watching at home. I reach the front of the line breathless, yet unscathed. Police officers stand on a wooden bridge that leads to Feyn's vessel—a naval masterpiece in solid, ostentatious gold.

After the elves revealed themselves, I expected leaves or tree trunks or other flora-related inspiration for their ships. I had made two mistakes: The elves have *one* ship—Tesoro del Mar— and it's shaped like a basket-hilted sword. The deck is long and narrow, but the opposite end is caged in golden bars that resemble a crown. A throne sits between the coiling steel. Tesoro del Mar floats beneath the orange and pink clouds, a weapon lying in wait. Unlike this port's ferry, the boat only has one deck. Ruby petals are strewn throughout. Foreigners believed they came from a common hibiscus, but the true source is La Flor de Maga, our country's national flower.

Jason and Ryujin are already onboard.

Prince Feyn stands at the edge of Tesoro del Mar's deck. His iron staff is perched on his shoulder. Unlike his little brother, he doesn't wear a velvet glove and he's *always* in black crop tops. He also loves makeup. Today he has silver glitter lining his eyes and a blend of creamy white and gray shadows below his brows.

I quietly approach Tesoro del Mar, bracing myself for his scalding glare. While Aro acts friendlier toward humans, Feyn is a glacier in leather boots. He doesn't seem excited to be hosting the Exchange. This is the first time he's doing it, as he's now the oldest royal alive.

Don't anger him. He could retaliate worse than his brother.

I hold out my invitation.

Feyn's eyes skim over it. "Why are you late, human?"

"I . . . I'm so sorry, Your Highness. Prince Aro chose me a bit late and—"

"You're blaming my brother for your insolence?" Feyn is fully glaring now. He tightens his grip on his staff, as if he's ready to swing it at my head.

"No! No, I would never. I'm sorry. I spoke out of turn, Your Highness."

The prince looks at the gathered crowd. "The third winner has finally joined us," he says, bored and bone dry. Feyn turns to Jason and Ryujin. "Take your seats. Eterna awaits."

———— ℓℓ ————

As I sit on the left side of the boat, Feyn walks down the length of his vessel, moving like a snake with no predators in sight—slow and comfortable. His staff remains slung over his shoulder. Only when he's seated in his throne does he lower it. Feyn taps the deck three times.

Tesoro del Mar shifts ever so slightly to the right.

It keeps turning, gaining speed in small increments. Feyn's throne now faces the port. The rest of the ship is aiming toward thick, spell-crafted fog.

Mami, I'm almost there. Hang on a little longer.

With another tap of his staff, Feyn commands the ship onward. It sails at a bearable pace; there's no need to grab onto the bench. The sea is cooperating, too. Waves crash against the sides of Tesoro del Mar, but they don't alter its path or threaten to topple it.

The farther we move, the less I hear people shouting for my name, the insistent clicking of cameras. I picture my face on gossip sites and newspapers. Returning to the mainland will entail further harassment, cracking my life wide open like a coconut fresh off the palm tree.

But that's a problem for Future Sevim.

Right now, there are two strangers staring at me from across the boat.

Only Jason is smiling.

"Welcome aboard!" He waves and knocks his backpack out of his lap. It's the only luggage allowed in Eterna, since the elves will be providing our complimentary wardrobe. After he grabs his backpack again, he says, "Whoops. Sorry about that. I'm Jason. What's your name?"

"Sevim."

"Cool. Nice to meet you!"

Wish I could say the same.

He points to the DSLR camera hanging around his neck. "Mind if I take a picture? It's for my personal collection." His eyes widen in horror. "Wait. That sounded weird. I'm not—"

"Yeah, go ahead."

I look into his camera before he keeps rambling. I'd give an arm and a leg to have privacy right now. Enough space to decompress from this hell of a morning. How are the elves treating Mami? Is she in pain? Does she know I'm going to save her? Or does she think I'm dead? The thought of her being holed up without food or water makes me sick. She should be in our dining room enjoying her café con leche and revoltillo. Dancing and humming Papi's favorite songs. Dreaming of forests filled with moth orchids and other flowers.

"I like your haircut," says Ryujin. She's in a pastel pink shirt, a short jean skirt, and white sneakers. Quite casual compared to Jason's emerald polo shirt and khaki pants. "Very beautiful."

"Thank you . . ." Her compliment makes me grin just a little. It's not enough to wash away the bitter taste of Mami's kidnapping, but it's something. "Your hair is, too."

"Oh. You're too kind." She runs her fingers through her waist-long brown hair. I think I read she'd had it short when she was still competing as a gymnast. Then she grew it out.

"Okay, here I go!"

Jason takes three pictures, thanks me for my patience, then aims his camera at the fog.

Tesoro del Mar cuts through it in a perfectly straight line. For a few minutes, the world is white. There's no sound, no movement. It's like sailing across a haunted sea in a Greek myth, with sirens waiting just beyond the white, ready to drag us into the depths.

But these depths would greet me with contaminated sea life.

It bustles among leftover bombs.

Culebra and Vieques appear at the edges of the fog—the former to the left, the latter to the right. My shoulders hang low as we draw closer to Vieques. My father was raised there. He lived on the main island as a college student and came back home for holidays. He only moved to Carolina after getting married. By then, my grandmother had already passed, and since she was a single mother, Papi had no more family to visit. He never offered to show me his old stomping grounds, either. Then again, he had a complicated relationship with his hometown.

Farther west is the demilitarized zone. Both in the western and eastern parts of Vieques, the U.S. Navy performed drills, tested heavy artillery, and stored thousands of munitions. Cleanup efforts are ongoing yet slow moving. The damaging effects on natural resources, wildlife, and the locals aren't fully understood. We *do* know Vieques has the highest cancer rate of all Puerto Rico. My father's symptoms were present in his twenties—chest pains, coughing, exhaustion—but he blamed work and academic stress. He was diagnosed with stage 3 lung cancer a week before my eleventh birthday. A thirty-nine-year-old man who never smoked.

"Oh my goodness!" Jason shoots out of the bench. He aims his DSLR above Feyn's throne; he completely ignores the gathered crowd on Mosquito Pier—Vieques's dock—to his right. Not even the Viequenses' own camera shutters can snap him out of it. *"We're here!"*

The fog is gone.

I cringe at the gold waters by Eterna's shores. This isn't bioluminescence, which is one of our archipelago's true marvels. There's nothing natural about this metallic glow. It's an enchantment designed to mimic said bioluminescence. A cheap parlor trick. I wouldn't be surprised if it's further contaminating sea life.

The island's saving grace is its sand, which is as dark as the one in Vieques's Playa Negra. Everything else—fronds on towering palm trees, ferns dancing in the breeze, even the hefty lagartos crawling across—is gold. There's a slight translucence to the vegetation. It's like the island couldn't decide between being a vibrant dreamscape or a grim haven.

Tesoro del Mar slides onto the black sand. Once the whole boat is on land, Feyn taps the deck three times again, and his vessel moves no more.

I made it, Mami. I'll be with you soon.

Feyn leaves his throne behind. "Everyone out."

Jason is the first to follow him off the ship. He's shaking his head like he can't believe this is real. Ryujin clutches her backpack straps tight and moves in silence.

I trail behind them. There are no royal guards in this area, which could definitely lead to rebel ambushes. Even though humans travel to Eterna aboard Tesoro del Mar, elves access their home by conjuring bridges. That's how Raff can drive Aro onto the mainland—they hide within ensueños that span the iron structure's length. Rebels cast bridges, too. Before their deaths, the king and queen announced they'd built a magical shield to keep their enemies out. But what good has it served when they're both dead long after its creation?

Feyn doesn't seem fazed, though. He walks toward the trees without a care in the world.

The harsh pounding of drums travels down the sandy path ahead.

It weaves between the trees, growing louder with every step I take. Jason is even *dancing* to the hectic beat. I can't see anything beyond gold leaves and palm fronds, but I've witnessed past welcoming ceremonies on social media. The elves are throwing us a party.

Fireworks launch into the sky. They crackle and glow as I follow the elf prince deeper into the island. Jason takes pictures as if the world will end if this isn't documented. Ryujin barely looks up, but she's nodding along to the drumming.

After a few minutes, the sandy path grows wider and wider, pushing the trees aside.

There are elves on the branches. Some are older. Others are younger, but none younger than me. Everyone wears black and gold clothing that's comfortable for summer—guayaberas, drawstring pants, and sandals. They strike giant gold drums with two sticks. Behind them, winding iron bridges connect to each tree. Spiked iron gates wrap around trunks that have been hollowed out to fit the elves while they slumber. There are silver orbs pressed against the bark, which makes me feel like I'm wading through a diamond-powered forest.

I don't know when the other elves arrived. They have leather vests, forearm braces, and iron staffs slung behind them—the royal family's bodyguards. They're quick to flank us. One by one, they kneel at our approach, gripping their staffs tight.

"Oh my God . . ." Jason's recording everything on his phone now. He keeps aiming the camera at his baffled expression, then back at the bodyguards. "This is amazing!"

"Is it?" I whisper.

Jason gasps. *"Oh my God!"*

There are five cottages to my left. Each has three stories,

sloping roofs, iron verandas, and no windows. Their gold walls have the Iron Staff sigil painted on mahogany doors—the royal family's private quarters. The humans' lodge is directly across from the middle cottage. Ours is similar in design but only has one floor. We have windows, though; white curtains are shielding the interiors from view.

But the main attraction is the garden. It separates the royal houses and our lodge. Grass peeks out from beneath the sand in small patches, then overruns the area with ferns and petals that glow like stardust. This is where they're launching fireworks. It's also where massive orbs of water float among the trees. Each orb has an elf at its center. Only their black silk robes sway back and forth—the elves are frozen like paintings, glancing up at the sky with yearning.

"They're alive, right?" I ask.

"Of course!" says Jason. "Magic helps them hold their breath. It's just for entertainment."

How are living elves posing as water statues supposed to entertain me?

A dining table cuts through the garden. Fruit wreaths lie in each corner, but there are tightly covered silver platters everywhere. The smokiness of cooked bacon wafts over to me. I groan. Why must my mouth start watering over elf-made food? The glass trays aren't helping. They're stacked with an assortment of pastries—cupcakes with coconut frosting, thick pies stuffed with cherries and blueberries, cream-filled donuts, quesitos with flaky golden crusts . . .

"¡Bienvenidos a Eterna!"

The elf looks like a plus-sized Afro-Boricua in her twenties. Her brown curls are braided on one side of her head. She has golden petals threaded in her hair. Tiny jewels frame her eyes in the shape of a sun. But the best part is her gown. The bodice and puffy skirt are a combination of black lace and tulle; her V-neck is embroidered with the same jewels as those on her face.

"It's a pleasure to finally make your acquaintance." She rushes over to Jason and kisses him on the cheek—the official Puerto Rican greeting. "My name is Ciel. I'm the—"

"Royal Advisor and Head of Diplomatic Affairs," Jason finishes her sentence.

She was also the dead prince's fiancée, but I don't think Jason will bring that up.

Ciel's laugh is honey-smooth as she kisses Ryujin and me. "It's an honor to serve as your host for the week. I'll be your main contact for any and all requests you may have during your stay. Don't hesitate to ask for whatever you desire!"

How about you tell me where my mom is?

Feyn raises his index finger.

The fireworks cease.

"I presume you know my brother," the prince says lazily. "Aro, come say hello."

I stiffen. Surely I've misheard him—how can he be here already?

Then I see the youngest prince shaking hands with Jason. He kisses and hugs Ryujin.

He hugs me, too. He leans in close enough for our hearts to pound against each other.

Close enough for him to whisper: "What are you doing here?"

ΠΙΠΣ

ITH ALL EYES ON ME, I have no choice but to return the hug.

And it's . . . nice. Aro's hands gently hold my back; they send a rolling heat wave all over me.

I clear my throat. Whatever the hell he's making me feel doesn't matter right now. Not when he's trying to embarrass me.

"I'm not in the mood for jokes, Your Highness," I whisper. "Surely you can understand."

"This isn't a joke. What are you doing here?"

"You invited me."

"No, I didn't. I haven't seen you since you escaped."

"Wow. You're really determined to piss me off, aren't you?"

"Sevim, I swear that's not what this is about. I honestly have *no idea* why you're here."

My heart repeatedly slams into his chest.

"You don't, um . . . remember . . . our last conversation?"

"Right before you sped off and left me to die? I remember that quite well, actually. It still doesn't tell me how you arrived to Eterna. Now what's going on?"

He has to be messing with me. He's trying to pulverize my spirits, especially since I can't drive away from him again. I might not be behind bars, but this is still a prison.

"You made me come here, Aro. We made a deal."

He takes a deep breath as he slowly releases me. "Pretend you need to use the bathroom. We can't talk here," he says.

When he pulls out a chair for me, he nods, as if to cue my lie.

I don't want to be alone with him. Least of all if he's keeping up this pretense of not knowing what the hell I'm talking about. And especially not when I'm somehow wishing for his hands on my back again. Why would I ever fucking crave an elf's touch?

But even if he's just trying to play me like a fiddle in public only to give me more instructions privately, maybe he'll still provide an update on Mami.

I'll have to take my chances.

"Excuse me, Your Highness? Where's the restroom?"

"This way."

Aro tells Feyn we'll be back in no time. Three guards escort us to the main house. Once Aro closes the doors, he weaves a path along the cottage, which is a poor name choice for what this really is: an arboretum with gold furniture, thorny wooden pillars, and a glass ceiling.

Sunlight chases me as I walk past a family portrait in the foyer. The three princes had been children when it was painted. King Arón stands behind his seated wife. Prince Lexen clasps her hand. He was killed paying his respects at their graves. That child didn't know he had no future.

Just like Mami didn't know I'd put hers in danger.

"Tell me every single detail about this alleged deal between us," Aro says sternly. He crosses his arms as he leans forward. "Spare me nothing, Sevim. Nothing at all."

"So you're really going to deny kidnapping my mom?"

He freezes. Maybe it's the way he isn't blinking, or how his mouth hangs slightly open, but there's something about his reaction that feels genuine.

Aro is a better liar than I feared.

"Who said your mom had been kidnapped?" he asks.

"You did! Why are you acting totally clueless?"

"Because I am. I swear I haven't taken her, Sevim. I don't even know what she looks like. And I'd never do something so low. It's honestly offensive you'd think me capable of that."

"Then who took my mom? Who can turn themselves into a prince and would use their appearance to trick me into participating in this ridiculous excuse to steal human dreams?"

Aro's jaw falls. "Did they threaten to hurt her if you didn't? Was that the price?" He draws nearer, as if he's hoping to comfort me with another hug. Thankfully, his arms remain folded. I don't need the enemy touching me again. "The more you tell me, the more I can help you."

"Help me do what? How am I supposed to trust anyone on this island? You keep saying you don't know what's going on, so why would I waste time talking to you?"

My thoughts are back at the Burger King parking lot, where I spoke to an elf that may or may not have been the same one standing before me. Where my fate had been redesigned into a vicious mind game. Maybe that's the point of today's events—to spill patience out of me like wine in a broken glass. I don't mean to cry. But I can control my tears just as well as I can control the rest of my life. Why must everything this morning be scribbled with question marks? I've never trusted Aro and every minute I spend with him only proves I never should.

"Don't cry. Nothing will happen to your mother." Aro's forehead is *inches* away from mine. He holds me captive without touching me. Just the warmth of his breath on my skin, the smell of leather and sand, the starved, narrowed gaze peering down at my lips. Then he backs away and clears his throat. "But if you want to save her, you need to cooperate with me. What did the impostor tell you?"

I wipe the tears off my cheeks. "He told me to successfully complete the Exchange's challenges, hand my dreams over to your kind, and Mami would be released on my last sunrise in Eterna. So that's exactly what will happen. I don't have a choice."

Aro looks away. He seems lost in thought; his lips are pursed tight. "Did he mention the corpses?" he asks. "Is that why he chose you as the third winner?"

"He didn't mention them, but he acted like he was the same Aro from the mall. He knows." My throat closes up as I gulp down. "This is my punishment."

The prince looks back at me. His unblinking gaze bounces from one eye to the other. It grows wider. "Punishment," he repeats. "Raff, my bodyguards, and I are the only ones who know what you've done. I wanted to interrogate you before sharing my findings with Feyn. He's less . . . compassionate. This Fake Aro must've been following you, too."

"Any ideas about who could've been following me?"

"Rebels. You've been stealing *their* bodies. They're the ones who make deals with your kind anyway. Our enemies never keep their promises, and their victims usually end up killed."

I think of Papi lying in that parking lot. Whatever he was asked to do, he failed, but did it ever matter? Was he always going to die just for striking a deal? Or did he truly stand a chance?

"I won't fail my mother," I say. "I won't."

"And I don't want you to. But now *I'm* involved in your troubles. Raff was supposed to bring my real pick for our third winner. Since you're here, Feyn must've left before their arrival." Aro stares at the wall behind me. "I just hope nothing's happened . . ."

"Maybe he's the one pretending to be you."

"Raff uses American Sign Language. Was that how this other Aro spoke to you?"

"No, but—"

"Then it wasn't him. Raff is powerful, but he's not as strong with ensueño creation yet. He can't make another version of me even if he wanted to. *And* he's incapable of touching a hair on humans. He's a good egg." Aro shakes his head. "This was a rebel. Mark my words."

"Forgive me for not trusting the guy who set up a trap to catch me." He's about to speak, but I raise a hand. "You said I need to cooperate with you if I want to save my mother. Why on Earth would you help me, Aro? What's in it for you?"

"This isn't about *me*." Aro points to the family portrait. "I know what it's like to miss someone you love. I don't wish that kind of pain on anyone, especially when that person is the only family they have."

So he remembers what I said about Mami. How it's just the two of us at home.

A thin layer of hope spreads over my heart. It'll take far more than empathetic words to convince me he's telling the truth. That he cares about saving the woman I'd die for. But I'm curious if his plan is as bogus as his promises.

"Besides, you owe me answers," he says. "The dreaming sessions will be easier. You fall asleep and your mind lets loose. But the magical challenges are grueling. As Eterna's ensueño master, I'm creating that specific ability's challenge, but I know what the strength, stealth, and combat tests look like. I can give you clues for each . . . *if* you tell me who your employer is."

I slide one boot back, then the other. "My employer?"

"The person who hired you, yes."

"I know what employer means."

"Good for you. Tell me their name."

"You said it yourself. I've been stealing rebel corpses. This doesn't concern you."

"Oh, really? Why were you stalking me at the mall? Why were you staring at my dead bodyguard while I begged you to drive away? You're only taking rebels because you haven't had the chance to take an Iron Staff yet, but that's what this employer wants, isn't it? They're probably offering you more money to deliver someone from my clan, right?"

Fuck.

I chose Mami over Doctor Ramírez by coming here. But I never expected Aro to blatantly ask me about him—I was dreading the dream sessions more than I should have.

Willingly giving him information is different. It's an *active* form of betrayal. Then again, the doctor betrayed me first when he fired me. He kicked me out of his house like I'm some meager street rat, not his dead friend's only child. His objective might be the same as mine, but we're not valuing the same things. Does it still count as betrayal if there's no longer loyalty?

"Just tell me their name and I'll give you a clue for the strength challenge."

"Why would I even need a clue when most humans can pass this challenge? And if it's really that hard, what about the other challenges?"

"Oh, I'll have more questions for you. There'll be other chances to win the remaining clues, but like I said, you have to—"

"Cooperate." I sigh. "Okay. I'll give you a name." As Aro nods, I scratch the back of my neck, even though it doesn't itch. "Doctor Alberto Ramírez. He was, um . . . a friend."

"Was?"

"You only wanted his name. I gave it to you. What's my clue, Your Highness?"

There's a knock on the door.

"¿Todo bien, Su Alteza?" a guard says.

"¡Todo bien! We were just heading back now!" Aro lowers his voice. "The strength challenge is tonight. Meet me at my beach house an hour before showtime."

"Wait, no. Why do I have to wait that long? You promised—"

"We'll have enough privacy for you to receive the first clue there."

"But—"

"Let's get back to breakfast. And don't worry about it getting cold. It's been enchanted to stay hot, like me." He smugly walks to the doors and holds them open for me. "After you."

What a way to signal the end of this conversation.

I storm outside, wiping my tears away, wishing I knew what Aro has in store for me at that beach house.

TEN

MY RETURN TO THE GARDEN GOES largely unnoticed.

Aro's does not. Jason snaps so many photos with him. Ryujin asks Aro to do something called aegyo, which she explains as acting and speaking with an emphasis on cuteness. She and Aro cup their faces and pout like adorable babies for Jason's camera.

Once they're finished, I sit next to Jason, who's eyeing the lavender cupcakes like they're his reason to live. Royal servants place a silver papyrus scroll next to our plates. It has a list of daily activities. Our week has been divided like so:

DAY ONE

WELCOME BREAKFAST & LODGING

STRENGTH CHALLENGE

DAY TWO

DREAM STUDY SESSION #1

DAY THREE

STEALTH CHALLENGE

DREAM STUDY SESSION #2

DAY FOUR

COMBAT CHALLENGE

DREAM STUDY SESSION #3

DAY FIVE

ENSUEÑO CHALLENGE PART 1

DREAM STUDY SESSION #4

DAY SIX

ENSUEÑO CHALLENGE PART 2

DREAM STUDY SESSION #5

DAY SEVEN

FINAL CHALLENGE AT SUNRISE

SAIL TO MAINLAND

Reading the list is exhausting. We have leisure time scheduled, but can we move around without guards tailing us? I search the map for forbidden areas or blocked roads; nothing is marked off-limits. I won't find Mami with this map. I need something to show me whatever's underneath the pomp and circumstance. This island has to be more than meets the eye.

The food is as hot as Aro promised. I cram a variety of puff pastries into my mouth—the perfect excuse not to engage in conversation. Technically, this still counts as participation in the day's event. But no amount of sugary sweetness, flaky crusts, and fluffy dough will let me enjoy it. This paradise is just a prison to me.

An hour or two passes; I can't keep track of time anymore. Prince Feyn finally claps and declares the welcome breakfast over.

"The winners' lodge awaits!" Ciel exclaims. "Come see your new home!"

OUR NEW HOME SUCKS.

It looks like a foreigner's idea of the Caribbean as a paradise for rest, relaxation, and just enough luxury to prevent them from exploring further.

The same lavish bungalow decor I saw in the main house has been copied and pasted here. There are wooden pillars and plants everywhere. We also have a glass ceiling; sunlight keeps our floorboards toasty. One difference is our Flor de Maga garden. It faces the black sand and sparkling waters beyond the palm trees. Hand-woven hammocks swing in the breeze.

"And now for the best part!" says Ciel. "Your rooms!"

When I enter mine, dark paint replaces the wood's natural brown. A black carpet unfurls beneath my shoes. The bedsheets are the same shimmery black as the vanity. My closet is entirely composed of an asphalt-colored wardrobe. And I finally have wrought iron bookcases. Their bookends are shaped like human skulls with a black bow on top. Bram Stoker's *Dracula*, Emily Brontë's *Wuthering Heights*, multiple editions of Shakespeare's tragedies, Edgar Allan Poe's poems, and the complete works of Oscar Wilde grace most shelves. One bookcase has graphic novels from my wish list: Cullen Bunn's *Death Follows*, James O'Barr's *The Crow*, and Kentaro Sato's *Magical Girl Apocalypse, Volume 1* are just some of the titles available.

"The rooms transform into the haven of your dreams. They will stay like this for the rest of the week." Ciel offers me a thumbs-up. "Do you like it? Is it comfortable?"

How can a room built with your trickery ever be comfortable?

"Yes, everything's good. Will we be required to attend anything else before the strength challenge?"

"Not at all. You are free to spend the day as you wish!"

"Perfect."

I lock myself in my room.

———— ℓ ————

THERE ARE NO SECRET PASSAGES in the walls.

Discovering them would defeat their purpose, but after hours of pressing and pushing every inch of wood, of sliding books out of their shelves, I have nothing to show for it.

So much for dream haven . . .

I sneak around the winners' lodge in search of maps, letters, and hidden chambers. Aside from my personal library, there's nothing to read around here. There are also no locked doors; I stumble into two extra bathrooms and a small gym I'll never use. I'm grateful for whatever's keeping Ryujin and Jason distracted. I can hear Jason talking loudly from outside his door, as if he's on the phone or livestreaming, but Ryujin is silent. Maybe she's taking a nap or listening to music. I move quietly anyway.

In the end, my search efforts lead me back to my bedroom, where I lay an obscene amount of clothes on the bed, mixing and matching different items for today's first magical lesson.

"Strength practice will probably be better without sleeves . . ."

I choose a tank top and a sheer Maxi skirt. The skirt comes with shorts underneath; they'll be comfortable enough to run in. My finishing touch is the choker. Black beads dangle from the lace band. They're shaped like teardrops, sitting beneath a rose at the choker's center. The rose is made of the softest velvet I've ever laid hands on. Metal chains work fine, but this style would make me feel like a vampire queen at a royal ball—it adds drama to a simple summer outfit. I slip on the choker and check myself out on the full-body mirror. Blood-red petals are the only dash of color in my ensemble. I might roast under the sun, but at least I'll feel powerful.

The challenge will begin in a little over an hour.

It's almost time to meet with Aro at his beach house.

I *need* to ace the strength test. I just can't shake the fear of being tricked again. What if all his clues are lies, though? Aro swore he wants to help me. But why ask me to visit him this long after I gave him what he demanded? Is he digging up information on Doctor Ramírez? Could he be out there personally looking for him? Or is something else at play here?

Either way, inviting me to his secluded beach house gives off warning signs of a trap. Aro knows where I'm staying. He could easily visit me instead; I doubt there's anything strange about a prince entering the winner's lodge for a quick chat. Now he's forcing me somewhere I've never been, away from prying eyes, most likely so I can be at a disadvantage. Just like in the parking lot. Whether this is what he really wants or not, I certainly don't.

Then again, I have no idea what awaits me in the challenge. What if Aro's clue *is* real and I fail without it? Or even worse, will Mami be punished if I ignore his request?

I sit at the edge of my bed. There's no right answer.

And it's not like I can call Doctor Ramírez to tip him off. I'm the one who put him in this position. I hope he fled the moment I didn't show up with Aro at his doorstep. That if the elves find him, he knows I did it for my mother. For the family he stopped helping me protect.

The clock keeps getting closer to dusk. Aro must be waiting.

But there's another person on this island who could help. Someone who knows Eterna better than me. Most important, he's someone I wouldn't confuse for a trickster.

Maybe he's privy to a few secrets, too.

LUCKILY, JASON IS IN THE kitchen.

Ryujin drinks a matcha latte in the living room. She waves hello. I wave back.

"Hey, hey, hey!" Jason greets me as he pours almond milk into his black coffee. I don't know why he needs it. He's jazzed enough to power the whole island. "Did you rest well?"

"Um . . . yes. You?"

"Oh, I fall asleep the second my head touches a pillow. But I spent most of the day FaceTiming my little sister, Carol. It's my first time leaving home, so she's not handling it well."

At least you're here by choice.

"Speaking of leaving home," I say, "what do you think of Eterna so far?"

Jason puts the almond milk in the fridge. "I don't mean to

be cheesy, but it's just magical. And we haven't even seen every-thing yet." He heads to the living room; I trail behind him. "I mean, we're mostly expected to hang out here, but Feyn hasn't forbidden us from gallivanting around the beach. We could take a splash at night if we want."

"Sure." I sit next to him. We're facing Ryujin, whose latte has her full attention. "Aside from the beach, are there other places you'd like to visit?"

"The main cottage, obviously. How was it?"

"Nice. It was similar to this lodge."

"They share the same aesthetic, but the cottages are much cooler."

"Really? Why?"

Jason sips on his coffee. He smacks his lips like he's tasted ambrosia, but I doubt that latte holds a candle to food of the Greek gods. "Underground tunnels connect them," he says. "All my editions of Eterna's history book mention how vast they are for an island that's just four miles long. Exchange winners have said it, too. It's where the dream studies take place."

"Have you ever seen pictures? I don't remember finding any-thing online."

"Humans aren't allowed to record or take photographs in the tunnels. It's the only place that's off-limits." Jason caresses his camera. "Sadly."

"So do you think they have more than dream study chambers down there? Like . . . I don't know . . . treasures or other precious belongings? Maybe even prisoners?"

Ryujin chokes. She coughs out green droplets; they slide down her chin and spray the air between us. Then she wipes them off and continues to drink.

"Are you *okay*?" Jason asks.

"I am. I was just drinking too fast. This matcha is delicious."

She's not looking at me, though. And she seems to be shrinking on the couch, hunching lower and lower as if she's hoping to disappear.

Leave her alone. She must be embarrassed.

"Okay, just be careful." I turn to Jason again, even though he's still paying close attention to Ryujin. "So is it possible? Do elves keep prisoners underground?"

"Not that I know of. They don't disclose how they deal with rebels, but I'm assuming they'd bring them back for questioning and a proper trial. Although I think those tunnels are weird places to put them. Why would they lock their enemies under their own homes?"

"You said the tunnels are vast."

"Yeah, but it's still a risk, isn't it? Especially after *three* royals were murdered."

I nod. "Prince Lexen was killed at his parents' graves. Where are they located?"

Jason points at the wall behind Ryujin. "Other side of the island. They're pretty close to the royal beach house. That's where Aro has been filming his interviews and diplomatic speeches."

And where he must be seething at my absence.

"But I think you're forgetting that elves are way more cautious than humans," says Jason. "They wouldn't build an underground fortress for prisoners. Ensueños would be their best bet—somewhere easy to access yet remote. Somewhere their enemies could never escape even if they knew exactly where they were going."

Doctor Ramírez's elixir should still be working. I could track an ensueño anywhere on this island. And I could've tested its efficiency on the path to Aro's beach house today. What if Jason's right? Mami might be stuck in an ensueño. She's somewhere out there watching her worst nightmares unfold while I stress over trusting an elf prince. I've been worried that she's simply behind bars, but what if she's trapped in a hellscape?

Prince Feyn's voice booms from a loudspeaker.

"Winners, exit the lodge now. Your strength challenge is about to begin."

ELEVEN

THE ELVES TOOK OUT THIS MORNING'S dining table and floating water orbs.

Raff is in the garden now, too. He briefly glances at me but shows no emotion whatsoever. Aro must've warned him I was here.

Or he really is the one who tricked me.

I don't care what Aro believes. If elves can turn against their monarchs, they can surely sever ties with best friends. Raff could be a rebel spy—what better way to know where the prince is than by always hanging out with him? He could've developed his ensueño powers in secret and mastered the art of pretending to be one of the most insufferable creatures on this island.

But if he *is* loyal to his clan, I feel even worse for him. I wonder how much time he wasted with the real winner. How he felt after realizing Feyn had already sailed away. Did Raff escort whoever was chosen back home?

Then I realize it's rather quiet.

"Will Prince Aro join us today?" I ask Ciel.

"Of course! He's running late with his UNICEF meeting. We haven't shared the news, but I'm proud to confirm we're launching our first campaign together. Aro will be its ambassador."

Jason gasps. "That's amazing!"

"Thank you! He'll be announcing at the Global Mental Health Summit this year and—"

"Enough."

Feyn brusquely motions for Ciel to move aside. She bows as she follows Raff closer to the rose hedges. Once they're both far away, the prince taps his staff against the grass.

A marble table rises.

It keeps growing until it reaches Feyn's waist. There's a slab of iron ore on top—another gift the elves use to manipulate humans. In addition to creating the Exchange, the royal family offered flower seeds and their cherished mineral to foreign governments. Museums display gold petals encased in glass. Special exhibitions are held in arboretums across the globe, where elves design sprawling gardens. Every contribution is purely aesthetic, but some foreign powers believe their iron holds magical properties that will eventually bend to humankind's will. Thankfully, this has yet to be proven.

Feyn pulls out a crumpled scroll from his pocket. He reads it aloud. "Welcome to your first magical challenge. Today marks the beginning of a tradition my parents started ten years ago.

It was once simply an idea in my mother's head, a desire to connect with those we'd spent far too long hiding from, and now we honor her wish as reality. We thank this year's guests for their generosity and for accepting ours in return."

Listening to him is as riveting as a sloth climbing a tree. It's good that he doesn't rush through speeches, especially since Lexen had a bad habit of rambling. But Feyn's low energy makes it unbearable. What should I expect from the child who hid behind his father when the cameras first arrived? A tiny, pouting elf that only spoke at his mother's patient requests and granted reporters one-word answers? Having strangers in your home—an entire species you've never spoken to in your sheltered bubble— would definitely unsettle a nine-year-old. Aro had been two years younger, and even though he coped well, it does no good comparing spring to winter. "My mother, the queen, created these challenges to welcome in a new age of connection with humans. She wanted to share the elven experience with the worthy. We honor her and our promise for connection with the Exchange. Our magic has been passed down to us from the great ancestor, the first elf here before Vieques was called by that name. He knew nothing about his origin except that his power came from the sun, and so does ours."

Jason whispers just as Feyn speaks the same words.

But Feyn doesn't notice. Of if he does, he pretends not to.

Together they share the only myth I've heard of Eterna's origin.

"One day, he made a wish to the burning morning star. *Send me a companion.* They created a family of elves that grew to the clan we have today. Though our ancestors lived in Vieques, they saw the growing power and greed of humanity. In 1942, the elves launched their light into the water. It split into thousands of golden specks. Wherever they landed, something new was born and soon joined forces to create Eterna, an island home free from interference."

Feyn stops to quickly read through whatever he has left on the scroll. He exhales.

Jason is no longer speaking, either. Even when the prince continues, he stays quiet.

"But now we open our home to you, our worthy guests, each chosen for your purity of heart. The first elf granted his children four abilities, and his strength is our strength today. And now we will share it with you."

I've spent ten years thinking this story is a joke. How can you not know where you come from? Humans have long debated their origin, but whether it's evolution or creation myths, at least we have conviction. We don't hide our beliefs and theories from elves. Why do they insist on doing it to us? Acting ignorant feeds into my suspicions that they're worse than meets the eye.

"You have a strong memory." Feyn cocks an eyebrow at Jason.

So he *was* pretending not to hear him.

"Oh, thank you, Your Highness! I've read this story *so* many times and—"

"I didn't ask you to elaborate." Feyn rolls his eyes as he pockets his scroll. "The first elf gave his children four abilities. You will receive them now in their most raw, basic form. You won't be able to use them properly until each challenge is won. By completing our missions, you'll level up in strength, stealth, combat, and the crafting of illusions. You need to master all four in order to win the last one without injury. If you fail *any* challenge, you're officially eliminated from the Exchange and will be sent home."

Jason, Ryujin, and I nod. He's not telling us anything new. In the past ten years, six winners have been kicked off the island. Two had been way too drunk from a party the night before to complete their stealth mission. The others simply sucked at the challenges.

Feyn points to the iron ore. "These abilities shall be provided through the stone you see here. This will temporarily transfer my powers into your bodies. Are you ready?"

"Yes!" Jason basically shouts.

"Yes, Your Highness," says Ryujin.

"Oh, sorry! I meant, yes, Your Highness!" Jason amends.

"Prince Feyn, won't that weaken you?" I ask. "Even if it's temporary?"

"I'm far more powerful than you'll ever be," he replies with a sneer.

I bite my bottom lip to keep from talking back. This asshole thinks he's better than me? No surprise there. His deflection might mean he *will* be weaker. Hopefully, becoming weaker doesn't also make him crueler to compensate.

Please give us the magic and go. We don't need you here.

Light shoots out of the ore.

I'm struck in the chest, but I don't feel anything. This is a breeze compared to the ensueño Aro cast in San Juan. My flesh boiled when I passed through cars like a ghost. Now the hairs on my arms stick up like needles. Small bumps appear on my skin. Each glows as if the light is pushing against it, searching for an exit. Then the bumps flatten. The light disappears.

"Woo!" Jason shakes his arms as if he's drenched in water. "That was *cold*."

"It was?" I say.

He turns to me. "You didn't feel that?"

"I wasn't cold, either," says Ryujin. "But my skin pulsed."

"Bodies react differently to everything," says Feyn, "including magic." He taps the altar with his staff, and it sinks back into the grass until it's gone. I wait for him to push out a weary exhale, to request somewhere to sit, to even limp a little—any sign that us taking his power has outward effects on him. But he seems fine. "Now that you're powered up, here are your instructions. You have thirty minutes to bring me the child's heart."

I lean forward, wondering if I've just misheard him. He can't be referring to a *real* heart. Allegedly impersonating Aro is one thing. But elves can't cast human-shaped ensueños; they're incapable of replicating our likeness, voices, or even shadows. That's why they need our consent to look into our subconscious; their magic prevents them from tampering with our bodies. Maybe they're much closer to achieving human ensueños and have been keeping it a secret. Or they've fully succeeded. If it's not an ensueño, what could substitute a living human's blood organ? And what does bringing him this "object" have to do with developing our magical strength?

"The past strength challenges haven't been about retrieval, Your Highness," I say. "Also, you said *heart*? As in, shaped like a heart, right? Not the real thing?"

Jason laughs nervously. "Why would it be the real thing? That's ridiculous."

"The rules are different now. I think it's important to double-check."

"Yeah, but why would we retrieve an actual beating heart?"

"Ask the prince."

Feyn swiftly slams his fist on the altar.

He splits it right in the middle, where a thick crack widens from top to bottom. Chunks of marble fly every which way. Jason, Ryujin, and I flinch, even though he's only looking at me. His glare is much colder than when we first met.

I was wrong about him growing weaker.

He *is* getting crankier.

And I don't want to know how much crueler he can be.

"Your challenge begins," he says.

Tall mirrors slide out of the grass. The edges are slanted like a guillotine's blade.

One by one, the mirrors wrap around the entire garden, trapping us in a glass maze.

TWELVE

"**B**RING ME THE CHILD'S HEART," SAYS Feyn.

He, Ciel, and Raff stand on a floating glass stage. They look down at us a few feet ahead, as if to keep away from whatever we're about to endure.

What the hell is going on?

"We only have thirty minutes, so we should get moving," says Jason.

I point to the mirrors right in front of us. "There's nowhere to go."

"Everything is an illusion, remember? Let's keep our hands outstretched and feel for anything that could be softer than glass. Or maybe something will open if we touch it."

"This is a *strength* challenge, Jason. Why would anything be soft or easy to open?" I turn slowly, checking every inch of our surroundings, but all I see is my reflection too many times to count. "I think we have to break the glass."

"But we'll get cut," says Ryujin. "We're supposed to bleed through this challenge?"

"We're wasting time!"

I run to the closest mirror ahead, then take a deep breath. I slam my fist against glass.

It doesn't shatter.

My knuckles aren't throbbing, either. It's like I didn't punch *anything*.

I turn to Jason and Ryujin. "Guess we can't break this, after all."

They gasp.

"Sevim," says Ryujin, "look."

The glass is melting.

It drips down like beads of water on an ice cube. Then it braids itself into shimmering threads of liquid. I stand back as they pulsate faster than my racing heart. A small burst of light emanates from the once-melted glass, and a brand new object reveals itself.

A sword.

Its hilt lands on my left hand. There's an inscription around it:

FOR THE CHILD'S HEART

"What in God's name . . ." I whisper.

"I think that's yours now," Jason says unhelpfully. "And again, the heart won't be real, so don't take it literally. We just have to decipher what this means before moving on."

"Or we can keep punching mirrors and getting more clues."

"Let's hold back on the punching, okay? We have to—"

"The clock is still ticking!"

I take the sword. It's as weightless as a feather. How can something so light in my hands be used for such a heavy task? I pretend I can't see its inscription on the way to other mirrors. I hit them with both fist and sword, but they don't melt.

"Why isn't it *working*?" I yell.

"Maybe if you listened to me, we could figure something out!" Jason yells back.

A child's laugh echoes around us.

It sounds like a little boy—thrilled and carefree.

"Did . . . did you hear that?" I ask.

"Yes," Jason and Ryujin say.

The boy laughs again.

All the mirrors start spinning. Then they shift like chess pieces being pushed into different squares. I make the mistake of blinking. Once my eyes settle on them again, nothing is moving.

There's a clear path ahead. The mirrors are placed at the sides like lopsided silver walls. My reflection is multiplied too many times. It shows my sweaty forehead and low-hanging jaw.

With another laugh, the little boy sounds like he's down that newly opened clearing.

"He sounds real." I don't even know I've said it aloud until Jason taps my shoulder.

"It *could* be a real person," he says. "I still think we don't have to take out their heart. The child could give us something that represents it instead. Something they cherish, for example."

I hate how gullible he is. Trusting people like him gets others killed in horror movies *and* in real life. "Whatever it is, there's no turning back now."

I bolt down the pathway.

"Sevim, wait!"

Jason and Ryujin's footsteps are close behind, but I don't stop. Neither Mami nor I have a single second to spare. I dash toward the stranger I must hurt in order to save her. The farther I run into the maze, the more silent it gets. Only my reflection keeps me company—it's like that thrilled and carefree boy was never here.

The mirrors melt. I skid to a halt as the maze disappears.

Now I'm in a sandpit.

Something slithers past my skirt. Loud hissing shakes the pit; hundreds of light brown tendrils are stacked on top of one another like coiled ropes. Their necks are shielded with small hoods made of their own flesh. Even though their mouths are tiny, their fangs carry enough poison to kill us instantly.

"Oh my God . . . cobras . . ." Jason says breathlessly.

He's panting hard, but the way his eyes dart from one snake to the next, growing wider each time, and how he's crushing his hands to his face, I'm surprised he hasn't fainted.

"Hey. You're all right. Just stay calm." I'm not particularly fond of snakes. However, I'm not terrified like Jason. "Focus on my voice. We have to—"

"Those are *cobras*!" He's panting even harder and rubbing his chest like he's trying to stay warm. "I can't . . . I can't breathe . . ."

"Jason, I need you to calm down, okay? Just focus on my voice!"

"THERE ARE COBRAS EVERYWHERE."

"Didn't you say it's all an illusion? They're not going to hurt us!" Ryujin shouts.

Jason chokes on his own spit. He's crying, shaking, struggling to breathe.

Fuck this. I have to keep going.

"You're holding us back, Jason! Hurry up!" I sprint and kick as many cobras as I can. They fly across the pit. Every second that passes is a second closer to Mami, and my burning legs are working overtime. "This is just an illusion! They can't hurt us! It's all a stupid trick!"

Fangs latch onto my wrist.

A large cobra bites me like I'm its first meal in weeks. Its fangs sink deeper until they scratch bone. Then the cobra whips its head back. It tears my skin right off.

Heat binds the wound tight . . . a bandage made of searing, unbearable pain . . . my ears ring with screaming . . . hissing . . . the gargled sounds bubbling out of me . . .

I drop as the world goes dark.

THIRTEEN

I WAKE TO THE SMELL OF FUDGE, coconuts, and lime.

"Good. I *knew* you'd react to this glorious frosting."

Aro sits next to my bed. There's a tray of donuts on his lap and dark circles under his eyes. They're barely cracked open; not even the sugar rush can fully awaken him.

"How are you feeling?" he asks. "Do you want a bite of this? Do you need to go to the bathroom? I can get a female guard to help you. I'd carry you myself, but I charge five million dollars for piggyback rides and I don't think you can afford it." Aro smiles.

"Why are you . . ."

Memories of the sandpit crash down like a tidal wave of screams and hisses. The last thing I remember was passing out after the biggest cobra bit into my wrist. I search for the wound. Someone has wrapped a thick bandage around it; I must still have ugly bite marks or dried blood on my skin. Thankfully, there's no searing pain when I touch the cloth. But now I know better—if I get hurt during a magical challenge, the injury will remain outside of it, too. Injuries that are much more lethal than I could've imagined. I shudder at the thought of getting another cobra bite. What if there are even more terrible things waiting for us in these next challenges? Were the cobras just a prelude to something much worse?

Then I remember Feyn's words.

If you fail any challenge, you're officially eliminated from the Exchange and will be sent home.

"Oh my God. I haven't lost, have I? Am I going *home*?"

I push off the bed. The quick motion makes me nauseous. It feels like someone is drilling through my skull, so I lay back against my pillows.

Aro holds out a hand. "Hey, hey. Easy. Our nurses healed you, but you might still get a little dizzy. You've been unconscious for a very long time."

"How long?"

"Well, it's officially the second day, so you—"

"*What?* Did Jason and Ryujin complete the challenge? If they found the child's heart, I'm not going home, right?" I shake my head. "I can't go home, Aro. You know I can't."

Aro puts the donut tray on my bedside table. He moves slower than usual, as if his muscles are tight with soreness. "All three winners must work together in order to finish a magical task. If you fail to work as part of the team, you're the automatic loser simply because you can't be trusted. It's not a direct competition between humans, but if you don't obey the rules, you're out. I'm told you forged ahead without helping or waiting for the others."

He grabs a donut and licks a bit of its frosting. He sighs like he's experiencing the closest thing to euphoria. Then he frowns. "Jason has ophidiophobia. Snakes are his literal worst nightmare. He was never going to react the way you wanted him to, and your impatience got the best of you."

"We were short on time!"

"He wasn't in a position to think rationally. That includes dwelling on how much time you had left." Aro bites into the side of his donut. At least he chews with his mouth closed. "More important, you wouldn't have been in a losing situation if you'd visited me like I asked."

Seeing him remember the invitation to his beach house is promising. Chances are this is the same Aro that spoke to me during the welcome feast. But if he'd been busy with his UNICEF meeting, when exactly would he have had the chance to give me the winning clue?

"To answer your question," he says, "you *are* going home. Those are the rules."

"No! You can't do this to me!"

"You did this to yourself."

"Okay, then I won't do it again! Just give me a chance. *Please!*"

"If you stopped yelling, maybe I could get a word in." Aro yawns into his gloved hand. Then he shakes his head like he's trying to keep himself awake. "The rules say you have to leave Eterna. Feyn is more than ready to send you home. So am I . . . unless you do what I ask."

Another deal? Is he serious?

Then again, I'm in no position to reject his bargain. If this will stop me from getting kicked off the island, so be it. Aro is just one prince, though. I need both to be on the same page.

"Feyn is okay with this?" I whisper. "He'll let me stay if I follow your command?"

"I convinced him to let me speak with you. He doesn't know what I'm going to request, but my brother trusts me." Aro glances at his ring. "I've confirmed Doctor Alberto Ramírez's identity. We have guards stationed throughout the mainland in case of rebel attacks. I ordered a few to visit the doctor's house and his workplace." Aro looks back at me. "He's gone."

So he made it out, after all. That shouldn't surprise me. He's a crafty man. I don't know what's in store for him. If he'll continue to live as Alberto Ramírez or if he'll change his name. If he'll ever wonder how *I'm* doing and try searching for his friend's only child.

The pit in my stomach tells me he won't. Eight months working for a man who never cared about me. I was merely an instrument to him. The one who did all the dirty work. Now I'm trapped on the elves' island while the doctor books the first flight to God-knows-where.

"Do you know where he could be hiding?" says Aro.

"No. We were close, but . . . well . . . I *thought* we were close."

"Giving you money doesn't make someone your friend."

I cock an eyebrow. "I know that. But he was my *father's* friend. And after he was murdered, I wanted to—"

My words hang in the humid air between us.

Words I didn't expect to speak in the prince's presence.

But he watches me like we're speaking of the weather. Something normal. Either he doesn't want to turn this into a big deal, or his experiences with murdered relatives have stripped him of the shock and awe that anyone else would show. And my third theory is . . .

He already *knew*.

"You researched the doctor," I say. "Did you find anything about my father, too?"

"They went to school together. I recognized your surname in the class photos. It's not an uncommon surname in Puerto Rico, but I did some digging anyway, especially since you resemble Eduardo." Aro closes his eyes and bows his head slightly. "I know what it's like to have rebels take those you love. I'm sorry you know how it feels, too, Sevim. And I'm sorry that someone you considered a family friend took advantage of your grief."

I never expected him to put the blame on the doctor. I approached him with the offer, after all, and even if Aro doesn't know that, he knows I'm capable of making my own decisions. He's seen me act selfish before. But pointing the finger at the adult . . . acknowledging I was being used . . . it shows me a sensible side to Aro. Like he just gets it. How can he understand me so well without knowing anything beyond the most basic things? And how has he always been so comfortable around me? It's starting to make me feel comfortable around him, too. It's more than feeling seen. I feel . . . safe.

He could still be tricking you.

"Thank you, Your Highness," I say drily. "Sometimes we trust the wrong people because there's no one else left, and our grief won't let us find the right ones. They could come to us with neon signs hanging around their necks and we still wouldn't see them."

"True. Also, things like loyalty, friendship . . . it's all complicated," Aro whispers.

"Actually, they're quite simple. Those loyal to you would do everything in their power to keep you safe and to not betray you. If they do, they were never loyal."

The prince stares off into the distance. "That's how you see it?"

"Yes."

"Hmm."

He falls silent, still looking away. It's like he's lost in thought or deep in memories.

"And to answer your question," I cut through the awkward silence, "I don't know Doctor Ramírez well enough to suspect his current whereabouts. He doesn't have a family of his own. He doesn't work for other institutions outside of Puerto Rico. I don't remember him mentioning destinations he'd like to visit, either. If you say he's gone, then he really is."

"What was your last conversation about?"

"He offered me five thousand dollars to bring him your body."

"*That's* what I'm worth to him?" He waves at his chest like it's the main dish at a royal banquet. "Others would pay millions for all this. And that still wouldn't be enough."

I bite down to avoid bursting into laughter.

"You can admit it." Aro waves even faster. "This is as high value as it gets."

"So can I stay in Eterna, Your Highness? I answered your questions. Or is there anything more you're curious about?" Maybe swerving to a different topic is rude, but Aro is wasting precious time. Besides, I'd like to avoid any opportunity to praise him.

He takes forever to speak again. But when he finally does, he smiles.

"You can stay, Sevim."

"Oh, thank God! And thank *you*. I won't make you regret it, Prince Aro. I'll be more patient with Jason and Ryujin and complete each mission accordingly!"

"Don't make promises you can't keep."

"I can keep this one. I *have* to. And I'll listen to you next time, Your Highness. I'm so sorry about not visiting you at the beach house." I shrug. "What, um . . . what did you do when I didn't show up? You look exhausted, if I may say so."

Aro coughs. He wipes his lips with the back of his hand. "I apologize for my rugged appearance. I barely slept. There was a little scuffle before the strength challenge. Some rebels had been hiding near my beach house and attacked. Everything's been handled, but it drained me, so I sat out the challenge. I didn't want anyone to worry about me, though." He looks straight into my eyes, grinning shamelessly. "Were you worried about me?"

"No."

I scoot to the other side of the mattress. Not only is his flirtation cringeworthy, but this is the first time I'm alone in my room with someone of a different gender—one I'm attracted to. And I'm in *bed*. So what if I was in need of medical assistance? Ciel or one of the nurses could've watched over me. Even though he somehow makes me feel safe, there's no excuse for allowing Aro into my bedroom, especially when I'm in such a vulnerable state and—I cannot stress this enough—*in bed*. Thank God I'm still wearing yesterday's clothes, which includes the rose choker Aro is blatantly staring at.

"Velvet suits you," he says softly. "You should have more in your wardrobe."

"In the tropics? Are you kidding me?"

"No. I wear it all the time." He raises his gloved hand. "It's quite comfortable."

"And sweaty."

"Sometimes. But I can handle it."

"Well, good for you." I quickly look to the door, wondering if anyone is going to barge in and put a stop to this nonsense. "So you said you were fighting rebels?"

"Yes."

That's not what Ciel told me. She could've lied to avoid causing concern—a rebel sighting could mean more are on the way. Or maybe this isn't the same Aro I'd spoken to yesterday.

Then how does he know about the invitation to his beach house?

I hate how easy it is for him to confuse me. How I can go from feeling slightly comfortable to not knowing what the hell is going on within seconds. But the elf that tricked me into coming here would want to punish me further, right? He wouldn't give me hints that help me save Mami—just make me think I'm being helped in order to fool me again. I should still take the risk and learn whatever it is this Aro has to say. If it's fake, I'll never listen to him again, and if it's true, he'll prove himself as the closest · thing to an elf ally I have on this island.

"Now that we've agreed I can stay here," I say, "you can tell me the clue."

"You're sure you want it?"

"Of course."

"Like, *really* want it?"

I scowl. "Yes, Your Highness."

Aro's laugh bounces off the walls. "Fine. You failed the strength challenge because you weren't a team. Humans need to find strength in *each other* so they may overcome their fears and doubts. You acted solo instead of listening to Jason and Ryujin, and also by leaving Jason to suffer through the cobras alone. That's not how this works."

"We need to be a team? Is that your big clue?"

"Only part of it." Aro tries sitting up straight, but he winces like his back is on fire. He settles into a slouch. "You'll have a second chance at the strength challenge today. It'll have the same obstacles, but the final leg must be solved with knowledge only you possess in the group. You should think about the inscription's message carefully before making your choice."

"I have to choose between . . ."

"That's all I can reveal. You're welcome."

I won't thank him yet. I still need to see if he's telling the truth.

The bedroom door slams open.

Raff barges inside.

"Oh, hey," says Aro. Then he signs something to his best friend. I read his lips: *I was about to come get you. I think she's feeling better.*

Good, Raff signs back, but he doesn't smile or show any type of positive emotion. His expression is colder than a lonely winter. *We're ready for her.*

"Ready for me?" I ask. "Am I doing the strength challenge right now?"

"That'll be in the afternoon. Raff is talking about your first dream study session." Aro slowly pushes himself off the chair. "It's time to dig into that mysterious mind."

FOURTEEN

WALKING TO THE MAIN COTTAGE LASTS forever and yet no time at all.

I appreciate Aro and Raff escorting me in silence, but they move too fast. The guards behind me are rushing along, too. We enter the royal manor as one.

Elves in plain clothes are leaving fruit and vegetable crates. Coconuts, pears, apples, tomatoes, and cabbage make up the majority of the goods. For the most part, elves are vegetarians, but they're obsessed with lionfish, which is also brought in. It's the only known animal in their diet. Count this as *one* good thing the elves have done. Without the ravenous lionfish invading Caribbean and Atlantic waters, our coral reefs can thrive. The elves are mostly concerned with how good the lionfish tastes to them, but their eating habits also benefit the environment.

"¡Wow, qué bueno verlos! ¡Muchísimas gracias por su ayuda!"

Aro takes his time to shake each hand vigorously. He tells everyone to claim hot meals in the kitchen. If we were in another country, farmers and fishermen would receive monetary compensation, but Eterna doesn't have currency. Sunlight replenishes soil and sea, too. Just like houses can store energy through solar panels, rays are the island's magical power source. They provide whatever the community requires for sustenance. Running, purified water; medicinal plants; fruits ripe for the picking; their precious iron. Commoners simply collect the island's gifts and receive equal shares of everything—perks of being 1 out of 835 inhabitants.

"I think they'll love the donuts I picked out this time. I hid the glazed ones for myself, of course, but they always choose the ones with filling anyway," says Aro.

"That's what you call a hot meal?" I say.

"No. Sugar is just for dessert. But if I had it my way, we could—"

Raff presses a hand on his back, rushing him through the servants sweeping the floors and watering the plants. He signs something quickly.

"I know we're late, Raff. Let's hurry up before Feyn throws a fit."

We go from one archway to the next. Most of these chambers are sitting rooms, dressing rooms, galleries with smaller portraits and other artworks. There's even a chess room; a board covers the entire floor with human-sized pieces. I can't imagine Feyn and Aro having the patience for such games. This must've belonged to their parents or older brother.

One archway leads to a wooden staircase. It's lowering deeper and deeper into a cavernous, dimly lit corridor. Iron torches hang on both walls. The flames flicker as if in order, starting from the very first torch to the last. The wooden steps creak under my boots. A cave's entrance lies at the end of the stairs. Jagged rock walls envelop me as I follow the prince and his best friend.

This is farther underground than I thought. And it's also quite barren. I stay alert for any sign of gold light, even if it's just the slightest flicker, but there are no ensueños down here. Dirt and stone keep me company all the way to the study chamber. The handful of guards present are facing its very center, where Feyn and Ciel are lost in conversation.

There's an empty bed between them.

It's king-sized with black cotton sheets—comfortable enough for me to sleep on. But the closer I get, the more awake I become. How am I expected to sink into peaceful slumber with all eyes on me? Knowing my innermost thoughts will be poked and prodded like lab rats? That I'm powerless against how my own mind works?

I can't think about the doctor and the bodies. They could show up in my dreams. Aro knows about them, but Feyn doesn't. I don't want to see what happens if he finds out.

"Sevim! How are you today?" Ciel waves me over. "Do you feel any pain? Discomfort?"

"No. I'm all patched up."

"Excellent. Right this way, mi vida."

I avoid the lingering stares as I approach her. She patiently watches me sit down first, then lie as stiff as a slab of wood. Even though Feyn is also beside me, I only focus on the smiling elf in her dark floral dress. Ciel offers me a hand. I take it.

"First of all, thank you so much for participating in our studies, Sevim! Prince Feyn will give you an elixir so you can fall asleep. Usually, humans enter the dreaming state at once, but this isn't always guaranteed. Whenever your dreams start, everything you see will be projected on these walls." She points to the rocks around us. "I'll be conducting the extractions. This process won't hurt you *one bit*, ¿está bien? You have no reason to be nervous."

Easy for you to say.

"Since dreams can't be removed without consent, it's important for you to answer clearly," says Ciel. "Do you grant us permission to access your subconscious?"

She says it like I actually have a choice.

Like my hands aren't tied to a fate I never asked for.

"Yes," I reply. "But just as a caveat, I don't really dream. You might not be able to find anything. And if I do have dreams, I never remember them."

"We'll take our chances." Feyn brings a glass vial to my lips. Pastel blue liquid swirls inside. This is definitely not Doctor Ramírez's golden elixir. "Drink."

Clear your mind, Sevim . . .

I grab the vial and down it in one go. Feyn snatches it back, then storms off to where Aro and Raff are watching me intently. I rest my head even lower on the pillows, waiting for my skin to tingle or burst with heat. But all I feel is my chest rising and falling with every quick breath.

Then the room blurs. I can barely keep my eyelids up.

Clear . . . your . . .

I'm sitting alone on the beach.

The sun is hot and bright enough to be close to noon. A light breeze ruffles my hair in different directions. Seagulls dive into the gold-specked water to retrieve their lunch.

I pick up a fistful of black sand. What we have on the mainland is much rougher; this feels like powdered sugar, even though the grains are just as big.

Something explodes on the coast of Vieques.

I flinch as another blast soon follows. Then another.

Heavy artillery drowns out the squawking of seagulls, the crashing of waves against shore.

Screams break out across the island.

I can't see anything except thick smoke . . . towering flames . . . the screaming rushes through the coastline until it finds me . . . louder with each sweep of breeze across my skin . . .

I run to the water.

I don't know who I'm running to—I just know they're dying. They need someone to stop the smoke, the fire, the pain. As soon as my waist is submerged in water, I swim toward Vieques in a rush of adrenaline and terror, wishing the current could propel me forward faster.

Someone grabs my ankle.

They pull.

I sink deeper into thrashing waves. Then I kick down to free myself.

But I can't see who's holding me. A steel grip crushes my ankle yet there's no hand around it. I'm flailing, trying to push myself back to the surface, and falling instead.

Laughter echoes nearby. It sounds like a *man*.

Then . . . a monstrous, bloodcurdling roar . . .

I release a scream that turns into bubbles. I swallow more and more water, filling my lungs until they're drowning and bursting in pain and—

"*Sevim!*"

I wake in the black bed again. I've locked Ciel in a hug I'm sure she never asked for. My wild eyes land on familiar sights—the cavernous walls, the bitter coldness of Feyn's scowl, Aro and Raff's matching furrowed brows—but none comfort me. The sheets are damp with my pouring sweat; I'm panting as if I've sprinted around the entire island.

"What was that? My dream . . . I don't know . . ."

"Dispose of it, Ciel. It's not useful." Feyn cuts me off without bothering to look in my direction. It's like the very thought of me disgusts him.

I keep my arms around Ciel. I've never heard of elves tossing dreams out like trash, and she's not going anywhere until I get answers.

"Why isn't it useful, Your Highness?" I say. "I have no idea what just let loose in my mind, but a dream is still a dream, isn't it?"

"Do you have a personal relationship with anyone from Vieques?" Feyn asks.

Every muscle in my body stiffens. "Yes, my father was raised there."

"And you've visited Vieques before?"

"No, but—"

"So he's the one who's actually been there?"

"Yes, but—"

"Have you ever drowned, Sevim?"

"Uh . . . no."

"Have you felt unsafe while swimming? Or at the beach?"

"No."

"Do you recognize the man's laugh?"

I grip the sheets tighter, heaving a defeated sigh. The only man's laugh I ever knew was my father's. It was a low yet hearty sound; not too gravelly and not too soft. Papi would pick me up and spin me around in our living room. He cracked up whenever I struck a flying Superman pose in the air. That's why he carried me often. My silliness made him happy.

"No," I reply. "Are you going to ask me if I know the monster, too?"

If looks could kill, Feyn would be burning me at the stake, bringing me back to life, then burning me all over again. "Let Ciel go. She needs to breathe." He hisses.

When I release her, she taps my forehead. I feel a slight rush of warmth.

It disappears a second later.

"All done!" she confirms. "You won't have the same nightmare during our next session. The moment it's extracted, its host may never experience it again."

"I still don't understand why it's useless."

"It's not personal enough," says Feyn. "Our magic requires something more aligned with your life experiences. Your emotions should drive whatever your subconscious is creating."

"But I was screaming. Clearly, I felt afraid."

"You were *reacting* to what was around you. You were never in control."

"It's a nightmare, Your Highness. How many nightmares can you control? Oh, wait. You can't even dream."

Should I be antagonizing the elf that creates our magical challenges? One with full access to my mind during its most vulnerable state? No.

He shouldn't treat me like I'm a disposable weakling, either.

Feyn stomps toward the cave's entrance. "We don't need your pathetic excuse of a dream. Your last strength challenge will be commencing shortly. *Don't* be late."

"I certainly won't be, Your Highness."

He picks up the pace as he exits.

"May I?" Aro offers me a hand. "I can back off, if you'd like." He looks down at the bed, reminding me this is the second time we've interacted while I was in one.

But all I can think about is Feyn.

Maybe the nightmare really wasn't as personal as he needs. There must be a reason why I had it, though—just like there must be another reason why he got rid of it.

And why he wouldn't let me dream more.

FIFTEEN

WITH AN HOUR TO SPARE BEFORE the second strength challenge, I grab a blank notebook from my bedroom shelf, open the very first page, and fill it with angry scribbles.

Then I write a brand new sentence: *The beach was on fire.*

I wish I had energy to add more details. My nightmare is never coming back. I should immortalize it on paper to dissect whatever the hell it means in secret.

But the words don't come. I reread the only sentence I can pull out of my rattled brain, wondering if I'll ever be worthy of calling myself a writer. Then again, I've just experienced the wildest dream of my life, and it was stolen. Maybe I should cut myself some slack and take a nap.

Another sentence sneaks onto the page: *The Garden Witch never liked to share.*

This is the villain Mami wants me to create in her image. So far, I only have her name—which will probably change tomorrow—and that singular fact about her personality.

I keep writing until I end up with a paragraph.

The Garden Witch never liked to share. She hoarded seeds and fruits the same way a queen held on to silk and diamonds. Men from all over the kingdom asked for her hand in marriage. Her beauty was legendary, but her psychic powers had a greater reputation. She could hear anyone's thoughts and pluck them out of their heads. She made their wildest dreams real—things the dreamer could see, hear, and touch. Most men wanted to take the gold coins in their minds and hold them in their greedy hands. But a few wanted to re-create a lost one's body, voice, personality. They wanted the Garden Witch to bring back the dead.

I don't know where this story is going, but at least the words are written.

They make me think about Mami even more. If she were here, she'd tell me this is good just because she's determined to keep me writing. Her feedback wouldn't be trustworthy from a craft perspective, but it would be the fuel I need to continue with whatever this story is.

There's no point in finishing it if I fail another challenge, though. I won't just be losing my mother—I'll lose the will to do anything other than mourn her.

And avenge her.

Prince Feyn speaks into a loudspeaker again, calling the

winners to the royal garden.

My second chance begins now.

—————— ℓ ℓ ℓ ——————

ONCE AGAIN, THE GARDEN HAS become a mirror maze.

Jason and Ryujin are already there when I arrive. We're barely exchanging hellos when Feyn repeats yesterday's instructions.

"You have *thirty minutes* to bring me the child's heart."

"Yes, Your Highness," we say.

Both princes nod to signal the start of our challenge. They watch us in silence from their glass stage in the sky. Aro nods again, as if he's trying to encourage me. Or maybe he wants me to remember the final leg will rely on something only *I* know. His vague clue isn't filling me up with confidence right now, but we have to start moving.

"We should each punch a mirror and get a sword," I say. "They'll help with the cobras."

"Now, now . . . Let's take it down a notch." Jason is already sweating.

"You need to stay behind us. We can fight them off. Right?" I ask Ryujin.

She looks from Jason to the nearest mirror. "I can try," she whispers. "I *want* to try."

"That's the spirit. Now go get your swords."

I run to the same mirror as before. After a swift punch, the glass melts again, then molds into the sharp weapon I once carried. Ryujin and Jason strike with softer blows, but they still get their swords. All three have FOR THE CHILD'S HEART inscribed around the hilts.

The little boy's laugh returns.

All the mirrors start spinning, then rearranging in brusque movements, as if an invisible giant hand is shoving them aside. We have an unobstructed path forward now. The boy is laughing louder. He still sounds like he's down the empty clearing ahead.

"Sandpit time," I whisper.

"You could've just kept that to yourself. I can still *hear you*," says Jason.

"Ryujin and I will protect you, but if anything jumps at you, make sure you don't stab *us*."

All he can do is keep his wide eyes ahead.

"We're going to start walking now, Jason. Stay close, okay?"

He doesn't respond.

I sigh. "Come on, Ryujin."

She squeezes the hell out of my shoulder. "Wait."

"For fuck's sake. Don't tell me you're scared, too."

"No. Look at the mirrors."

Full-length portrait paintings have replaced them. Each has a background in sheer, crinkled strokes of orange, similar to the woman's dress in Frederic Leighton's *Flaming June*.

Each painting features one of us.

But we don't have eyes.

There's no blood or torn skin—just empty sockets. Like dark holes to another dimension.

A shaking Ryujin releases me. "This wasn't here yesterday. Where's the sandpit? And what are we supposed to do with these horrible paintings?"

"I don't know, but I choose this over cobras any day." Jason pats his forehead dry. He's breathing steadier and faster. "We should focus on the missing eyes. Could it mean there's something we're not seeing clearly? Are we looking away from the truth?"

"Or is this a distraction?" I ask. "The elves could be toying with us so that we waste time. How are these portraits relevant to our mission?" I point my sword toward the clear path ahead. "We're searching for a child's heart. We're not going to find it in those sockets."

"What if we did? That's the last place you'd think of looking for it," says Ryujin.

"Elves would never make it this easy. Right, Jason?" I know they wouldn't, but confirming with our resident elf expert will validate my theory. Besides, the more I include others in my decisions, the stronger our teamwork becomes—the key to winning this heinous challenge.

Jason grimaces. "Yeah. It seems too simple. We have to approach this differently."

"And we have to hurry," I remind him.

"But I'm not entirely opposed to what Ryujin suggests. These paintings are important. We can't keep going until we're a hundred percent certain about their meaning."

I dig my nails into my scalp. Then I bite down to suppress a soul-ripping scream. Leaving them behind is nonnegotiable—I can't repeat yesterday's mistakes—but they're not making my choice to stick with them any more bearable. Why can't they *listen* to me? Humans shouldn't be this gullible! This is what the elves want!

"Sevim? Are you okay?" Jason draws closer.

"No. We need to go, and all we're doing is analyzing some damn holes. What on Earth are they supposed to mean, Jason? You're so convinced they're relevant. How are they relevant?"

"That's what I'm *trying* to figure out."

"Please don't argue," says Ryujin.

"We're not arguing!" Jason and I yell.

The paintings are hissing.

Cobras slither out of the sockets, then drop like brown ropes onto the grass. They keep falling and piling onto each other until the maze is overrun.

"Shit." I press my back against Jason. "Stay behind us!"

Ryujin hurries next to me. We raise our swords and block Jason from the loud, frantic snakes skittering around. They bump into my boots, ruffle the hem of my skirt, lick the air with those sharp tongues. I try counting them, but more pour out of the paintings.

"Watch their mouths," I tell Ryujin. "They'll bite us if we're not careful."

"You attacked them first. That's why you were bitten."

"No, it wasn't."

"Yes, it was, Sevim. You kicked and stomped everything around you. It was horrible."

"How else am I supposed to get past them *and* stay on time?"

Ryujin gulps as she peeks at Jason. "Whatever you do, don't let go." She hooks his arms around ours. It's much harder to hold my sword steadily, but knowing Jason won't be staying behind or fleeing makes me feel better. "We should move as one. Like this." Ryujin slides one sneaker across the grass. It lightly touches a cobra.

The animal slithers aside.

Three others follow suit, clearing up more of the moss-green patches ahead.

"You're joking," I say. "*This* is all it takes? We just tap them and they get out of the way?"

"Strength isn't always about force. I learned that early on as a gymnast. Sometimes our minds overpower everything else." Ryujin lowers her head. I'm about to tell her not to dwell on her past when she says, "And if that happens, we need to slow down, not push through."

"But we have powers. We even have *swords*. Why not take advantage of that?"

"Slow down. Don't push through," she repeats. "Trust me."

Humans need to find strength in each other so they may over-come their fears and doubts.

That's what Aro said. Teamwork isn't just about sticking together and being supportive—it's about accepting someone else has the answers you seek, even if you don't like it. I've never played sports. I can't even remember the last time I participated in academic activities outside of class. But trusting others is important in any group dynamic, isn't it? And if there's someone who'd know that well here, it's the only athlete in our trio.

"Okay, let's go slow." I squeeze Jason's arm tighter. "Close your eyes."

He immediately obeys.

Ryujin and I move first, then pull him forward. My boots slowly rub against scales. I stop once the coiled ropes push off the grass, fearing another lightning-fast strike, but they hurry out of our path. Whenever I tap a snake, it slides away as if it's late for a hunt. Only a few tense up and expose their forked tongues. I hold my breath and aim my sword down in case they jump.

None retaliate.

"We're doing good," Ryujin whispers. "Remember. Slow down."

"Don't push through," I finish.

"Yes."

It takes an eternity to get past them—Ryujin is *determined* to go at a snail's pace—but seeing these fanged predators ignore us gives me the confidence to continue. It reassures me we're going to win even if we're much closer to the thirty-minute mark than intended.

Mami, I won't let you down again.

Once the last cobra speeds off, I breathe a sigh of relief. "We fucking did it."

"Whatforrealwedidit?" Jason speaks way too fast.

"Yes. Open your eyes."

He looks out at the empty maze. His whole body relaxes like a deflated balloon. Ryujin and I have to prop him up, but we're smiling through it.

"Oh, my sweet Jesus . . . They're really gone," says Jason.

"Now what?" I say. "Can you hear the child? I feel like he disappeared once the snakes—"

The paintings are spinning.

They sink deep underground as if Hades beckons them.

Cavernous walls rise in their place. We're surrounded by the same jagged rock that wraps around the dream study chamber. I can barely see anything in such a dimly lit cave.

But there's no hiding the three wooden coffins ahead.

They're big enough to fit a toddler.

SIXTEEN

"ARE YOU . . . SEEING . . . THREE COFFINS, TOO?" Jason asks.

"Ne. Oh, sorry," says a flustered Ryujin. "Yes."

I can't push out a single word. Do they have real children inside? Or are we supposed to put children *in* them? Both options are disturbing, mostly because it reminds me of the rebels. How can Feyn and Aro stand against human murders and design such a twisted challenge?

There's an inscription at the edge of each coffin.

Two sentences I keep rereading.

STAB THROUGH THE WOOD. HURT NO LIVING THING.

"This is why we needed swords," I whisper. "Does that mean there are kids inside?"

"I don't think those coffins will open until we follow instructions," Jason laments.

Maybe there aren't any children in danger. But I can't shake the feeling real kids *will* get hurt if we don't decode whatever this inscription is talking about. I memorize it and move on to studying the different animals carved into the wood. The first coffin has a ladybird, a butterfly, a moth, and worms spread around them. There's a bat, a cricket, a gnat, a beetle, and a grasshopper in the middle coffin. And on the third one, a frog, a tiger, a bear, and a goat sit side by side.

"Is there a pattern with these animals?" Ryujin asks.

"Aside from the fact that they're animals? Nothing's coming to mind," says Jason.

I tune their nervous chatter out as Aro's words flood my thoughts.

You'll have a second chance at the strength challenge today. It'll have the same obstacles, but the final leg must be solved with knowledge only you possess in the group. You should think about the inscription's message carefully before making your choice.

Stabbing is just a command. We can't act before understanding the second part.

"Hurt no living thing . . . ."

"What?" Jason and Ryujin say.

"That's our clue. We can't hurt whatever is alive from this group of animals."

Jason cocks his head. "But they all exist. They're actual species that—"

"Hurt no living thing," I repeat. If this *is* the challenge's final leg, then it's my turn to save us. Biology isn't my strength—I must look at these carvings through the eyes of Victorian poetry and literature. None of the books I've read come to mind as relevant, but there *is* one poem that begins with the same words in the inscription's second sentence.

"Have you heard of Christina Rosetti?" I ask Jason.

"That's the 'Goblin Market' lady, right?"

"Yes, it's the poem she's mostly known for, but she wrote another that starts with this." I aim my sword at the inscription. "She mentioned specific animals we need to protect. I think those that aren't in the poem are the ones on the coffin we should stab through."

Jason and Ryujin raise their eyebrows.

"Please tell us you remember all the animals correctly," Ryujin whispers.

"Whoa, wait a minute. How can you be sure this is about that Rosetti poem?"

"It's literally the same verse and creatures, Jason. The first and middle coffins." I take turns saying their names aloud. "Those are featured in her poem. But the frog, tiger, bear, and goat," I move toward the third coffin, "are not."

"Yes, but——"

"Three minutes left." Feyn's voice spills down toward us like a blast of cold water.

"It's this one, you guys. We have to stab it now." I'm already holding my sword up.

Jason stands between the coffin and me. "Wait! Are you *a hundred percent* sure?"

I can't blame him for not trusting me. My first challenge will haunt me forever.

But I'll never make the same mistakes again.

I nod. "It's this one."

Ryujin lifts her sword, too. "I trust you." She looks at Jason. "We have to do it together."

He glances up at Feyn, sighing hopelessly. "Let this be right . . ." Jason stands next to me and raises his sword just as high as I am. "Count us down, Sevim."

"One. Two. Three!"

We stab the third coffin.

Blood spills beneath the wood.

SEVENTEEN

E'VE FAILED THE MISSION.

Despite my best efforts, my expertise, we've failed.

And even worse, we *stabbed* someone. Why else would there be so much blood? It keeps pooling out so, so fast, a river rushing out of the doomed coffin.

"Did we just kill . . ." I can't even finish. The thought of harming anyone, let alone a child, devours my conscience inch by inch. This was supposed to work, unless the final leg of the challenge hasn't even started yet. Have I acted prematurely again?

"You told us to pick this one!" Jason yells.

"Stay calm. Let's get these out now." Ryujin taps her sword.

I quickly yank mine out alongside her and Jason. The three of us step back, trying to escape the red liquid, but it fills the cave in the blink of an eye.

We're drowning.

I brace for an overwhelming taste of copper, but it's as bland as water. Much thicker, though, and wild like the waves in Thomas Hope McLachlan's *The Isles of the Sea* painting. I choke and cough and flail around for something to hold, but the current moves too fast.

Ryujin's screams are muffled whenever she goes under. But she breaks for air again, screaming loud enough to shake the Earth's core. "I can't swim! Please help——"

She's pulled down.

"Hang on!" Jason dives toward her.

I swim, too. The rolling waves won't loosen their grip on me. They knock my sword away.

Then swallow it to the depths, where it'll rest forever.

"Fuck!" I burn everywhere from swimming against the current. I spit out each drop of red flooding into my open mouth, frantically searching for Jason and Ryujin. Whenever he pulls her back up, they're mercilessly dragged underwater. He can't save her by himself. "I'm coming! Just hold on, okay? I'll be right there!"

Something glints at the opposite end of the cave.

I gasp—a small red jewel floats by itself. It doesn't have veins or valves; I don't think it was ever inside a real human's chest cavity. But its shape is unmistakable.

The child's heart!

We had three minutes left when we stabbed through the wood. I won't have time to collect the heart *and* save the others. It's not just about winning the challenge—whatever happens to Jason and Ryujin here will affect them outside, too. Will they be unconscious like me? Or will they drown in real life? Jason is *barely* pulling Ryujin up as another wave sinks them. It's like our magical strength is no match for whatever this blood is made of!

The tide keeps rising.

The ceiling will pin me underwater in three seconds . . . two . . .

I punch down a wall.

The crimson sea spills out as if it were a waterfall—now there's a hole that leads down. I can't see what lies beyond. All I know is that it's draining the cave of blood. As it rushes in the opposite direction, I break into a furious swim. Aches and strains burden me, slow me down, but I don't stop until I'm close enough to Jason and Ryujin, who are barreling toward me.

I seize Jason's shirt. Pulling him is easy.

But I've forgotten how strong I am.

He crashes into me, pummeling all three of us to the hole.

"Hold on to the wall, guys! I found the child's heart! I'll lunge for it once it floats here!"

Ryujin is closest to the edge. With a scream, I lift Jason's upper body, and he does the same to her. Once she secures her grip on the wall, Jason stabs the rock, abruptly stopping us from spilling out of the hole. I dig my fingers into the rock, too, clinging for dear life.

"You said you found the heart?" Jason asks.

"Yes! It's right—"

The glinting jewel floats past me.

"THERE!"

I'm too far, too slow to catch it. Jason can't let Ryujin or his sword go.

Ryujin unleashes a desperate scream. She leans forward as far as she can, then drives her sword toward the child's heart.

Her blade pierces the jewel.

It doesn't shatter or crack. The heart remains in place as Ryujin pulls her sword in.

"You did it!" I yell. "You fucking did it!"

I land on grass.

I'm blood-drenched among roses. Jason and Ryujin lay next to me, shielding their eyes from the scorching sun. The cave walls, the coffins . . . it's all gone.

As we try to stand, wind blows over us, bringing with it more heat and a hint of crackling energy. Skin and muscle tighten together, then press down as if they're coating an additional layer on top—thick enough to withstand any blow. Even though I don't have a flat stomach, it's crunched hard and feels like I'm poking an armored truck. The air entering my lungs smells fresher, too; I can inhale twice as much now and it comes back out even crisper. I feel myself getting stronger, capable of carrying any building on my back and racing up a deadly mountain.

We're powering up . . .

"¡Felicidades!" Aro and Ciel say. They clap and whistle as if the clock has struck midnight on New Year's Eve. Raff is smiling, too, but he doesn't meet our gazes.

Feyn is the only one who stays behind. His glare could poison every root, stem, and petal in this garden. "Congratulations. You've won the strength challenge. Now you may move on."

I'm no stranger to his bitter tone.

But why does he sound like he wanted us to fail?

EIGHTEEN

THERE'S EVEN MORE FOOD TONIGHT.

Specifically, double the amount of dishes reserved for humans—our reward for today's victory. Seafood paella, braised chicken legs, seared scallops with lemon sauce, grilled pork spare ribs, coconut shrimp skewers, and eggplants stuffed with zucchini fill the dining table. Ryujin hoards the tofu wraps. She and Jason also share a butternut, chestnut, and lentil cake.

Fire breathers surround the table, spitting flames toward the clouds. Once again, the floating orbs are behind us, but the elves swim around water with a metallic sheen. Pinks and reds are the most prominent colors, as if silver paint is mixing with cotton candy and blood.

I quietly bite into a chicken leg. The meat slides off right away. It is *so* tender, seasoned to my heart's content with salt, pepper, and my beloved adobo.

Eating makes Feyn's coldness more bearable. He didn't speak again after declaring us the strength challenge's winners. He *is* staring at Jason. I don't know if it's because Jason won't shut up about his amazing cake or if he's checking him out. I've never heard about Feyn's love life, so if he won't even date his own species, the odds of him finding a human attractive are lower.

When the fire breathers leave, musicians take their place. They effortlessly play flutes and harps. Ciel sways to each note. The stars in her hair glint one by one. She clinks our water goblets and drinks, then returns to her seat next to the sourpuss prince.

"Raff wants to know if you're enjoying the chicken."

Aro sits to my right, signing to Raff what he's just told me.

Raff vigorously shakes his head. *I never asked that.*

Yes, you did. Don't lie to Sevim, a smiling Aro signs back. Then he looks at me. "He also wanted to congratulate you on solving the coffin's puzzle. That was amazing."

"Why are you using Raff as an excuse to talk to me?" I chew on my chicken leg.

"I'm not! He's been warming up to you ever since today's victory. Haven't you, Raff?"

The fast-driving elf rolls his eyes, but it's nowhere as disdainful as Feyn would be. It's more like he's embarrassed. Maybe he *is* warming up to me and doesn't want me to know.

"He officially thinks you're cool now." Aro pats him on the back. "An intellectual."

"Thank you, Raff. You're cool, too," I say.

He reads my lips and nods as if he's always known he's cool. Then he stuffs a handful of lettuce into his mouth.

"Since there's barely any chicken on that leg, you *are* enjoying it," says Aro. "Am I right?"

"You are, Your Highness."

"What does it taste like?"

I squint as I remember the elves don't eat meat. Still, I can't be the first person to describe the taste of chicken to Aro. "No one's ever told you before?"

"They have. I've actually had a bite or two. I had a somewhat rebellious phase."

I almost laugh at the thought of eating chicken being considered rebellious. "Then why are you asking me?"

"Because I want to know what it tastes like to *you*." Aro meets my gaze only for a second, then puts all his focus on the glazed donut on his plate. "I want to see the world through your eyes. They seem fascinating." Aro grins. "*Annoying* and fascinating. Just like the rest of you."

Insulting and complimenting me at the same time. Suddenly I feel like I'm back in middle school. Boys never treated *me* this way. Loners in black clothing, heavy makeup, and chains don't often receive a lot of date invitations. I mostly observed them using these tactics on other girls. Some still use them in high school. It's like normal conversation isn't complete until a cisgender straight boy jokes about your appearance or personality.

I watch him savor the hell out of his donut in silence. He's probably waiting for a smartass comment. The last thing I want is to lower my frequency in order to match his—he can keep his middle school tactics for someone else. Right now, all I care about is his help. I should thank Aro for today's clue, but I also need him to *keep* giving me more. Today's challenge was still confusing. I'm guessing the remaining ones will be much harder. The more

I go into them with a clear head and confidence in what I'm doing, the easier it'll be to win.

But I can't be hasty or harsh with my demands, least of all in public. I can still butter Aro up, though. Being kind to him could get me what I want without ever asking for it.

I whisper, "Thank you for today, Aro. I couldn't have done anything without you."

"Are you serious?" His whisper is much lower than mine. "You could've solved that puzzle by yourself. All I did was speed up the process. If you hadn't known the answer was found in a poem, it would've taken you longer to figure out, but *your brilliance* earned you that win. Have you loved Victorian poetry and fiction for long?" He speaks that last question louder, as if we're in the clear to let others overhear us.

Not the change of topic I was hoping for, but I'll have to oblige.

"I started reading it because of my mother. School isn't my strong suit. I was failing most classes by seventh grade. I couldn't concentrate or give a shit about anything. All I did was draw terribly and daydream. I watched music videos for hours, too. Lots of German prog metal."

"Hmm. Do you speak German?"

"Not at all."

Aro laughs. "I'll have to teach you one day."

"*You* speak German?"

"Seven languages, actually. My older brother, Lexen, could speak eleven. We don't have your schooling system in Eterna, and we mostly learn how to develop our magic, but we educate ourselves in whatever interests us about your species, too. For example, Raff loves engines, so he scares half the population by racing at odd hours of the night. He stops during Exchange week. We don't want our guests to suffer heart attacks." Aro laughs again. "And I, as you know, love——"

"Donuts."

"Sugar," Aro clarifies. "But mainly donuts, yes. And foreign cultures. Being able to communicate with others is rewarding to me. I'm also fascinated with historical linguistics." He taps his fork against the plate. "Back to you, though. German prog metal."

"Yes. I was just trying to distract myself. *All* the time. But when Mami told me about her favorite poems and how they helped her focus better, I asked for recommendations."

Aro sips on his water goblet. "What were they?"

"Mostly works by women. Christina Rossetti, Mary Shelley, Emily Brontë, Elizabeth Barrett Browning . . . But there was a lot of Oscar Wilde. He's probably my favorite male poet."

"Probably?" Aro cocks an eyebrow as he leans closer. His grin is very much still present. "You should speak with conviction, Miss Burgos."

I hate how my cheeks flush when he calls me that.

I hate it even more that I can't remember what I was saying.

There should be a limit to how many times we can be this close, especially after he's watched over me while I slept. Not even an act of God could erase the awkwardness of seeing him just . . . there. It's been hours and I'm still hung up on it. What the hell is wrong with me?

Then again, he never stepped out of line or made me feel like a piece of meat. His genuine care for my well-being was quite . . . attractive. My fingers start itching for his skin. The warmth that only he can offer me without truly understanding what makes it so . . . enticing.

"Tell me a fun fact about any of these poets," he says. "Something you find lovely and bizarre at the same time."

Is this a test? Will he relay this information to Feyn for the next challenge?

"Well . . . One thing that shocked me was how many love letters Elizabeth Barrett Browning and her husband wrote to each other." I fail to see how this would be useful in a magical task, but I'm choosing honesty over strategy. Aro might see right through me if I try to outsmart him. "Robert Browning was a poet, too. He met his wife after reading her work and writing to her about how much he loved it. They exchanged the most romantic letters even after marriage."

"How many letters?"

"Five hundred and seventy-five."

Aro squints. "That's it?"

"Are you kidding? That's a *lot*."

"No, it isn't. I'd write much more than that to my love."

I let out a laugh. There's no way he's serious. He's just trying to sound as impressive as the whole world thinks he is. "Then I feel bad for your wrist," I say.

"Did your father write love letters to your mother?" Aro asks.

I stare at him blankly. "What?"

"I'm sorry. Is that inappropriate? You don't have to tell me anything."

"No, it's just such an unexpected question."

Aro blushes as he puts what's left of his donut down. He fixes his shirt even though it's in no need of fixing. "I shouldn't have asked, Sevim. I'm overstepping."

"You're fine. He . . . didn't write love letters. But he brought her flowers a lot. And he took her to botanical gardens. She *loves* them. When they met in Istanbul, my mom was visiting for the annual tulip festival, but she couldn't choose a park. My dad overheard her talking to herself in Spanish and asked if she needed help. After telling him she couldn't choose where to go, she asked him to pick for her. That was her way of flirting, I guess."

Aro and I laugh.

"What happened then?" he asks.

"My dad offered to take her to as many as they could visit in a day."

"And that was *his* way of flirting."

"Yes."

Aro nods. "A plant lady. She sounds wonderful."

My heart skips for a second. "She is," I whisper.

"And I might be biased, but seeing as your father and I are both from Vieques, I also think he was pretty amazing." Aro picks up his donut again but doesn't take a bite. It's like he needs to hold on to something while he loses himself in his thoughts. "I know my brother would never condone the rebels' atrocious acts against humans, but he agrees with them on Vieques. They don't see a future in which elves return to their homeland. They don't want to be part of a place that is no longer what we remember. A peaceful, lovely island before the U.S. Navy's arrival."

Aro sighs. Then he eats his donut as if he'd rather lose himself in sugar than whatever's running through his mind.

"And you?" I coax him. "What do you think elves should do about Vieques?"

He carefully sets the last chunk of donut down. "A lot," he says.

"Such as?"

"My campaign with UNICEF is important, but I have another goal I'd like to meet. I *do* want us to connect with our roots. I want to go back to Vieques, heal our land, and help the people who need us. This whole idea that we turned our backs on them makes me sick. I'd love nothing more than to show our neighbors we haven't abandoned them. We never will."

I turn to my half-eaten chicken leg, my cheeks burning even hotter. It doesn't matter how many love letters Aro can write. His compliments mean nothing. But hearing him speak of doing the one thing I've hoped for—the one thing his entire species *should* be doing—sets a thousand butterflies loose in my stomach. I never thought I would respect Prince Aro. That I would support him and wish for his goal to be met. That I would want to praise him for being selfless.

He can't resurrect my father. But if he can stop more Viequenses from becoming ill, if he can keep contamination levels at their all-time lowest, it would do more good than anyone has ever attempted in the history of his tiny island.

"You're really planning on helping them?" My voice can't rise above a whisper anymore. It's as if a spell has lowered it, and if I force it to sound louder, it'll fade forever instead.

"I have to," he says. "We can't leave our people. I don't care how long it takes. Our home will either be what it once was or much better. It can't continue the way it is now."

My body is an oven set to its highest temperature.

I *need* to ask about the next clue now. We can't derail this conversation any longer, but I can't let Aro see me blushing or acting like a little kid with a crush.

Because he is *not* my crush.

"Your Highness? I believe we're ready for your toast!" Ciel

speaks to Aro.

"Everyone! Time for a toast!" Aro stands with his water goblet and fork. He strikes it gently enough to alert the table. "I'm about to blow your minds with my eloquence."

Jason is the first to follow Aro's orders, of course. Ciel and Ryujin are next. Raff and I take a bit more time, moving as if an unknown force is pushing our limbs down.

Feyn doesn't raise his goblet.

"To the guests!" Aro speaks as if he can't see his brother being a jerk. "Today you showed courage, patience, selflessness, and teamwork—the very things required to win. Your reward was leveling into greater magical strength, but you truly deserve so much more. Without a doubt, you're our most admirable winners in Exchange history. It's an absolute *honor* to share my gift with you, and I'm excited to see you grow into these magical abilities."

"Calm down, Aro. This is uncalled for." Feyn seethes with indignation.

If a pin dropped, every inch of this island would hear it. Everyone stares at the angry elf, then at his frozen little brother. The only thing moving is Aro's chest as he breathes slower.

"But they did so well . . ." says Aro.

"After a horrible first challenge. They barely finished, too. What you call teamwork is just being dependent on someone else to take you away from fears you can't face." The elf prince snorts, then lets out a long, cruel laugh. "An athlete who can't swim . . . and Jason . . ." He doubles over. "His face when he saw those cobras! I've never seen anything more pathetic."

Jason slumps, putting his glass down. "I'm *not* pathetic, Your Highness." He says it firmly, but he's not looking at Feyn, as if eye contact would prove too high of a risk.

"Your behavior has shown me otherwise."

"Then pay more attention?"

I stop myself from gasping, but Ryujin lets it out. I wish Jason would keep going. That he hadn't said it like a question and had yelled at the top of his lungs. Feyn needs to be humbled, especially through someone he's underestimated.

But the elf prince's laughter only grows louder, crueler. "You can't even talk back without avoiding my gaze, Jason. Please. And Sevim—"

"Why the fuck are you so bitter?"

I've never sassed at Mami. Not even in my angriest moments. I just stomp around, slam doors, and shove things aside. My rage wouldn't let me communicate properly anyway—I don't have clever comebacks in my arsenal. Besides, my mother isn't *mean*; everything she's ever scolded me about has been because she knows I can do better. Because she loves me.

But Feyn is only full of hate.

He stops laughing. Then he knits his eyebrows as if he's struggling to accept what I've asked. To understand that a human cut him off and called him exactly what he is to his face.

"Su Alteza . . ." Ciel tries getting his attention, but he's only looking at me.

"*What* did you just say to me?" he barks.

"She didn't mean it!" Aro turns to me. "Right?"

This is my chance to drop it. Change the subject back to Aro's speech and carry on with what had been a relatively pleasant night—the first one since my arrival. But I catch another glimpse of Jason frowning at his cake and I want to wrestle the elf that made him feel like less.

"I apologize for speaking out of line," I say.

Aro sighs in relief. "There you go. She was just——"

"But you're out of line, too," I continue. "Jason can't control his phobia. Ryujin can't force herself to swim. And whatever you were going to say about me surely improved during our second opportunity anyway." Each word rushes out like the same crimson waterfall we almost drowned in earlier. "I've heard you don't like humans, Your Highness, but you could've canceled the Exchange if you weren't in the mood to tolerate us. What's one year without our help? Are you in *that* much need of dreams? Also, since you did invite us, shouldn't you be pleased with our performance? The better we are at these challenges, the better quality our dreams will be. So why are you acting like you *don't* want us to master your gifts?"

The image of Feyn kidnapping Mami overpowers my mind. He could be punishing me, after all. Why else would he be this furious with someone he's never met? Someone he's trying to sabotage by shattering her self-confidence. And he's targeting Jason and Ryujin, too, as if he knows hurting them hurts us all. We won't make it through the week if he kills our spirits.

Tears stream down Feyn's cheeks.

Actual tears.

"Hermano, por favor." Aro moves toward him.

"Déjame quieto." After asking to be left alone, Feyn pushes off his seat, avoiding his brother's pleading gaze. "Dinner is canceled."

He storms off.

He viciously shoves a guard aside, knocking him down. The guard takes it like a champion and doesn't even grunt, but when he gets back up, he's limping.

"Feyn!" Aro puts his goblet on the table. As all eyes are on the eldest prince, Aro sneaks in one last whisper into my ear. "Meet me by the garden's fountain an hour before the challenge."

Then he runs after his brother.

A staff flies to the back of Feyn's head.

He falls. I can't tell if he's still breathing.

I hear Ryujin and Ciel scream, the sound of pops and blasts . . . One by one, the floating water orbs are blown apart. Ashes mix with silver, pink, and red liquid, which splashes the grass.

Dozens of golden motorcycles rush into the garden.

Their riders shoot spells at the guards, Raff, and Aro . . .

The rebels are in Eterna.

NINETEEN

"¡**M**ÁTENLOS A TODOS!" ONE REBEL SHOUTS.

Soon others repeat the same message: *Kill them all.*

"¡Eterna es nuestra isla! ¡Eterna es nuestra isla! ¡Eterna es nuestra isla!"

I don't give a fuck if this is their island. They're not taking more lives.

A motorcycle is fast approaching me. Even though its rider is aiming balls of fiery light at the guards, he'll be close enough for me to knock off of his bike. I angle myself so that I can land a jab through his gilded helmet. Surely my newfound strength will obliterate it.

"Get down!" Ciel drags me under the dinner table. I don't know why her strength and speed shock me—no one's ever moved me this quickly in my life. Ryujin is already hiding down here, too. I search for Jason and see his khakis moving away from us . . .

Toward Feyn.

A rebel is trying to pick the prince's unconscious (dead?) body up. Another is shielding them from Aro's persistent blasts—the youngest royal barrels onward alongside Jason and Raff.

"What is he doing?!" Ryujin yells right in my ear.

I flinch. "Jason and Aro need backup! We can't just hide!"

"But the rebels will kill us!"

She's trembling. Her teeth are even chattering. It's one thing to face cobras that won't strike unless provoked. To let someone keep you from drowning and stab a crimson jewel in the nick of time. It's another entirely to launch into battle.

Especially when you're protecting a land that's not yours.

"They won't kill us, Ryujin. We're too strong for them. Besides, what are we going to do if they murder everyone who's on our side? You think we can stay under this table forever?"

"You haven't fully developed your fighting skills yet." Ciel's voice is still soothing despite the loudness erupting left and right. "It's a risk to let you go out there."

Ryujin says something I can't make out—each blast pierces my eardrums until there's only an incessant ringing. The coast is clear at the dinner table; there are seven rebels left. Two are drawing back the royal guards. Five are attacking Aro, Raff, and Jason. Feyn lies at Aro's feet.

He's awake.

He glares at the rebels circling them in their bikes, a whirl-wind of flying sand and smoke.

Feyn might be horrible, but he doesn't deserve to die like this. Neither does Raff. I'm not letting anything happen to

Jason or Aro. The former is one of my allies here. The latter
is . . .

Someone I need to complete the Exchange.

I turn to Ciel. "Watch me beat them up anyway."

"No! I'm not underestimating you. I'm *protecting* you, Sevim.
Please let me protect you."

"Your royals are literally about to die and you care about
me?"

"I care about everyone on this island. But my instructions are
clear. I won't leave you alone and that's positively final. Get closer
in case a spell flies in this direction!"

Ciel will never be my mother—she's not even old enough for
the role—but the way she's pleading with me makes me think of
the woman I'm here to rescue. This isn't part of her job. Guards
could've been assigned to do this. Did Aro tell her she needed to
serve as our magical shield in case of an ambush? Because I doubt
Feyn gave her such a kindhearted command.

Now's not the time! Go help Jason and Aro!

"Closer, Sevim," says Ciel. "Hurry."

"Okay."

I shove her as hard as I can.

When she's finally down, I slide across the grass, then pull
myself up. I charge deeper into the garden, searching for those
five motorcycles.

Three are in flames. Their riders' bodies are lost in the fire.

Jason holds the last two bikes high. He shakes them hard
enough to topple both riders and their staffs onto the grass.
Then he smashes metal against metal. Fire and smoke burst
into the night sky as the motorcycles are turned to scraps. Jason
lets the flames fall from his hands, landing on the screaming

riders. Somehow they're too slow to cast spells or run to the beach.

They burn.

Jason closes his eyes and turns away. It's like he can't look at them while they die.

And an open-mouthed Feyn stares up from the ground at him.

TWENTY

"**W**HAT DO YOU MEAN YOU DIDN'T see his face? Jason, listen to me. Feyn was *impressed.*"

"Absolutely not. That never happened."

"It did!"

"Okay, Sevim, you can stop being nice to me now."

"I'm not being nice. You were outstanding. I think Feyn would agree."

"Well . . . thank you . . . ." Jason suspiciously covers his mouth. He must be smiling.

But he swears he didn't catch Feyn's reaction after he smashed those bikes into scraps and flames. Right after the ambush, Aro and Raff grabbed the lone rebel that was left alive (one of the two that had been sparring with the guards). Aro told us they're keeping him for questioning. I overheard him telling Raff about securing perimeters and destroying the bridge these rebels made to access Eterna. He also needs to contact guards on the mainland to see if there were casualties from trying to stop them. This will definitely be a long night.

Aro did take a second to ask if I was okay.

"You ran to us. Why would you do that, Sevim? You could've gotten hurt or worse."

"Have you told Jason the same thing?"

"That's . . . different."

I'm still wondering what he meant—I refused to ask.

Especially with Feyn glaring at me. He *tipped his head*, though. Not in a formal bow, of course, but in appreciation? Acknowledgment? Maybe I'm reading it wrong, and he's mad that I disobeyed Ciel? On top of already being furious with what I told him at dinner, I mean. If he *is* pleased with my efforts to save him, I hope this is the start of better treatment for the rest of this hellish week, but I won't hold my breath. I need actual confirmation.

I catch up with Ciel at the front of our line. She's leading us back to the lodge and scanning the pathway, most likely in case we encounter additional rebel surprises. She took us away too fast for me to ask if I could apologize to Feyn. I haven't apologized to *her* for that awful shove—even though she was wrong for hiding like a coward, I had no right laying my hands on her.

Not a bone in my body feels like groveling, but as soon as I step inside our new house, my actions tonight, coupled with the thought of tomorrow's challenge, falls like a ton of bricks on my conscience. I need to make sure Feyn won't lose his entire cool if Ciel tells him I disobeyed orders and pushed her. Otherwise, he'll sabotage us worse than whatever he'd initially planned.

Aro's next clue might end up being useless.

Ryujin quietly hangs back with Jason as I approach Ciel.

I speak in my softest tone. "Hey. I'm really sorry about earlier. That was out of line. I shouldn't have touched you or run off like a child."

"Oh, don't worry about that. I know you didn't mean to harm me and you were just trying to help out. That was incredibly brave of you, Sevim."

Ciel pulls off the kindest smile I've seen yet. Either she's the type to suppress how she's truly feeling and put on a brave face, or she's unbothered. How could she ever be unbothered by this, though? I understand she brushes off Feyn's rudeness, but that's her boss. It makes a little more sense for her to go along with whatever he's game for. There has to be something deeper to Ciel. Something that explains why she's so *okay* with everything.

"Thanks, but I don't think that was acceptable. It was in the heat of the moment and—"

"Exactly. Your impulses got the best of you. Most humans have the same problem. You're not the worst example of such a thing."

"I'm still sorry. And I want to apologize to Prince Feyn."

"That would be *lovely*, Sevim. He'd appreciate it so much. I'll let you know when you can speak with him. It'll most likely be tomorrow at the stealth challenge, though."

"Makes sense. I can leave him alone till then."

Ciel nods, then addresses the three of us. "If any of you have questions or concerns, please don't hesitate to contact me. Send a guard my way and I'll be here in no time. I want to ensure you feel safe because *you are*. What happened tonight won't happen again."

Didn't Aro fight off a smaller ambush near his beach house? This will definitely happen again. I just don't want it to hinder my chances at saving Mami. But if the rebels can attack whenever they want, something is seriously amiss with royal security. Or maybe there's not much they can do aside from fighting back? I get that this elf war spawned from the king and queen's decision to open up the island for human visits. I also get that they banished all those who opposed and threatened them. What I don't understand is why the rebels insistent on claiming Eterna went as far as murdering the king and queen, but still haven't overrun the island.

"Why do you think the rebels won't return?" I ask Ciel. "All they do is kill humans and try to reclaim their home."

"This was *never* their home. We don't share anything with those monsters."

"You did live with them once. Both on this new island and in Vieques."

Ciel walks slower. She's nodding along to every word. "My mistake. We do share something with them. History. That's pretty much it."

"And magic. I think that's important to note." I wait for Ciel's reaction to my sarcasm. She just keeps walking. "Take those helmets, for example. Why do rebels even wear them? No one else in Eterna has anything like that."

"They designed those helmets in a futile attempt to resemble crowns. It's supposed to represent their superiority over humankind. I've also thought they're separating themselves from us further. Not only are they better than humans, but they're also better than the elves they betrayed."

"And the motorcycles?"

LAST SUNRISE IN ETERNA

Ciel takes a breath, picking up her pace again. "The rebels were once royal servants. They were mostly in charge of working with our iron and other minerals. Some were quite fond of engines and anything that could go extremely fast. Our dear Raff trained under them. He outraced every single competitor he ever faced. He built and repaired at a faster rate, too. But he and Aro were inseparable. When the rebels tried taking him, Raff fought back."

"You've never suspected him of being a double agent?"

The question *flies* out of me. I desperately wish I'd framed it in a different way. That I could've figured out how to ask it without making it sound so accusatory. But if Raff has any ties to these hateful elves on motorcycles, why wouldn't I doubt his allegiance?

"Whoa. That's a heavy thing to ask." Jason scratches his shoulder. "Raff doesn't give me traitor vibes, though. I think he's a cool dude."

"That's what a traitor would want you to think," I say.

"Okay, true. Still, he seems . . . good."

"He is," Ciel speaks firmer than before. "You should have no doubts about him or anyone else on the island."

Then tell me who the fuck has my mom.

I'm trying to figure out what to ask next when Ciel waves at something ahead.

The lodge's entrance.

"We're here!" she says.

"Thank you so much for escorting us, Ciel," says Ryujin. "Get some rest."

"You do, too. You deserve it. And Jason? I'm in awe of your bravery tonight. What you did will never be forgotten. I can promise you that."

"That's very sweet of you, Ciel. Thank you."

I nod. "Ciel, please remember to tell Feyn—"

"¡Buenas noches!"

She rushes to the main cottage.

TWENTY-ONE

"**I** *REALLY* HOPE I GET TO TALK to Feyn before the challenge," I say as I drag my feet into the living room. "He needs to know I'm sorry, and I need to know he accepts my apology. There's no way I'm heading into that stealth mission with a furious elf prince pulling the strings."

"Don't stress too much about it, Sev." Jason sits down first. "Can I call you Sev?"

"Sure. No one's ever called me that before."

"What? Not even your friends?"

"I . . . don't have them."

Ryujin and I claim the couch in front of Jason. They're both staring at me like I'm in dire need of a hug—a sweet yet baffling gesture. Not everyone goes to school and clicks with their classmates, right? These two surely know what outsiders are?

That we can't control who likes us and wants to spend time with us? Or have they been popular their entire lives?

"Well," Ryujin speaks softly, "you have them now."

"Oh." I don't know what else to say. Feeling like I'm the only person in a room full of people my age has always been annoying. Ryujin calling herself my friend simply because we've shared the most harrowing experience of our lives is mind-blowing. Of course I consider her someone close to me now. We trusted each other. We *survived* together. But isn't it too early to consider us friends? We literally just met. Unless she's the type of person to form bonds easily?

Wish I could relate.

"You sound surprised," says Ryujin.

"Well, it's just . . . strange. I've never clicked with anyone this fast."

"I'll be honest with you. I wouldn't have been mad if I never saw you again after that first challenge," Jason admits. "You were the actual worst."

I frown. "I know."

"No, but the *actual worst*."

"Okay, I heard you the first time, Jason."

"But after the second one? And after what you *just* did with Feyn at dinner? The way you defended us reminded me of my little sister, Carol. She loses it whenever people use my deadname." Jason raises his fists. "Imagine an eleven-year-old threatening to punch transphobic seniors."

"Sounds like my new best friend," I say.

"You both stay ready and I appreciate it. Feyn is super hot, but he's intolerable."

I slap a hand on my forehead. "You do not find that asshole

attractive, Jason."

"Excuse me? Have you *seen* him in those crop tops?"

"Oh my God . . ." I pretend to throw up, which makes Jason and Ryujin laugh. "So why do you think he's angry? What's the point of having us here if he's so mad?"

"Maybe he misses his parents and older brother. He's not known to cry easily, but the Exchange could remind him of the people who supported it the most," says Jason.

"It feels insidious, though. Like he wants to hurt us. This doesn't scream nostalgia to me."

"We don't act logically when our hearts are broken." Ryujin picks at her nude nail polish, chipping at its corners, and watching it fall onto her lap. "And even though everyone's heart can break, we won't put it back together in the same ways."

So they're sticking with the sob story. Fantastic . . .

Jason and Ryujin might be the closest things to friends I've ever had, but telling them about Mami is risky. I don't want to involve anyone else in my mess, especially after such a chaotic dinner, even though sharing my theory about Feyn keeping her hostage might sway them into agreeing with me. The longer they center Feyn's behavior as a result of painful losses, the more I want this conversation to be over.

And I have the perfect change of topic.

"We haven't discussed our dreams during the study sessions. Mine was a nightmare."

"I had one, too." Ryujin plays with her hair now. She looks at the perfectly healthy ends as if she's considering snipping them off anyway. "I was at my final gymnastics competition in Seoul. The day I missed the beam and fell. I lost my focus while I was in the air."

"The twisties," Jason offers. "That's the English word for it."

"Yes," says Ryujin.

I consider asking for more details, but I don't want to upset her. "I'm sorry."

"Me, too, Ryu. Can I call you Ryu?" says Jason.

That gets a smile out of her. "Yes. And thank you."

I turn to Jason. "What about you?"

He sits comfortably again, his whole face lighting up. "I was at my first book signing. My Exchange memoir was a bestseller, and I was already a famous, prize-winning journalist."

"Are those your plans? To write about your experience here?" I ask.

"Mm-hmm. The odds of getting into a journalism program will be much higher with a personal account about Eterna under my belt. I'm hoping it wins me a full ride to an Ivy League, but my dream made the whole thing so much better. People came to see me from around the world. They used my real name and pronouns. And my book had my name on the *cover*."

It doesn't surprise me another ticket winner has ulterior motives, but I wasn't expecting this from elf-obsessed Jason. I can't fault him—college in the U.S. is outrageously expensive. I don't know anything about his academic career or home life. But I do know what it's like to need money. To take financial matters into my own hands. At least Jason is doing it in a more ethical way.

"I hope you know what it feels like for real soon," I say.

"Thanks, Sev."

"What was your nightmare about?" Ryujin asks me.

"I was sitting by the shore when bombs and screams went off in Vieques. I dove into the water, but something pulled me under.

As I was drowning, I heard a man laughing—a voice I didn't recognize—then a monster roared. Feyn forced me awake before I could understand what was happening. He told Ciel to toss the nightmare away because it wasn't personal enough."

"So you don't know anyone from Vieques?" Jason asks.

"My dad."

"Oh! Then it *is* personal."

"That's what I thought, but Feyn said it was just a pathetic excuse for a dream. I couldn't recognize the man laughing. I've never heard the roars before. I'm only aware of what the bombs were alluding to."

Jason nods. "The navy's drills?"

"You know about that?"

"Medical and environmental issues have always interested me."

"What happened with the navy?" Ryujin asks.

I explain how Vieques was used as a military training facility from the 1940s until 2001. How the Navy officially abandoned the island in 2003, leaving behind toxic waste and active explosives deep beneath soil and water. A federal wildlife refuge is now where they once trained, but the barrage of signs alerting locals and tourists to watch out for munitions, the government's embarrassingly slow cleanup efforts, and high radiation don't provide a sliver of solace.

"Residents have found astronomical levels of heavy metals in their blood, too, especially uranium. The navy used uranium bullets in their firing drills," I say. "People have also been diagnosed with different types of cancers. Some are fully metastasized upon discovery. My dad . . . he, um . . . had lung cancer. Never smoked a day in his life. But he was from Vieques."

Jason's frown is deeper than mine. "My grandma had breast cancer. She passed away, too. I know it's not the same situation, but losing someone you love is horrible. I'm so sorry."

Part of me wants to clarify how Papi really died. Hiding the truth feels like lying, too. But that's a can of worms I'm not ready to open. Talking about the rebels will undoubtedly lead me into my corpse-snatching days, then Mami's kidnapping.

In any case, it's refreshing to know I'm not alone in my pain.

"I've never talked to anyone else who's been through this, too," I say.

"Neither have I." Jason starts to smile, even though he's tearing up. "I wish we didn't know what going through this feels like."

"Agreed."

"I'm sorry for you both." Ryujin shudders. "But *why* would you dream about those navy bombings, Sevim? You didn't witness them, did you?"

"No, but I've never had a nightmare like that before. And it's not like I had plenty of time in the nightmare anyway. Feyn was quick to pull me out. Why wake me up if it's not a big deal? You think he's hiding something?"

All three of us exchange worried glances, as if we're searching for answers in each other, but we don't have them.

"We need more information," Jason finally says. "I don't want either of you stressing over this tonight, though. Our day was rough. Tomorrow will be rougher. We should get some rest and stay fresh for the stealth challenge. Lord knows what Feyn has up his sleeve."

More torture, probably.

We say good night and head to our respective rooms. I shower again even though I cleaned myself thoroughly after swimming in crimson. Hot water always reinvigorates me, and after a night fighting rebels, I require a boost.

Afterward, I slip into my pajamas and get into bed, ready for exhaustion to take the reins.

⌁

I'M STILL AWAKE AT THREE in the morning.

I dwell on Feyn's tears, his insistence on ridiculing us at dinner, on belittling my Vieques nightmare, trying to control what I can and cannot see in my own mind . . .

But most of all, I think of Aro.

How he ran after a brother who's probably never shown him the same sympathy. A brother who ordered that he be left alone, yet Aro fled after him anyway. I could never care for someone that volatile.

I balk at the absurd comment Aro made about the Brownings. Would he really write more than five hundred and seventy-five letters? If I ever fell in love, I'd be dissuaded after a handful of correspondence—the relationship itself would be all the commitment I could deal with.

Then I picture Aro sitting in a corner by himself, scribbling in everything from notebook pages to fancy papyrus scrolls, searching for the perfect words to impress the unfortunate soul who owns his heart. I've never had a boy give me anything remotely indicative of their feelings for me. I can't remember the last time I was stared at like I was *beautiful*.

Other than Aro at the mall.

And every single time we've spoken.

I wonder what it would be like for someone to gift me verses.

To write more than five hundred and seventy-five love letters reserved for my eyes alone. But whenever I try imagining a human boy, someone I can actually build a healthy future with, I see him.

No. Just . . . no.

I pull the covers off and go for a walk. Stripping my mind of the youngest elf prince will surely take me less than ten minutes. Outdoors is a better option. I can listen to the waves and let them lull me to sleep in a hammock. I tiptoe around the house, praying Jason and Ryujin are lost in pleasant dreams, then open the double doors to our backyard.

Ryujin sits on a marble bench alone. Her back is to the doors. She whimpers, sniffles loudly, and whimpers again.

She's crying.

"Oh, sorry." God, I *hate* myself. She wasn't even looking at me. I could've slipped back inside without her ever noticing!

Ryujin jumps off the bench. "Sevim . . ." She pats her cheeks and eyes dry as if she's blending her makeup. "You don't have to apologize. I was just having a hard night."

"You're not still thinking about Feyn, are you? He's not worth your tears."

"This isn't related to him."

"Good." I take a slow step toward her. "Do you need someone to talk to? Or would you rather be alone? It's fine if you want me to leave."

"You can stay." Ryujin sits again. "Are you struggling to sleep, too?"

"Horribly." I join her on the bench, noticing she's removed more nail polish. Only three fingers left until it's all gone. "Why are you awake? Did something happen back home?"

She stares blankly at the rolling waves ahead. "No. I just miss my mother."

Her words drive wooden stakes through my heart. It's not the same to miss someone who's patiently waiting for you. Someone who'll open the front door, run into your arms, and show you that home isn't only a spot on the map. Ryujin *knows* she'll see her mother again. They'll be reunited and comforted with each other's love. *I* don't have that guarantee.

Then I remember the press has only mentioned her father, an accountant in their hometown of Gwangju. How he raised her as a single dad.

"Tell me about her," I say.

Even when she slouches, Ryujin still looks more graceful than me. I suppose athletes have no choice but to make everyone else seem awkward in comparison.

"My mother left me when I was six," she says. "I was waiting for her to pick me up after gymnastics practice. My father came instead. He said she was on vacation. That she'd be back soon. But I heard him crying in the bathroom that night. He cried for months. Years. I grew up thinking she'd willingly abandoned us. I thought it was her choice."

I'm tempted to place a hand on her back, to offer any sort of physical comfort, but I doubt it would make much difference. "What really happened?" I ask.

"She told my father she didn't love him anymore. The truth was much darker." Ryujin lets out a long, tired breath. "Last year, a few days before my final gymnastics competition in Seoul, there was a knock on my door. It was my mother. Her clothes were covered in blood."

"*What?* Was she okay?"

"No. My father fainted when he saw her. I asked her where she'd been. She told me she . . . met someone who could help me. She was obsessed with my career. Her desperation to see me become the best only grew when I started underperforming during practice."

"Fuck. She made a deal with an elf?"

Ryujin nods. "He promised I would become the greatest gymnast our country has ever seen. The price was to leave her family—the elf demanded her at his side. But he never kept his promise. And one day, he didn't want her anymore. He cast her out of Eterna and dropped her into my bedroom like she was nothing. My mother came home, but her mind, her heart, were still with him. He brainwashed her into thinking she was truly happy without me."

I can't fathom how she's sharing this so calmly. If this were *my* mother, I'd still be in therapy, rife with abandonment and trust issues. No wonder Ryujin is so quiet. A mind chased by painful memories holds no space to process much else.

"Did she try to mend your relationship?" I ask.

"She swore everything was fine, that I should go back to sleep, and that we'd talk more in the morning. Then she hanged herself."

Waves and wind no longer register in my ears. It's like someone unplugged the island's sound system and left me with echoes of Ryujin's confession. Now I understand why she failed her competition days later. Such a tragic loss would've kept me from being productive, too. I still can't recall the press ever covering her mother's suicide, but I'm grateful it hasn't been the focal point of Ryujin's life story. Exploiting anyone's past for clicks and views disgusts me.

"I'm so fucking sorry, Ryujin. I didn't know she . . . I'm *sorry*."

She just sits there quietly.

Then she says, "I'd like to sleep now."

It's four in the morning when we head back inside. I watch her disappear into her bedroom, hoping she gets enough rest, knowing she probably won't.

And neither will I.

TWENTY-TWO

THE NEXT MORNING, RYUJIN DOESN'T TOUCH her breakfast.

She doesn't contribute to my conversation with Jason, either, resorting to frequent nods and blank stares at her ice-cold omelet. All of her nude nail polish has been chipped away. After I shower and get dressed, I find her repainting her nails in the living room, still in her pajamas. A group of thirty-something men is singing in Korean and dancing in perfect sync on her phone.

"Who are they?" I ask.

"Super Junior."

She continues painting in silence.

I ponder asking more about them, but she clearly wants to be left alone. That doesn't bother me, but I fear her head won't be in the game today.

I need Aro's clue more than ever.

So I stay in my private quarters until an hour before the stealth challenge begins. When I return to the living room, Ryujin is still watching K-pop videos on her phone, this time featuring a four-member girl group. They sing about love being on fire as I slip outside.

None of the guards stop me on the way to the garden. I feel their eyes on me, though, and sure enough, they're all watching me closely.

I quicken my pace.

Doves chirp overhead. Some find shade in the golden palm fronds before flying away. Flower beds coil around me in pink, red, and yellow pastels. Farther ahead, seven trails diverge before a moss-covered wall. A marble fountain lies right in front of it.

Aro is already waiting for me.

He sinks his ungloved hand into the fountain's base, swirling the crystal-clear water around. My heart does a little leap at the sight of his back, his wide shoulders . . .

"I'm here," I speak before my daydreams run wild.

"Oh, hey . . ."

This is the palest I've seen him. It's as if he's being drained of his very life force. When he walks away from the fountain, he has a limp that wasn't there last night. Did Feyn lash out at him because of *me*? Were rebels hiding near his beach house again? The more he moves, the slower he breathes, but he's pushing out a poor excuse of a smile.

"How are you, Sevim?"

"What happened?"

Aro stops. "I tripped on the way here and hurt my ankle. But it's fine."

"We should sit anyway. You don't want more pressure on it."

I grab his side.

He winces.

When he tries moving away from me, I drift closer.

His chest presses against mine.

Our heartbeats match in tempo—swift and unstoppable. "Don't." His breath warms my skin, raising the hairs on the back of my neck. But the heat only lasts a moment. Chills catapult down my spine like falling stalactites. I doubt Oscar Wilde referred to this when he wrote about the Mountain-Torrent being kissed by the Ice-King in "The Star-Child." Yet the prince has turned me into a snowcapped landscape dressed in black. How can someone make me feel hot and cold at the same time? And why does it have to be *this* someone?

I back away. "Sorry. I shouldn't have touched you." Heat blooms underneath my skin again. Somehow I'm burning *more*—I'm an ember that will soon engulf this entire island in flames. "You hurt your ankle *and* your ribs. That must've been some fall, Your Highness."

"I said I'm fine."

"And I don't believe you. Why haven't you been healed? I had a cobra bite taken care of and I'm a human peasant. Surely a prince requires immediate medical attention."

"Surely." Aro looks behind me. Even though he's calm, his eyes remain glued to the path toward us. "I haven't gone to the healers yet. You're my first priority."

If he's expecting me to swoon, I'm thrilled to disappoint him.

But let's hope he stays far enough away to not feel my bouncing heart.

"Tell me the truth, Prince Aro. You're too graceful to drop so easily."

Aro breaks into a much wider smile. "Was that a *compliment*?"

"Don't derail the conversation."

He chuckles. "All right. It was another rebel battle, this time on the mainland. My guards got word of an attack in the mountains of Humacao. They broke into a home and tried kidnapping children for a live execution." He pauses, tilting his head as if he's thinking how best to phrase whatever comes next. "Raff and I made sure the kids are safe. I'm just in a bit of pain."

A part of me wants to know how the rebels died. Hurting children—using their bodies as *props*—should've earned them a long, painful death. Then I think of Aro risking his life for these strangers, and how he swept into action to save his best friend in San Juan, and I'd rather cling to the image of him being so courageous than waste another second on these killers.

"Why did they choose kids?" I ask.

"My mother was one of our best magical instructors, but she was also a budding historian on all things humankind. She loved reading your species' textbooks to our island's children. It was her mission to educate them with empathy and respect for those who were different. And she was very fond of human children, too. She saw them as future leaders our kind could be great allies with. She raised my brothers and me to feel the same way, but we had royal guards protecting us. The rebels were too scared to attack us first. So they chose the defenseless."

I wish I hadn't asked. Not because it's tough to hear—as heartbreaking as it is, I can stomach it. But it's surely much more difficult to relive for Aro. I don't want him feeling as horribly as he looks. I need to pivot from whatever amount of pain he must be hiding from me.

"And the mountain attack happened after speaking with Feyn?" I ask.

"During, actually. The guards interrupted our chat." I'm about to ask how Feyn is doing when he looks over my head like he's checking for eavesdroppers. "My brother will be creating another maze today. This one is designed like a vast desert. There will be landmines hidden everywhere. The keys to deactivating the mines are the ravens that will fly overhead. You and the other winners will have to decipher how best to use them together."

This is the clue.

Ryujin's usually patient enough to handle a desert full of landmines, but after speaking with her last night and seeing how distraught she really is, her mind could be focused on other things. It'll be up to Jason and me to get her across without giving up. We'll need her to figure out those ravens, too. I'm already thinking of Edgar Allan Poe—the key to success could be hidden in his verses. Neither Jason nor Ryujin strike me as avid Poe readers, so maybe the answer lies elsewhere. Or it could be a combination of my knowledge of "The Raven" and other things they're familiar with?

"Were you listening?" Aro asks.

"Yes. Sorry."

"It's okay. You're cute when you're spaced out." He smirks. "Repeat it so I'm sure."

"We'll be put in a vast desert. There'll be ravens flying overhead. They're the answer."

"Perfect. It's especially important that you—"

"¿Qué carajo estás haciendo?"

Feyn darts toward us.

This is the first time I've heard him cursing. Even though he demands to know what the hell Aro is doing, Feyn doesn't wait for his response. He steps between Aro and me like a soldier protecting his general. Gone is the elf crying at the opposite end of the dinner table. The elf fleeing as if tolerating another second in my presence would've robbed him of breath forever.

Now he's the elf shrinking me with his menacing glare.

"How can you betray me, Aro?" he says.

"I didn't betray you! I was just—"

"YOU TOLD HER WHAT THE CHALLENGE IS."

I flinch and retreat, but Feyn closes the distance between us. Aro tries pulling him back. He's too weak after whatever happened with those rebels. Aro whispers something unintelligible. But I do catch Feyn glaring at Aro's ivory ring, then at his little brother.

"Por favor no te desquites con ellos, Feyn. Es mi culpa."

I don't care how many times Aro says this is his fault, or how hard he begs his brother not to take out his rage on us. Feyn will never listen.

"You're a cheater," he tells me.

"I'm sorry, Your Highness."

Enduring his silence is like walking in a forest at midnight. I can't see where I'm going. I don't know what lurks among the trees and brambles. But one wrong move is all it takes for danger to welcome me into its fold. Will he shove me like he shoved that guard last night? If he tries, he'll get smacked hard across the face—my reflexes won't let anyone push me around.

"I'm changing the stealth mission now," he finally says. "You'll regret ever crossing me."

TWENTY-THREE

DON'T DARE SPEAK WITH JASON AND Ryujin.

Even looking them in the eye drills a hole in my stomach. They arrived a few minutes ago, confused with my refusal to engage in conversation. I haven't said a word ever since Feyn left the fountain area. Aro tried staying with me, but his brother ordered him to leave, too.

"You and I need to talk!" Feyn had yelled. "*Alone.*"

And like a good little brother, Aro quietly limped behind the eldest prince.

Fifteen minutes later, Jason and Ryujin found me.

Now we're back in the main courtyard. Feyn has cast the same glass stage, taking Aro, Ciel, and Raff to overlook the garden at a safe distance.

"Our apologies for the brief delay!" Ciel is in a green midi dress with puffy sleeves; bronze leaves shimmer all over the tie-up bodice and skirt. Her hair is up in a topknot today. Little stars and thin silver thread cling onto most strands. "His Highness, Prince Feyn Herrera, requested alterations after a winner was caught cheating."

"What?" Jason and Ryujin say.

I stay silent. Feyn could take my excuses as yet another slight. I'm not about to turn this challenge into something much worse.

"Your challenge starts now," Ciel proclaims.

"Wait!" I finally speak. "What are the rules? Do we have thirty minutes, too?"

Darkness wraps around us.

Almost at once, the light returns.

The glass stage is gone. It's like the elves were never here.

I'm in an electric chair.

Rusted metal chains lock my arms and legs. I can't move no matter how hard I try.

"What is this?" Ryujin's strained whisper fills me with greater dread.

She and Jason are also chained to electric chairs, but they're each in a separate prison cell. We're in an abandoned prison. Grime and graffiti cover the walls. The lamp swinging overhead flickers on and off; thick cobwebs hang from the light bulb. I feel like I'll get tetanus just by looking at my prison cell's bars.

Then there's the statue.

A hooded elf in polished marble stands outside my cell.

It's holding a papyrus scroll with a short message.

THE UNSEEN ITS TRUTH REVEALS

Maybe it means something different to my friends.

But I recognize it as a verse from Emily Brontë's "The Prisoner." This was the first of Emily's poems Mami read. She discovered it long before she touched *Wuthering Heights* and despised its characters. I remember her telling me not to consider Heathcliff the man I should aspire to marry. I had no interest in spending my free time buried in more books back then, though, so I had no idea what she was talking about.

I have to tell Jason and Ryujin about the poem. It'll help us develop a plan.

"You guys, that inscription is from—"

I break out in spasms.

Thousands of electric shocks burst all over me. I arch my back. Grind my teeth. I become lightning. Thunder. *Fire.* Everything feels like it's burning, falling off, and turning to ash . . .

The shocks stop.

I'm drooling. Sweating. I hack a cough and fold into a bundle of pulsating limbs.

"Sevim!" Ryujin yells. "What happened to—"

She screams.

She's being electrocuted, too.

"No!" Jason and I shout.

My chair unleashes more shocks—this time with double the strength. Jason, Ryujin, and I endure a relentless stream of white-hot bolts. By the time they're gone, I'm hunched over and spitting out wads of saliva, wondering what the fuck is provoking these sudden blasts.

Ryujin lets out a sob.

It earns her another round of torture.

"Stop this!" Jason begs.

He earns another, too. Just for speaking up.

I hold back a gasp—I was electrocuted after trying to say something. Jason's plea, Ryujin's sob . . . We were all making noise. Could the shocks return whenever we produce sound?

One potentially mistaken theory is better than none.

Since I can't call on Jason and Ryujin, I shake my head slow enough not to brush strands of my hair against my shirt. It takes them a second to notice; they're sweating and drooling even more than me. I barely lift my finger, pointing to my lips, and curling them inward—a warning not to speak.

Ryujin is on the verge of tears, but she doesn't open her mouth.

Neither does Jason.

Feyn never gave us a time limit. He threw us into the dark without a match. More darkness is surely on the way if I don't decipher whatever this poem is meant for.

Jason and Ryujin sit perfectly still as I go over Emily's verses in my addled brain. "The Prisoner" is about a literal captive who's threatened with death and despair. However, her faith in God acts as her shield against all evil, rejecting any kind of pain as something worth fearing. In the end, the captors quit trying to shatter the prisoner's will and leave with their tails between their legs. This isn't someone they can easily torture.

But if we're supposed to mimic that same attitude, what does *speaking* have to do with it? There's nothing that stands out in regard to noise in Emily's piece!

Then I remember the first two lines:

> *In the dungeon-crypts idly did I stray,*
> *Reckless of the lives wasting there away.*

The captors visit their prisoner in order to torment her. They have no respect for anyone they've doomed to life behind bars. Despite this captive's wounds, her soul remains untarnished, her faith unbroken. She doesn't need others to release her—she's already free.

Aro has always stressed teamwork. We can't win if we're selfish.

What if Feyn's new challenge *does* require selfishness? He erased what his little brother hoped I'd succeed in. Wouldn't that include switching the methods of winning, too? Getting out of here will demand self-preservation. I reread the inscription: THE UNSEEN ITS TRUTH REVEALS.

There are secrets we bury like corpses, rotting in our souls instead of six feet underground. Stealth isn't just about concealing our bodies. It's also about lying. Moving around in a world that would cast us away if they knew who we really were, what we truly thought and felt.

This challenge demands confession.

It won't be something we fear or hate. Feyn already knows that.

But the things others would judge us harshly for, the things weighing down our hearts, cut deeper. If selfishness is the key to leaving this prison, we must give up what we've gained by being selfish in the past. My pulse quickens. Feyn isn't just trying to torture and humiliate us—he wants information. If he *is* tricking me, he seeks confirmation in front of everyone.

And I'm not in a position to deny him.

I press my eyes shut. "I've been stealing elf corpses for money!"

The electric chair doesn't shock me.

My rusted chains are still bound tight.

But I've set myself free.

Jason and Ryujin stare at me like I've just driven a truck through a house. Like I've demolished every single brick in its familiar, comfortable foundations. I don't know what kind of person *seems* like a corpse thief, but they don't give me the impression that I ever looked like it.

I can deal with their surprise, their disappointment, later.

Now I have to get them out in one piece.

"You have to confess. Think of something unethical or illegal you've done. It could be something you're planning on doing, too. Whatever would make you a shitty person."

Ryujin might as well be dead. She's sitting even *more* still.

Jason fidgets. He's sweating a little harder, looking at the statue, then the grimy floor.

Neither speaks.

"I know it sucks, but it's the only way. You have to confess."

Silence is the only response.

"You can do it! I won't judge either one! And whatever it is, there's simply *no way* it's worse than getting paid as a body snatcher." I shake my head. "I'm a fucking thief."

Jason is tearing up. His upper lip quivers, then he shakes from head to toe.

"No judgment," I say. "Not from me. And you shouldn't care about—"

"I worked for the rebels."

Whatever I was about to say is lodged somewhere deep, deep down.

Serving as a double agent for murderous elves . . . Those who kill *your own kind* . . .

He doesn't get shocked.

He's just confessed something terrible and *true*.

I want to ask him everything—what exactly did he do, if it was all worth it . . .

"Ten seconds!" Feyn's voice rips through the air like a comet.

Jason and I gasp.

"Come on!" I tell Ryujin. "You have to hurry!"

"Nine, eight, seven . . ."

Ryujin isn't blinking. It's like staring at a red-eyed mannequin.

"Six, five, four . . ."

"COME ON!"

"Three, two . . ."

"I'm in Eterna to kill my mother's murderer!" Ryujin shouts.

TWENTY-FOUR

OUR CHAINS FALL OFF.

Familiar heat courses through me. So does that burst of energy I experienced after the strength challenge. It makes me feel light, as if my restless soul isn't attached to a body. As if my footsteps will never make another sound, and I'll never cast shadows again.

My stealth has leveled up.

The bars slide open. Guards swarm inside my cell.

More sweep into Ryujin's, their staffs aimed at her throat and chest. Only Raff enters Jason's cell. He quickly presses a finger to his lips. Whatever happens next, Jason shouldn't interrupt.

"Don't hurt them!" Aro is outside my cell, but he looks from me to Ryujin to me again, as if the message is for both sets of guards. "We'll get to the bottom of this without violence."

"That's not your call. And I promise *nothing*."

Feyn steps out from behind the marble statue. Each pound of his boot against cement is a thunderclap. It warns us of a perfect storm's approach.

He chooses Ryujin's cell first.

Ciel follows him, but Aro stays closer to mine. He keeps inching toward hers, though, as if he's torn between stopping two certain dooms.

Feyn rushes up to the shaking, crying girl. He bends so their foreheads are almost touching.

"Who killed your mother?" he asks.

I hate that I feel entitled to this answer, too. Ryujin *lied* to me. Was she so desperate to vent that she made up a suicide in order to release the pain eating at her last night? And if she's *here* to find her mother's killer, that means . . . could it be . . .

"I don't know his name," she says. "An elf made a deal with my mother. She agreed to abandon her family in order for me to have success as a gymnast. But he tricked her. His voice was always in her head. And when she tried returning to me, she hanged herself."

"You believe he made her do this?"

"No. She was *fighting* his voice. But he said she'd always have him in her thoughts. So she . . ." Ryujin breaks down even more, fully bent over. "She's gone. Personal belongings. Family portraits. School and legal records. Everything was erased. It's like she never lived."

She sobs into her trembling hands.

I want to run up and embrace her, but a hug won't heal her pain. Even a little bit of comfort is better than nothing and I need it, too. Especially after learning an elf used her mother like his personal plaything. This *must* be the same elf that kidnapped Mami. What if he's using my wrongs as an excuse to use her, as well? He's tossed me into enemy territory, making me think this is all about punishing me, but he could've also crafted a scheme to replace Ryujin's mom.

"The elf you seek is dead," says Feyn.

Ryujin and I gasp.

"He . . . he is?" she whispers.

"Yes. He was the rebel clan's leader. He always hated humans, but his hatred grew once we moved to Eterna. It was his belief that we should rule over your kind. That hiding on a remote island was a waste of our potential. Our former Royal Advisor . . ."

Feyn's upper lip twitches.

He takes a deep breath, then exhales. "He discovered the rebel leader's crimes against women, specifically, and told my parents. They imprisoned him. Unfortunately, his followers broke him out before his execution. He drove a dagger through my father's heart, and a year later, he ambushed my mother. My older brother's murder was a year after hers." Feyn gives a small nod, even though Ryujin isn't looking at him. "I stole his dagger and returned the favor."

I press my lips tighter, suppressing a groan. The elf that has Mami isn't this clan leader, after all. Hearing Feyn confess to murder unsettles me, too. No one should take lives as payment. He shouldn't be so calm and collected about it. Especially at nineteen years old.

But if I were in his shoes, would I do the same?

I hate that I almost say yes. How easily I imagine a world where rage and grief blend into a single shadow that covers my once-blue skies. If Mami suffers the same fate as Feyn's family, Ryujin's mother, I'll never be the Sevim she raised ever again. I wouldn't even be the Sevim who lies and steals behind her back; those crimes would be tame in comparison.

I won't become that Sevim, and that won't be Mami's fate.

"You killed him, Your Highness?" Ryujin asks.

"Slowly," Feyn admits.

Ryujin drops her hands. She's bright red, but she's not crying anymore, as if she's emptied her entire reserve of tears. "Tell me his name, Your Highness. Please. I need to know."

"Names hold power. We refuse to speak his ever again." Feyn stands tall as he retreats. "I'm sorry for your loss, Ryujin, but I hope two things comfort you. I made sure he suffered a great deal. And if you're crying *this* much, you were never meant to kill."

He exits her cell.

And steps into mine.

"Feyn, please . . ." Aro speaks without moving a muscle. I don't know if he's in more pain now, or if he fears his brother retaliating against me if he intervenes.

I don't move, either. I'm not about to put us through another last-minute mission.

Feyn stops mere inches from my chair. He doesn't bend over now. He wants me to look up at him.

"Have you stolen any Iron Staff bodies?" he asks.

"Never. Just rebels."

"How many have you stolen?"

"Thirteen."

Feyn smirks. Is he impressed? Grateful I'm disposing of his enemies? Or does he think I'm exaggerating? That a human girl would never be capable of snatching that many bodies?

"How many buyers do you have?"

My eyes flick over to Aro.

He doesn't move. I can't tell what he wants me to say. If it's okay to betray Doctor Ramírez's identity again, this time to a much crueler prince. Would he command his guards to hunt him down and kill him? Or would he want to personally execute him?

"How *many*?" Feyn repeats.

Aro's lips barely open, but I can read them: *Lie.*

He must have a reason to hide the truth from his brother. Maybe he's close to locating the doctor and wants to interrogate him before bringing him to the island. Aro's hesitance is more than enough confirmation that Feyn could lash out before extracting useful information. Or he could simply not want human blood on either pair of royal hands.

Either way, I need to trust him.

"Sevim Burgos, I asked you a question." Feyn takes a step closer. "*Twice.*"

"I don't know, Your Highness. They were all drop-offs. I always grab the envelope full of cash at the delivery site and leave before the bodies are collected. It could've been multiple clients for each transaction, though."

"How did these buyers contact you?"

"I posted in online forums. The first client contacted me using a burner phone number, then I suggested it to others so that everything stayed confidential."

There's no sure-fire way to know whether Feyn believes me or not. He's just watching me like a headmaster who's caught his least favorite teacher behaving badly. Like he's grateful I've validated his disdain and wants me to continue.

"How did you see the bodies?"

"They weren't in ensueños, Your Highness."

"Thirteen elf corpses left uncovered in streets and alleys? Where bystanders could've easily photographed them and shared the images around the world? Where I could've found them long before you ever had the chance to steal them?"

Fuck.

That first elf—Papi's killer—had been the only one exposed. Whoever killed him *wanted* him found. All the others were hidden. But how do I keep the lie going? Feyn will never believe the rebels suddenly dropped their ensueños during fights.

"Take Ryujin to the study chamber. She's ready to dream," Feyn tells Aro over his shoulder. "Keep Jason here. We'll interrogate him once I'm done with her." Then he glues his narrowed eyes to me again.

I squeeze the armrests and lean away from him. The fact that I'd rather stay in an *electric chair* than let Feyn take me wherever the hell he desires is outlandish. Yet here we are.

"Your Highness?" Ciel approaches Feyn. "Should we move Jason somewhere else? I can take him to a more comfortable chamber and help him clean up before—"

"He stays here, Ciel."

She hangs her head low. "Yes, Your Highness . . ."

This is the first time I've seen her going against Feyn's orders. It's not a huge act of defiance, especially seeing how easily she gave up, but it gives me hope to know she's trying to steer her boss into kinder ways of dealing with us. Maybe she'll grow more insistent soon?

"You're going to follow me, Sevim," Feyn commands.

"Yes, Your Highness," I mumble.

He's off.

As I quietly trace his steps, I hear him say, "You've got more cojones than I thought."

He's speaking to Jason.

The sad boy who turns away, blatantly refusing to acknowledge him, wiping his tears in shameful silence. The same person who said Feyn was super hot doesn't seem to care.

"It was a mistake," he says. "I don't work for them anymore. I wish I never did."

"That's why you couldn't look at them. It wasn't because they were burning." It takes me a moment to recall what Feyn's talking about. Then the raid during dinner overwhelms all other thoughts. "You knew those faces well. It hurt you to watch them die. To *kill* them." Jason opens his mouth to speak, but Feyn talks over him. "You'll get your chance to explain yourself. And I'll teach you what happens when you come to my home with a secret like that."

We march to his cottage together.

TWENTY-FIVE

FEYN'S PRIVATE RESIDENCE IS AN ARBORETUM with fewer plants.

He does have plenty of art. A star-filled mural wraps around his living room. There are tiny portraits of the island's black sand on coffee tables and bookshelves. Paintings decorate the walls leading down the main corridor. The sandstone floor is dotted with stardust. It shines even brighter than the glitter on Feyn's eyes.

"Through here."

The double doors before him are gilded—the only ones of their kind on the first floor. Feyn swiftly pushes them aside. The smell of yellowed pages wafts across the chamber, which is covered in wooden shelves from wall to wall. Feyn's idea of a home library consists of piling six desks together, dumping scrolls onto chairs, leaving crumpled balls of paper on the floor like breadcrumbs, and keeping a dusty chandelier that dangles on its left side only. I'm thankful all the windows are closed. A sudden gust of wind could snap that chain in half.

It isn't strange to have chandeliers in a library. A marble fountain proves less likely. Its tiers are Flor de Maga petals reaching skyward; stars, clouds, crescent moons, and ocean waves are carved into the base. Golden liquid sloshes around all four tiers—the same one I've dabbed onto my eyes.

This is the doctor's elixir!

"Do you recognize it?" Feyn could cut me into pieces with his tone alone.

"No, Your Highness."

"You've never seen this before?"

"Never. What is it?"

Feyn is quiet. I can't tell if he's withholding information to spite me or if he's truly afraid of confessing.

"Forgive me, Your Highness. I'm out of line again."

"This elixir is meant to untangle ensueños," he says abruptly. "It shows the truth behind illusions. My mother wanted me to be strong enough to create such a potent spell, but she also hoped to share it with humans someday. It was supposed to help them trust us more. If we gave them a tool to see through our magic, they wouldn't think we had anything to hide. I only perfected it after her death."

Feyn quickly turns to the fountain. I suspect he's hiding tears.

I disappointed my mother long before she was kidnapped. Even if she wasn't aware of my job, I knew she'd never support it. But Feyn did what was asked of him. He couldn't deliver in time, and he couldn't keep his mother's wish safe. I don't have to like Feyn to feel terrible for him.

"This is the only place you can find it," he says. "I cast a spell on the library's entrance. Only I may enter. No one would survive crossing the barrier. And since no uninvited human can step foot in Eterna," he turns to me, "how did you get my elixir?"

"Your Highness, I've never seen this liquid before."

"You swear it?"

"Yes, I—"

"On your father's grave?"

I bristle. How *dare* he mention Papi? I've never understood the insistence of referencing the dead whenever people need confirmation. Binding the ones we've buried to our truth is just as disrespectful as binding them to our lies. They have nothing to do with either.

"Something wrong?" Feyn teases. "It should be easy to swear on his grave."

"I disagree. We should only speak of the dead in memories. Not promises. But you're not interested in my views on the matter, so I'll leave it there."

Feyn's laugh chills me more than any of his glares. "I know you're lying. I know you—"

"Why don't you want us to win these challenges?"

It's a question blurted without forethought, a mistake I only acknowledge in hindsight, but I can't take it back. If Feyn demands answers, I'll demand some, too.

"You're in no position to ask. I should've kicked you out the first time you failed."

"But *why*? You've never met me. You don't know what I'm capable of. And you *invited us here*, Your Highness. So why are you acting like we're such a nuisance?"

Feyn walks briskly toward me. He presses a finger against my forehead.

My skull erupts into pulsating, bone-shattering pain.

I fall to my knees, writhing and gasping for air. Something slithers around my eyes. It coils around the sockets, hooking its tendrils tight. Romantic poets and playwrights were all wrong— there's no beauty in agony.

Feyn presses even harder, as if he's coaxing the tendrils free.

I topple like a sack of bricks. Only the fast-paced pounding in my chest hurts.

"There's . . . *nothing.*" Feyn stares at his empty hand like it's betrayed him. Like he was expecting a puddle of gold in his palm. "You weren't lying?"

"No, Your Highness."

"Or you're just getting stronger."

"I wasn't lying!"

Yelling is another mistake, but I'm so fed up. First he tortures me into confession. Now he's ripping my skull apart to steal the elixir. I don't know why it didn't spill out. Maybe I *am* getting stronger. Hopefully, it teaches Feyn a valuable lesson. He shouldn't fuck with me.

He watches me rise without offering help.

"Go to your study session," he hisses. "And don't you dare speak to Aro again. If I catch you talking to him, Jason and Ryujin will pay for your insolence."

"So you won't kick me out?"

"That rule is for normal winners who fail challenges. You're so much more than that, Sevim. You're a mystery and a threat to my kind. I'd rather keep tabs on you and uncover *all* of your secrets. And, of course, make you suffer." He exhales. "Stay away from my brother."

"What does that mean?" I hiss back.

He's already out the library door. "Disobey me again and find out!"

TWENTY-SIX

They wanted the Garden Witch to bring back the dead.

Mourners came every day, begging her to re-create the ones that were taken from this earth. To conjure bone, muscle, and memories for those who couldn't move on.

But they never had anything to offer in return.

"What's in it for me?" the Garden Witch asked.

They said, "What do you wish for?"

She couldn't think of an answer.

I reread the story's new lines. They're not as evocative or aesthetically pleasing as I'd hoped. I don't even know what I was hoping for. The plot still hasn't fully formed in my head. Pulling teeth would be an easier task than figuring out what the hell I'm trying to write.

But I need to keep my mind occupied. I can't think of the doctor, his elixir, or any part of my conversation with Feyn. Dreaming about them will unleash greater chaos—shit will truly hit the fan if Feyn discovers I *was* lying in his library. And since speaking to Aro is out of the question, I must only rely on myself.

Think of the Garden Witch. Think of bringing back the dead.

By the time the guards arrive at my room, I've memorized every single line.

Hopefully, today's dream will be more pleasant than the last.

———————

"Do you grant us permission to access your subconscious?" Ciel asks.

I settle on the familiar black bed. Seeing Feyn in this wretched cave is the most awkward experience of my life, especially since he won't talk to me again. It helps to know he's all the way by the entrance for this session. He and Aro are far enough for me to feel a twinge of peace.

Avoiding Aro was easy—Ciel whisked me to the dreaming area at once. He did ask how I was. I'm grateful he didn't ask again when I ignored him, and even more grateful I didn't turn to see his reaction. Feyn needs to break the news we can't interact anymore. I don't know how I'll win the remaining challenges without his clues, but I won't take that concern with me to sleep.

Think of the Garden Witch. Think of bringing back the dead.

"Yes," I reply. "Go ahead."

"Gracias."

The world goes black.

Then I sit alone by Eterna's shore.

Sunlight shines down on my dewy skin. Everything is quiet.

There is no garden. No witch. No mourners begging for their loved ones back.

I try to remember the lines I wrote moments before falling asleep, but there's only a blank page. It's as if I've never written a single word in my life.

Bombs go off in the distance.

The breeze carries loud, piercing screams from Vieques all the way to me.

There's no chance this is the same nightmare. Feyn told me it can never come back, didn't he? And if I *am* repeating it, he'll cut it short.

I dive into the water.

No one drags me to its depths. I don't hear a man laughing, a beast roaring . . . The swift current takes me to Playa Negra, where the sand is as black as the one I just sat on. I swim until my bare feet brush against it. Once the water only covers from my waist down, I run.

The screams stop.

So do I.

Should I call out? Is that monster waiting for me? Is there even anyone here?

There's no one on the cliff wall. It surrounds the beach like a jagged, honey-gold fortress. The distance between sand and rock is too short; my options for hideouts are low.

Bullets rain down around me.

I dash across the beach. Black sand soon becomes the same honey-gold on the rocks to my left. I'm fleeing from hundreds of live rounds, but there's no sign of either human or elf shooters. I search for crevices wide enough to slip into. Caves that will lead me to the other side of this island. Something to shield myself with. There's nowhere to hide . . . nowhere to run . . .

A monster roars.

Its giant shadow hovers right above me, as if it's chasing me in flight.

I look up.

My foot knocks into something solid.

"Ugh!" I land on top of what I tripped on.

I see the elongated ears first. Then I notice he's not breathing. It's a much smaller elf than the ones I've stolen. The more I stare at him, the less I understand what's right in front of me.

I've tripped on a little elf boy.

His eyes are missing. Dried blood sticks to his brown skin.

"Get her out!" Feyn's yell echoes above, as if he's hiding among the clouds. "Hurry!"

"¡Sí, Su Alteza!" says Ciel.

No. I need to understand what's going on.

As I slowly back away, more elf children appear on the beach. Twenty-six bodies. Their eyes are missing, too. My knees buckle as I wait for a pulse. For any sign these kids aren't actually dead. This is the first time I've seen an elf child outside of a photograph. The youngest elves before them had been Raff and the princes. Are elf kids forbidden from running around Eterna during Exchange week? Shouldn't I have at least *heard* them playing nearby?

"GET HER OUT, CIEL!"

"I'm trying!"

The little boy stirs.

I gasp. "Oh my God . . . Are you okay? Can you—"

He grabs my wrist with a freezing, clammy hand.

"You will never save her. She belongs to us now," he says.

One by one, the others start rising. The beach is no longer

a graveyard.

"You will never save her. She belongs to us now."

The elf children repeat his words in frail voices. They aim their empty sockets at me, as if they can clearly see the girl shaking before them.

"You will never save her. She belongs to us now."

"Shut up!" I yank my arm free. When I jump back, I crash into someone's chest.

The monster unleashes its loudest roar yet.

And it's right behind me.

I quickly turn.

I'm back in the dream cave.

I'm sweating, gasping for air, tossing the sheets aside. How can such a large chamber feel so tiny? My body vibrates with the most potent chills I've ever experienced. I can still feel the child's freezing hand on my skin. I still see the black holes where his eyes should've been.

Ciel and Feyn are on me, their rushed words blurring together. Aro is yelling, too. He tries pulling Feyn back, but his brother is as motionless as a statue. His lips are moving, though. All I can hear is the dead elf children's tinny voices.

You will never save her. She belongs to us now.

"Can't you see she's not okay? Let her rest!" says Aro.

Feyn speaks anyway. "Who were they talking about, Sevim? Who belongs to them?"

"Please let her take a break! She's not well!"

"ANSWER ME!"

"Feyn, you're being . . . you're . . ."

Aro lets Feyn go. His eyes roll all the way back.

He collapses.

TWENTY-SEVEN

I HAVEN'T SLEPT OR EATEN SINCE YESTERDAY.

Exhaustion isn't enough to make me slumber. I can't concentrate with Aro's fall replaying in my mind. And since last night's dinner was canceled, my stomach rumbles louder every hour.

After Aro passed out, Feyn and the guards rushed him away. Ciel escorted me to the lodge. She had no choice but to endure my constant freak-outs about Aro.

"Do you think he'll be okay?" I'd asked her.

"Of course! His exhaustion just got the better of him. How are *you* feeling?"

"Not great. Watching Aro faint is one thing. But right after Feyn was being a total dick? A girl can only deal with so much."

"I . . . I'm sorry for His Royal Highness's behavior. Your

nightmare was quite intense. He could've been much kinder to you. Especially since this year's challenges are so *abhorrent*. I've tried speaking to the princes about modifying the nature of your missions."

"Wait, you have?"

"Yes. Many times."

"And they're still choosing to torture us?"

"I'm so sorry, Sevim. I never want to see anyone suffer. But sometimes there's not much we can do to change the course of events."

"What's the point of being their royal advisor if they won't listen to you?"

She doesn't answer.

Since she dropped me off, I've mostly stayed in my room, wondering what happened to the youngest prince. It would be easier if I had someone to talk to, someone to discuss endless theories with, but my friends weren't in the kitchen during breakfast or lunch.

Ryujin has been crying in bed since I returned. She cries on and off like a faucet dripping fresh pain. I suspect Jason is either too embarrassed or guilt-ridden to show himself after his confession. The good thing is he's not in any physical pain. Whatever Feyn promised to do after his interrogation, it must've been more psychological. Or maybe Jason gave him all the information he had on the rebels and spared himself the ugly aftermath of Feyn's rage. Either way, Jason is in no mood to talk, and I don't blame him.

At this rate, the three of us won't be together until our combat challenge later today.

Ciel had left us a note with one of the guards. She'd confirmed my worst fear that Aro is too ill to attend the challenge. No other details were provided. Of course I want clues. Even if I didn't need them for the stealth task, narrowing down my options saves me time and energy. But more than advancing in the Exchange, I think of Aro's body hitting the floor, the way his eyes turned upward like a slow, spinning billiard. I see him drop in a loop of memories, too weak to run toward him and hold him close. Still too shaken from the nightmare. I hear the children's foreboding message of failure as the youngest prince collapses. As he fails to keep Feyn away.

I've spent all night wondering if those elves existed. If their small bodies ever washed up on Playa Negra's shores just like they did in my nightmare. Of course Feyn would keep elf deaths from humans, especially with such young victims, but why would *I* dream of children I've never seen? More important, why were their eyes removed? Our portraits in the second strength challenge also had empty eye sockets. Could there be any correlation between them?

My first theory tied the bodies to rebels. What if Feyn disposed of anyone associated with his enemies? The internet was no help in providing information about child casualties. None have been reported during the mainland battles or the royals' murders. But I also couldn't find evidence of elves younger than Aro and Raff. Considering they're both seventeen, Eterna has spent more than a decade without pregnant inhabitants. How will they continue as a species if no one gives birth?

You will never save her. She belongs to us now.

What if Feyn isn't tied to these deaths? Or—as much as I hate cutting him some slack—with Mami's kidnapping? Whoever took her could've also hurt the innocent kids on that shore. That could be why Feyn doesn't want me seeing deeper into the nightmare. He might not have hurt those victims. But he knows who did, and he's terrified.

I shudder and hug myself.

I imagine Aro holding me instead.

The root of my rage switches from knowing he's fallen ill to not knowing why. I want that clue for tomorrow's challenge. But I want to be there for Aro more. He's already stayed at my side while I was recovering. I never expected to willingly return the favor. To care about this overly chatty, reckless elf. As hard as I push the thought away, here I am opening a map of Eterna online. Aro's tree house is a little drawing by the northern seashore. It's nestled between palm fronds, reaching for the sky in a three-story wooden structure.

To hell with Feyn's threat. I've passed his stealth challenge. What better opportunity to practice my magic? Besides, if I approach Aro with both sympathy *and* cleverness, he might tell me more about the bodies. The monster. Whatever the hell it is Feyn is so desperate to hide.

The next challenge starts in two hours.

I tighten my bootstraps and head to the backyard.

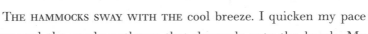

THE HAMMOCKS SWAY WITH THE cool breeze. I quicken my pace toward the sandy pathway that descends onto the beach. My boots are too loud, but I can't afford to move slower—I don't know how long it'll take to return. The last thing I need is elves barging into an empty bedroom.

After walking for a few minutes, beads of sweat already spring from my pores. I let the shoreline guide me onward, sticking close to the greener areas in case I need to hide. Luckily, my journey is filled with the sound of fluttering wings and rolling waves. Colibrís chirp side by side in elf-made feeders, as if its nectar nourishes both body and heart. Farther along the path, emerald-feathered cotorras are perched high on tree branches, repeating phrases such as "¡Bienvenida a Eterna!" and "Welcome to our home!" like robots. I wonder if they're doing more than just greeting visitors—could they also be used for surveillance?

I'd rather fight rebels than get ratted out by a parrot.

I expect elves to lunge at me from the bushes, to burst out of branches, or to shoot me with lightning from afar. Only wings and waves keep me company. The sun's rays grow warmer with each step. I'm bathed in sweat; damp hair sticks to my neck. I regret not bringing water bottles. Every time I gulp, sharp tacks slide down my throat. This unrelenting heat makes the journey to Aro's beach house feel eternal. Like I'll never know what air-conditioning is ever again.

Then I see iron walls high between the trees. Roses decorate the three-story structure; most are dangling from the roof like crimson ropes. The house is wrapped in lights. A mahogany stairwell leads to Aro's front door, where more bulbs shine inside mason jars. All the windows are open. None have curtains; I can't see anyone inside. No one is guarding the perimeter—shouldn't there be more security with constant rebel attacks? Is this a trap for rebels to think they can waltz into the beach house and find themselves ambushed once inside?

The royal family's graves should be nearby, but I don't see them anywhere. Shouldn't their tombstones be visible? A monarch's name would be carved in marble. Their years of birth and death would appear underneath. There should be flower wreaths, letters, trinkets that once belonged to them . . .

Worry about that after you find Aro!

I crouch as I make my way to the house. This side of the island is the same—black sand, glowing gold shores—but there's more salt in the air. It's also less windy, which doesn't help with the dripping beads of sweat. I carefully climb the stairwell. I fear the wood beneath my boots could break at any moment—it's creaking so loudly that it could either be too delicate or even booby-trapped. Still, I arrive to the front door without trouble.

I go around all three stories, peering into the open windows. There are more roses, more lights. There are couches and hammocks and bookcases and a small bed in the topmost floor.

Aro is on that bed.

Shirtless.

Well, the silk sheets cover half his chest. I can only see the bare, smooth brown skin on his shoulders and clavicles. He's writing in a leather journal. His brow is furrowed in intense concentration. Other than his sunken eyes and the bags underneath, he seems perfectly alert.

Which is why he sees me before I duck.

"*Sevim!*" Aro shouts. "What are you *doing* here?"

I groan as he waves me inside, moving much slower yet flashing a smile. Suddenly, my boots are anchored to the floor. Aro keeps motioning for me to join him. The point of me being here *is* to join him. But judging from how warm my cheeks feel, I wait until I'm not bright red.

"Raff is out doing laps! Come in before he sees you!"

"Ugh . . ."

I slide the window open, then enter at a snail's pace, imagining landmines under the floorboards. I must admit they're cleaner than expected. Aro keeps his beach home spotless and smelling like cherries. My appetite grows with each whiff of the fruity aroma. But there aren't any candles. The scent and tidiness could be a spell. Maybe his maids take care of it—princes would be too entitled to sweep and scrub. Not even the gilded mirrors have one speck of dust.

They don't show my reflection.

I move out of frame, then walk toward the mirrors again.

I still can't see myself.

"They only reflect me," says Aro.

"Oh. How vain."

"Actually, my mother made them. She said, *'So you can always see the most precious thing in the world to me.'* My brothers have ones, too." Aro hesitates. "I mean, Feyn has . . ." He smiles, but his lips don't quite lift as high. "Anyway, you need to leave. Like, right now."

"What happened in the study chamber?"

"I'm serious. The combat challenge starts in an hour and a half!"

"I'm not leaving until you explain yourself."

"Exhaustion. Stress. Those things get the better of you sometimes."

He answers way too quickly—a rehearsed excuse.

"Aro, that didn't look like exhaustion and stress. You seemed . . ." I don't even know what to say. I walk steadily toward the bed, stopping once I'm close enough to touch the sheets. I hope for the right words to pour down on me like spring rain. Something that will lead him to the bodies and the monster and whatever else Feyn is hiding. But all I come up with is, "Gone."

"I did lose control for a moment. I'd just seen what *you* saw in your nightmare."

"And it affected you?"

"A lot." Aro gazes at the wall. "A lot," he repeats, this time lower.

"Why?"

He squints at me. "There were dead elf children on the beach, Sevim."

"Yes, but did you know any of them? Were they all part of my imagination?"

"Of course they were imaginary. Why would you ever dream of faces you've never seen? And when they mentioned failing to save your mom, I was *so* worried Feyn would question you about her. That he'd throw yet another fit if you didn't tell him anything. I tried keeping him away, but he insisted, and my body couldn't handle it."

He pushes off the bed.

He's very much still shirtless. His bruises must've been healed; there's no sign of black or blue on his brown skin. He's chiseled in ways a seventeen-year-old human would be if he worked out often. Not that I've ever stood in front of a half-naked boy back home, but I've seen them practicing basketball and volleyball and jogging around the track field and—

Aro is walking toward me.

I open my mouth in vain. There is absolutely *nothing* coming out.

He makes a beeline for his closet and grabs a plain white shirt.

Thankfully, he puts it on. I'm still lost for words, but at least he's not half-naked anymore.

"As much as it hurt to witness your nightmare," he says, "it hurt much more to know your mind was forcing you to experience that. I wanted to wake you up, too. I never want you anywhere near horrible things again, whether real or imaginary." He's respectful enough to keep a good six feet between us. "Is there anything I can do? What do you need?"

No one has ever asked me that.

Mami always cheered me up with a sonnet or scene. With flowers she stole from other people's gardens. Promises of brighter, easier days whenever the universe and all the stars chose to grant her steady income. When Papi died, she would lay my head on her lap and read me books aloud, talking excitedly about adventures I didn't care for. She'd tell me to find solace in dog-eared pages, words underlined in red ink, but the only fiction I held dear was a world in which my father still lived. Mami's efforts were all rooted in *her* interests. She never inquired about mine, and I think she might've suspected how dark, how bloody, they were, especially whenever I spoke of finding my father's killer.

Sometimes people already know the answers you wish to give them.

They'd rather you never speak them into existence.

But Aro *thrives* on verbalizing every little bit of his being. Even when no one asks him. Even when no one cares. There's a certain power that comes with honoring your truth in words without expectations. Without waiting for someone to reach out and catch you. To hear him ask how he can comfort me . . . how he can grant peace without rooting it in *his* interests . . . He was lying about mastering seven languages. Clearly he's also fluent in Sevim Burgos.

"What's wrong?" he asks.

It's only when he speaks that I feel tears slide down my face.

I consider locking myself in Aro's closet. Somehow crying is much more intimate than his half-nakedness. It exposes me as the powerless girl I've fought so hard not to be. A girl who can't do anything well on her own.

"I'm sorry . . . I was just thinking about my mother. When you asked what do I need, I could tell you to bring Mami in one piece. To revive my father. To help me win these challenges and get me off this island without kicking me out. To speak with my friends without putting their safety at risk. And I want my life to finally mean something. The saddest part isn't that *you* can't grant me that. It's that I can't grant it to *myself.*"

"You're not supposed to, Sevim. Nobody is supposed to do everything alone."

"I know, but—"

"No, no, listen. Remember when we first met? What did I conjure for you in the car?"

My tears slow in their descent. "A rose . . ."

"That's what you remind me of. Roses are *commanding*. Even with larger, more colorful flowers around, they make you stop and admire them." He looks at the floor as he takes a step back. "Sometimes I dream of a rose garden."

I swear I misheard him.

But he's not speaking anymore. Not meeting my gaze. He lets silence reign over us, as if allowing me time to process what he's confessed.

"Aro . . . you can . . . *dream?*"

He looks up at me. "Yes."

Now it's my turn to let silence take over. How in the world can he dream? Has he always been capable of dreaming? Can all elves dream and have been keeping it a secret? If Aro is the only one with this ability, what's the point in using humans when he's around?

"Tell me," says Aro.

"What?"

"Your questions. I can see you're thinking about what to ask." He shrugs. "Say them all."

So I do.

Aro sits at the edge of his bed. He peers down at his ring, then at the floor. "I've only been dreaming for less than a year. No one else in Eterna can dream. At least no one's mentioned it. And I can't give my dreams away like humans. They won't leave my subconscious."

"Ciel can't extract them?"

"Not her. Not my brother. No one."

His problem is the opposite of mine. Even though I'm not supposed to have a recurring nightmare, let alone further develop it in subsequent sleeping sessions, I do. Maybe it won't matter how many times Feyn removes it. There's a chance it can still return. But Aro's dreams won't even allow for removal at all.

"What do you think is causing this?" I say. "If the other elves still can't dream, there must be something going on with you specifically. Have you been feeling ill or different?"

"No. It's just that sometimes," he glances at me again, "I dream of a rose garden. It's on a glass stage above the sea. I can enter along with anyone else I invite, but for the most part, I'm alone." He swallows slowly. "And when I'm not alone, someone is always hiding in smoke and shadows. I can't see or reach them. I try, but it never works."

Pangs break out across my chest. I don't know if seeing him so defeated is what's forcing one foot in front of the other, drawing me closer to him. Maybe it's the way he's completely dropped the charm and false optimism that comes with being a public figure. A *royal*. There's nothing regal about the elf sitting before me. Nothing put together or meant to impress.

Now he's just a boy.

He knows what it's like to be lonely, to miss what can never return.

"How often do you dream of this garden?" I ask.

"Every night."

"And if you could guess, who do you think is the person in the smoke and shadows?"

"My family. Papi, Mami, and Lexen. I like to pretend they take turns visiting me."

How I wish he hadn't said that. I would've preferred him speaking of some elf girl he's crushed on, or a sinister force bent on tricking him just like I was tricked. Wanting his dead loved ones to slip into dreams he's not supposed to be capable of having? He's ripped my chest wide open now—if I were in his shoes, I'd want the same thing.

"Wait, why am I wasting your time? Sevim, you *really* have to go. The challenge is—"

I lean in for a kiss.

Aro steps back, holding out his hands. "What are you doing?"

"I . . . I just felt like we—"

"Letting you in here was a mistake."

The first time I had my nightmare, someone tried to drown me.

Aro's words are the current sweeping me under. They're too strong, too sudden, to swim against. I'm not in love with him. But he still holds parts of my soul in his hands—ones he's carefully put together with kindness. Is this another trick? Have I fallen into a fuckboy's web?

"A mistake," I repeat gravely.

He won't look at me. "I shouldn't have an Exchange winner in this house. Especially one who's on the island with such a desperate ulterior motive."

I cross my arms. "Desperate . . . ulterior . . . *motive*?"

"Don't you want to save your mother?"

"Obviously!"

"You're more interested in receiving clues, right? You're showing me interest because you need to finish the Exchange. I want to help you, but not at my heart's expense, Sevim."

He's really throwing this in my face? Even though there's some degree of truth to his suspicions—I *have* prioritized the clues—he's letting his insecurities get the best of him. And he's conveniently telling me he doesn't trust my intentions *after* I try to kiss him?

I should've fucking listened to Feyn.

I should've stayed away from his brother.

"You could've said this before now." I hiss as my eyes well up. Wiping my tears is the only thing I'm capable of right now. Aro doesn't deserve to see me cry.

He *finally* looks at me.

And he's tearing up, too.

"Wait. You think I was tricking you?" he asks.

"You knew I was vulnerable. I've never dropped my walls with anyone else and this is what I get."

"Okay, but it's just that being with you . . . it makes me over-think everything."

"Then I'll help clear your head."

I walk toward the door.

"Sevim, wait! I can get you to the garden faster! I've been testing a new spell. You walk through a golden archway and arrive to your destination."

I almost stay. Give him chances he hasn't earned and never will.

"Keep your tricks and clues, Your Highness. I don't need shit from you anymore."

I bolt downstairs, crying all the way back to the royal garden.

TWENTY-EIGHT

I ARRIVE AT THE GARDEN THIRTY MINUTES late.

The challenge hasn't begun.

"I'm so sorry, Your Highness!" I tell Feyn, who's already on the floating glass stage. This is my first time seeing him in a long black shirt. I'm glad he owns more than crop tops.

His choice of wardrobe isn't as unsettling as his silence. He's barely even looking down.

I stand between Jason and Ryujin. "I take full responsibility for being late! Please take this out on me alone! Not my friends!"

"We're in no hurry today." Feyn turns ever so slightly to Ciel. He winces as if he's unable to move more. They chat privately, but the longer he speaks, the tighter his jaw muscles become.

Is he biting back pain? Is *that* why he's not in a crop top?

"Why haven't we started?" I ask Jason and Ryujin.

"Feyn said we had to wait for you. Where have you been?" Jason jumps right into it. "You wouldn't answer your door, so I thought you were asleep. But you weren't home, were you?"

"We can talk about that later."

"Not if it's gonna distract you from the challenge. You sure your head is in the game?"

"Yes, Jason."

"Then why do you look angry?"

"She always looks angry," says Ryujin.

"No, I mean more than usual, Ryu. Did something bad happen?" He lets the silence linger for two seconds. "Did you visit Aro?"

"I said we can talk about it *later.*"

"So this *does* have to do with him."

Ciel's clap saves me from further awkwardness. "Today you'll be tested in the art of combat," she says. "You must finish the challenge holding a staff. You have fifteen minutes."

Jason and I gasp.

"Fifteen?" Ryujin is the only one who's able to speak.

"Fifteen," says Feyn. "Use your time wisely . . . for once."

"Hey!" Jason catches himself, clearing his throat. "Sorry, Your Highness. It's just that we *have* used our time wisely before."

"Have you?"

"Yes, Your Highness. But go ahead. Finish whatever you wanted to say." Jason bows. "And I'm sorry if my comment offends you. That's not what I intended."

"The last thing you should be discussing is what you intend, Baxter."

It takes me a moment to process the fact that *Jason is glaring at Feyn.*

"What does that mean, Your Highness? If this is about my past, I've already apologized to you a hundred times. You can see into my subconscious when I'm dreaming. You *know* I'm sorry. I don't expect you to forgive me easily. Or even forgive me at all. But could you at least cut me some slack here? Nobody's perfect. Not even you."

Holy shit . . .

I wait for Feyn's brutal comeback.

"Those cojones have gotten bigger," is all he says. His expression is just as icy as Jason's.

The garden disappears.

We're trapped in a black paper forest.

It's burning.

Leaves, trunks, petals . . . they crinkle as flames engulf them . . . beads of sweat sting my eyes . . . I inhale smoke and cough out my lungs . . .

Jason pulls Ryujin and me behind him. "No wonder we only have fifteen minutes. This place will be ashes soon!"

"What are we searching for?" Ryujin asks.

"Anything to put the fire out?"

Jason's confusion is contagious. There aren't obvious tools around to extinguish the blaze, and my hacking cough won't let me focus.

"Maybe . . . the trees . . . have clues . . ." I say.

"Okay, but you stay here. That cough is . . ." Jason starts coughing.

Smoke burns my eyes; I can't keep them open for long. I still scan every tree as quickly as possible. Focusing on the higher branches only shows flames. So I stick to the base. Its paper is holding strong and tearing at a slower pace. I find nothing on the row of trees to the right. When I move to the left side, I can only crack one eye halfway.

It's enough to see the small print.

"There!" I point to the last tree.

When I'm close enough to hug it, I can finally decipher what's written on its trunk:

PASIPHAE

I read it aloud. "What does it mean?"

"It's Greek!" A series of coughs interrupt Jason, but he's walking to the tree. "I read about her for a literature essay on myths! Pasiphae is a goddess! She's the Minotaur's mom!"

"Is there anything about her life that relates to this challenge?" Ryujin asks.

"The Minotaur's dad was a white bull!" Jason speaks as if his words make any sense to me. He's even staring like he's waiting for my gratitude. "It was a trick!"

"The white bull was fake?"

"No! Poseidon sent it to her husband as a sacrifice. King Minos kept the bull, and Poseidon got mad so he made Pasiphae fall in love with the bull, and she disguised herself so they could be together and—"

"Okay, thank you." I don't need more information about how messed up the Greek deities were. Pasiphae gave birth to the Minotaur using trickery. Is that what we have to do here? Manipulate the burning forest into letting us live? How is that combat? Who are we *fighting*?

"Pasiphae." I speak clearly, slowly, as if the name is an incantation. "What do you know about her enemies? How did she fight them?"

"I don't know! She's not as popular as her sister Circe or her dad Helios! Everything I read about her was always tied to other people!"

"So if it hadn't been for them, she'd be forgotten?"

Three wooden chests land at our feet.

Each has a papyrus scroll on top:

FORSAKE FOREVER THE MEMORY

YOU REVEALED IN THE PRISON CELL

AND YOU SHALL RECEIVE YOUR WEAPON

"We have to trade . . ." I say.

"Fine by me!" Jason's cough is finally subsiding. "Do I just open the chest and think about the memory? Or, like, actively wish for it to be expelled from my mind?"

Ryujin and I are quiet.

Of course Jason would prefer to get rid of his memory. I don't need all the details to comprehend just how awful his selfishness was.

But Ryujin and I had our lives ruined.

There's no way she'll erase her mother. Ryujin has already suffered enough. Removing such an important piece of her personal history would invalidate most of it, right? Would she even be the same girl without knowing how she became herself?

And if I forsake *my* memories, am I only forgetting the body snatching? Would I also lose Papi's murder as a catalyst and Mami's kidnapping as a result? How am I supposed to save a woman I don't remember? I can't sacrifice my mother's love in my life's story. I can't abandon her to experience the same—or worse—torture Ryujin's mom went through. Winning that staff is important, but the risk is too high, too uncertain . . .

"I can't lose her again." Ryujin speaks for the two of us. "I can't."

Jason holds her hand between his. "You're not forgetting your mom, Ryu. You're only getting rid of the desire to kill her murderer. That's what you shared in the cell."

"How can we be certain?" I ask.

"We can't," Jason laments. "But we don't have a choice. Time's running out!"

Flames jump onto his arm.

He's burning alive.

TWENTY-NINE

WITH A DEATHLY SHRIEK, JASON ROLLS on the ground.

The fire won't die.

"Eight minutes." Feyn's voice ripples through me like chills.

"Did he just say *eight*?" Ryujin asks.

"Yes!" I yell. "Jason, stop! You have to let us help you!" I don't know how we're getting rid of the fire. Everything around us is already turning to dust.

"WAIT!" Jason is lunging for the nearest wooden chest. He flings the top open and shouts directly into it. "I FORSAKE MY MEMORY! TAKE IT!"

The flames shoot into the air.

They unfurl like long, thick wings, spreading between the paper trees. As Jason checks his arm for burn marks, another version of him appears in the fire. He's in a dark alley. A stranger

is pinning him against a wall. Three more stand a few feet back.
 Rebels.

"You thought you could spy on us and we wouldn't notice?"
the elf holding Jason asks. "You want a slow death. We'll give
you one."

"I'm not spying! I was on my way to the hotel and stumbled
upon your hideout!"

"Really?" The rebel pulls out Jason's wallet. He takes out the
room key. "Your hotel is two towns away, human. What's a tourist
teenager doing in Bayamón alone past midnight?"

"I wanted to sightsee as much as possible!"

The rebel slides Jason up the wall, forcing his legs to dangle
in the air. "Or you were tailing us," he snarls. "Did the royals
send you?"

Jason shakes his head. "I don't know them. I swear I don't—"

"Then what's all this?" Another rebel lifts an unzipped backpack. Books and notebooks are piled together inside. "You've
been documenting our every move in your journals. These are all
of the printed editions of Eterna's history. Clearly you have an
obsession . . . and a motive."

Jason flinches. "Okay! I *do* collect information, but I don't
work for the royals. I'm just curious about your species. I want
to know everything about your war against the Herreras. What's
your side of the story? No one's published a complete view of
your isolationism or your history in Vieques. What *happened*
there? Why are you so violent?" He gasps. "Wait, that was the
wrong word! I'm sorry!"

"Why are you here alone?"

"My family is back in Atlanta. My grandmother passed away
a few weeks ago. Everything's been a mess, so I . . . took a break."

The rebel nods. "Don't worry. You'll be joining her six feet underground soon."

"Wait, I—"

"Unless we strike a deal."

Jason's entire body slumps. It's like his skeleton has evaporated. "A deal?"

"Yes. You can have all the information you want from us."

"What do I have to do?"

"We're planning an ambush in Eterna. Someone with your extensive knowledge and analytical mind could prove useful. And you'll help us develop crueler ways to get rid of the fools on our island's thrones."

Jason closes his eyes. "You want me to hurt the royal family?"

"Yes. Unless you'd rather die tonight?"

"No . . . I can help . . . I'll do it."

The flames fold like a book closed shut. They enter the chest and are locked inside.

Jason's memory has been claimed.

White smoke swirls around Jason's hand. A flash of gold bursts between his fingers, then the light disappears. It leaves behind a tall, slender object.

An iron staff.

"I got it!" Jason roars. "Hurry up, you two!"

A new set of flames lunges at Ryujin and me.

We duck, narrowly escaping the blast.

Then we run.

Ryujin's pounding footsteps are right behind me. We *know* what we have to do. Neither willing to do it. There must be another way to beat this challenge.

"Five minutes," says Feyn.

I duck, dodge, and cough until my ribs ache. I don't know where this paper forest ends. I keep running and thinking about Pasiphae's trickery. Her disguise fooled the white bull. She'd been fooled into falling for Poseidon's gift in the first place. One spell begets another. *You must finish the challenge holding a staff,* Ciel had told us. The fire, the wooden chests . . . it's all designed to push our survival instincts into overdrive . . . to choose self-preservation . . .

But Pasiphae didn't run or surrender. She simply hid her true form. Poseidon made her act like someone other than herself— they both used *illusions.*

What if we don't have to receive our staffs?

What if we can just create them?

The next challenge is for ensueños. This could be the first step toward mastering them!

I throw myself at the ashen pile of paper before me. A fireball flies overhead as I search for the other girl fleeing. "Ryujin, we need to cast an ensueño! We can—"

She's crying into a wooden chest. It glows bright from the flames locked within.

She's surrendered her memory.

Ryujin puts the chest down. Her iron staff materializes a second later.

She's not crying anymore. Her face is a bland, blank canvas.

"No . . ." I whisper. She's given up so easily. Does she even remember she once had a mom? Is that why she looks dead inside right now?

Fire nips at my heels.

I push off into yet another run. The stronger my emotions, the more powerful the ensueño will be. I channel all my fear of burning alive. Never seeing Mami again. I remember the rage ripping my patience to shreds at Aro's beach house. How he dismissed me—*used* me.

Numbing heat surges through me. I'm dragged back as if by an invisible bungee cord. The fire wedges itself into my chest. It doesn't burn; it's *cold*. I'm sparking, but the smoke thickening around me is black. It swirls around my raised hand. A mighty breeze shoves the dark smoke away, taking the cold fire in my chest along with it.

There's a black metal rod in my hands.

It's wrapped in thorns.

They're dangerously sharp, but the middle has space for me to grip it safely. I swing the staff in front of me, over my head, behind my back. It weighs nothing. It doesn't slow me down. My very first ensueño isn't like the others' staffs, but it's exactly what I needed.

A weapon.

THIRTY

THE LAST WOODEN CHEST VANISHES.

So do the flames, the smoke, and the crinkling paper trees. We've returned to the royal garden.

"The combat challenge has been successfully completed. Congratulations."

Feyn speaks somewhere behind me. Knowing we've won another mission puts a smile on my sweat-drenched face, even if the confirmation is coming from him.

At least it's not his brother.

"I did it," I whisper to the thorn staff. "You're mine."

Feyn and Ciel are stepping off their glass stage. The prince heads off to his cottage. He moves as if putting one leg in front of the other shoots pain across his torso.

"Hey. Can we talk by the fountain again? Feyn could come back soon."

Aro's lips brush against my ear.

His warmth had once been a magnet. An invitation to ask for more.

Now I squeeze my staff tighter and stand far, far away.

"When the hell did you get here?" I ask.

"Just a few moments ago. I was hoping to—"

"I have nothing more to discuss with you. Good day, Your Highness."

I start walking.

"Wait, are you mad at me?" he says. "Why are you angry?"

I trip.

My staff props me up like a cane. With my balance regained, I wheel around and watch the flustered prince narrow the distance between us. He leans in close like he's about to whisper.

I speak first. "Are you kidding?"

"No. What's wrong?"

"You cannot be serious."

"I *am*. Why are you angry at me, Sevim?" His tone rises in despair. He doesn't pause, doesn't break eye contact. The dark circles are much rounder, deeper than when we had our fight—one he doesn't even remember.

Because he's not the Aro I fought with.

"It fucking happened again," I say. "He was there . . ."

"Who are you—" Aro's eyebrows are stitched into one. "You mean the trickster? Where was he? What did he do?"

Confirming it won't quiet the howling storms in my mind. The trickster will keep chipping away at my confidence—my very sanity—until I steal Tesoro del Mar and haul myself back to mainland. The thought of being fooled again . . . I can't even keep my eyes open, my fists unclenched. Each drop of blood coursing through me is hot enough to boil flesh.

I wish I could spill it on the trickster's face.

The same face that looks at me now as if it's waiting for an answer.

"He said you have dreams. Was that a lie, too?"

Aro gasps. "I can dream, but why did he tell you that? Where did you talk to—"

"Your beach house. He was alone in your room. Is that why nobody was guarding the perimeter? Because it wasn't you?"

"If it had really been me, I wouldn't have been alone. But *why* did you go over there?"

I almost confess I was worried. That I wanted to check up on him because I care. That I tried to kiss someone who looked like him and he rejected me. The real Aro just confirmed he has the ability to dream. The trickster knows him much better than I do. What if the true prince feels the same way about me using him to save Mami and has been hiding it all along? I'm in no mood to be rejected yet again. Most of all, I refuse to be toyed with.

"Get away from me," I snap. "I'm so sick of these games, Aro. I'm done."

"I know, but that wasn't me, okay? What else did he tell you?"

"It doesn't matter."

"Of *course* it does! I can't help you if you don't trust me."

"How am I supposed to trust you if something shitty happens whenever I do? Your brother wants us apart. This trickster keeps fucking with my emotions using your appearance. You swear it's not you, but where's the proof, Aro? Show me footage of you leaving the beach house. Let me see you searching for Raff on the mainland while I was at that parking lot. There's nothing for me to fall back on. So just stay away from me. I mean it."

"Please listen to me." Aro steps even closer.

I slam the tip of my staff against his chest.

Aro falls too quickly, too easily. He screams as if he's landed on a previous injury.

One that wasn't there before.

The guards circle him; I only notice Raff is in the garden when he furiously pulls me from the commotion. I read his lips as he speaks to the guards: *Get him out of here now.*

Then he drags me down the path to the winners' lodge.

Aro cries in the distance. I've hurt him so, so much worse. If Feyn hasn't heard him yet, he will soon. He'll make me pay for making his brother suffer.

But as each anguished note grows louder, as it cracks larger corners of my heart, I know this is punishment enough.

THIRTY-ONE

"**Y**OU WANNA TELL US WHY IN the Lord's name you shoved a prince?" Jason tails behind me. He looks from me to Ryujin to me. "Or should we start guessing?"

There's no way in hell you'd ever guess.

"Don't waste your time dwelling on it," I say.

Raff is still gripping my arm. In another life, I would've yanked it free. But I've already angered him. I don't need an additional reason to suffer through Feyn's wrath, either. Raff should know I wasn't trying to start a fight. That I didn't expect to hurt Aro that badly. I just wanted him far away, and he didn't listen. This is *his* fault.

"But you deliberately pushed him, Sev. What did he do?"

"Nothing." I turn to Jason, motioning to Raff.

Jason stares long enough for flies to enter his gaping mouth.

Then he says, "Okay." He's nodding like he understands this conversation is better suited for the lodge. "By the way, your staff is gorgeous. I've never seen anyone make their own before!"

"Thank you. It's—"

"What was my memory?" Ryujin asks. She's walking a little ahead of Raff, but she's watching me like I hold the keys to a locked door. Like I'm the only one who can get her out.

She doesn't seem to care that Raff can read her lips.

Or that he's aggressively pointing at the lodge.

"I can't ask about my memory?" Ryujin insists.

Raff shakes his head.

"But it feels so strange here." She rubs the very center of her chest. "It's . . . stirring."

"Is it the same for you?" I ask Jason.

"No. I'm fine."

"And you don't have any suspicions about what you forgot?"

"None." He pauses. "Was it really bad?"

Ryujin doesn't speak.

Neither do I. If they're not meant to remember, why should I remind them? Will their staffs disappear if I confess? The pressure of sacrificing my memory distracted me from understanding *I'd* still remember *theirs*. They have questions I'm not supposed to answer. If they catch me at the wrong moment . . . if I see them struggling with the weight of what was lost, I just might.

But humiliating Jason, breaking Ryujin's heart . . .

I can't let them go through that again. I need to be strong for all of us.

"There are things best left in the past," I say solemnly.

"Okay, but you can tell me if it was really bad," Jason urges.

"Yes. And that's all you need to know."

He falls silent. Maybe he's searching for clues of what he did wrong, but his heavy sigh tells me he's connecting dots in the dark.

"At least you're not in pain," says Ryujin. She's matching Raff's pace now, still rubbing where her chest is supposedly stirring.

I don't know if that's normal, especially since Jason seems fine. But if it were truly dangerous, Raff would've helped her by now, right? He can be mad at me all he wants. Ryujin has nothing to do with my outburst.

Yet all he does is lead us toward the lodge. Once we're near the front doors, he tugs at me a little harder, as if he's tired of my slower pace. He forces me to walk beside him.

He only releases me when we're inside.

Raff signs to us. I read his lips carefully. *No one leaves this house. I'll come back when it's time for your dream study sessions.* He gives me the dirtiest look I've ever received—and this is counting Feyn—before his sour gaze moves to my staff. *What you did to Aro is disgraceful. I don't care why he upset you. You shouldn't have touched him, human. Don't ever do it again.*

"You don't have to be such a prick."

The words fly out of me before I grasp their meaning. Their weight. My mind and mouth are no longer connected. My lips only move when all rational thought is dormant.

"I know he's your best friend," I plod on anyway, "but you don't even know why we were arguing. You're assuming I'm wrong just because of that shove? Fine. I shouldn't have hurt him. But don't act like he's an innocent *victim* all the fucking time, Raff. None of you are. Why was he even screaming like that? Did the rebels get to him again? Feyn's injured, too, isn't he? What are the princes doing behind our backs? What are you so determined to hide from us?"

Raff is already halfway out the doors.

I follow him, making sure he can see me when I speak.

"Why is Aro injured?" I ask.

He ignores me.

"You see? Everyone on this island is a liar. Aro especially."

Raff halts. He glowers at my staff.

He's tearing up.

I wish I could crack open his mind and scoop out the truth hiding within. That I could put all the pieces next to one another like the torn pages of a map. But the longer Raff looks at my weapon, the harder it is to read anything on his sullen expression. It's like he doesn't care that I can see him, yet he's not vulnerable enough to actually show me anything.

He signs one last time.

Aro is the best of us all.

I watch where he stood long after he's stormed off.

THIRTY-TWO

The Garden Witch had everything she could ever dream of. It didn't matter how many times the mourners asked her to choose a reward. Her mind couldn't imagine having more.

One night, a young man visited her on behalf of his widowed mother.

"Bring back her wife," he said. "They belong together."

"The dead can never return," said the Garden Witch. It became her usual response.

The young man shook his head. "The dead don't really leave. They stay in our hearts and dreams. Take what you see in mine and make her appear before us."

"What's in it for me?"

The Garden Witch waited for the young man to ask her what she wished for.

Instead he said, "I'll come live with you in this beautiful garden. I'll tend to it as if it were my own. You can command me as you desire and I'll obey. Just bring her back."

A knock on my bedroom door startles me.

"Sevim? May I come in?"

It's Ciel. She must be escorting me to the study chamber today.

Raff probably refused to be anywhere near me again. I wonder if he's with Aro right now, cursing the day I was born, hoping that his best friend heals quickly from the pain I've caused.

From the pain something else inflicted first.

There's no point in asking Ciel about Aro. All I can do is follow her to the study chamber and see who's in attendance. If both princes are heavily injured, they shouldn't be there. And if they are, whatever's hiding in my subconscious is worth more to them than their health.

"Sí," I answer.

Ciel rushes inside as I close my notebook. "Oh! What were you writing?" she asks.

"Not much." I set the notebook on the dresser, then head for the door. "Is it my turn for the study session now?"

"Yes, but I didn't know you're a writer! Or is that your journal?"

"I *kind of* write stories. I don't know what I'm working on yet. The words are coming to me slowly." I wave to the corridor, frowning. "After you."

Ciel looks from me to the door.

She shuts it.

"Don't we have to go?" I say.

"We do, but . . . Have you written for long?"

I don't understand why she's so interested in this, but I'm not in a position to defy yet another elf, regardless of her rank. The easier I can make bearing my presence for everyone on this island, the better my odds of keeping things as calm as possible.

"Um . . . It's a recent hobby. I'm mostly a reader, but there's a character I've been meaning to develop for a few months, so I'm trying to see if her story becomes anything."

Ciel's smile could thaw frosted glass. "My fiancé wrote stories, too. Beautiful ones."

So *this* is why she's interested. Prince Lexen's reputation mostly relied on his maturity and gentlemanliness—he was the most polite member of the royal family. I have vague memories of being impressed by how well-spoken he was in interviews. Even as a child, when the cameras first came to Eterna, he greeted the human reporters as if he were already king. The last thing I expected was for him to spend time away from diplomatic endeavors to focus on creative ones.

"I had no idea," I say.

"He didn't exactly talk about his work. Lexen was confident in many ways, but his art kept him doubting at times." Ciel's smile starts to subside. She's looking at the doorknob. "But he loved writing. And I loved *everything* he wrote. Even the things he considered trash."

I nod. "Your support must've meant a lot to him. My mother, um . . . she encourages me to finish my story all the time. It's like she doesn't know how to stop being my cheerleader."

Ciel and I share a soft laugh.

"It's important to encourage those we love," she says.

"True. Was he already writing when you started dating?"

"Sí. Obviously I knew who he was, but I'd never spoken to him. My mentor . . ." Ciel grows quiet as she looks back at me. Her smile is officially gone. "The royal advisor before me was a writer, as well. He taught Lexen most of what he knew about writing."

I remember what Feyn said back in Ryujin's prison cell. How that same royal advisor told the king and queen about the rebel leader's wrongdoings. I've never met this brave elf that also wrote. And if Ciel has replaced him, he must either be retired or dead.

"Where's your mentor now?" I dare to ask.

"He's gone," she says.

"Gone as in no longer alive?"

She nods.

"Oh. I'm so sorry. Was it the rebel leader? As payback?"

Ciel opens the door. She's halfway outside, peering into the empty corridor. "We should leave. Prince Feyn must've arrived at the chamber already."

I can't put one foot in front of the other. Maybe the rebel leader did kill him. Or maybe his death is even more tragic than anything I could suspect.

"Sevim? We really should go."

"Yeah, sorry. I'm right behind you."

She exits my room faster than me, as if she's hoping the more distance she puts between us, the less I can figure out what she's hiding. The answers are all in my nightmare.

In the little island Feyn doesn't want me seeing while I'm asleep.

And I'm determined to visit again.

I THINK OF VIEQUES.

Playa Negra's shores. The dead elf children. The monster's roars. I focus on having the same nightmare so I can remain unconscious longer. If I can start where Feyn cut me off last time, I can find out something useful before he wakes me up again. Even if my punishment far outweighs the nightmare.

I prepare to face Aro, too. Will he acknowledge me? Should I expect to see him at all?

Concentrate on the nightmare.

A few minutes later, I'm back in the study chamber. Aro isn't here, of course. Raff doesn't acknowledge me. It allows more time to picture myself among the rising dead. To anchor my mind deeper into the black sand as if removing me will also strip the beach clean. Playa Negra and I will be one and the same.

Feyn sits on a chair that wasn't here before. He must be hurting too much to stand.

I wait for him to berate me. Punish me even worse.

"Sleep well," he says.

I hurry to bed. Surely he knows what I did to his little brother. He's aware that I broke the one rule he gave me. But I won't question his indifference. He might be avoiding confrontation to get me to dream about something more pleasant? To keep me away from whatever took so many young lives? Is he afraid of pushing my buttons and unlocking more images?

Concentrate on the nightmare.

Ciel touches my forehead, sinking me into slumber.

I'm at the beach again.

But I'm already on Playa Negra.

The children are still here. No eyes. No pulse. Detonations are going off above the cliff walls, growing louder, as if they're getting much closer.

The little boy who grabbed my arm doesn't stir today. He's as dead as the others.

I hear his frail voice behind me anyway.

"You will never save her. She belongs to us now."

Then the monster roars.

Muffled sounds follow. I vaguely recognize Feyn's shouting, Ciel's frenzied responses, but the roars are far too loud.

I turn.

Feyn kneels on the sand. He's shirtless. His chest is bleeding from thick, diagonal slashes.

Claw marks.

"GET HER OUT! HURRY!" The real Feyn's shouts are crystal clear now. They echo way up high in the clouds, as if he's standing directly over my unconscious body. "DO IT NOW!"

Cold rushes through me. My boots levitate a few inches. It's like I'm being summoned toward the sky. In a few seconds, I'll be awake.

I picture myself holding the thorn staff. How sturdy, how warm, it feels in my grasp. How it weighs the same as the air breezing past me.

"GET. HER. *OUT!*"

I'm levitating higher. Piercing light creeps at the edges of my vision. I shut my eyes in vain—it shines brighter than a starry night. I groan and grind my teeth and push all my energy into dreaming of the staff. With a blast of black smoke, it appears in my hands.

I stab it into the sand.

Then I pull myself back down.

"NO!" Feyn yells farther, farther away. The tighter I hold my staff, the less I can hear him.

Dream Feyn looks at me. He's sweating, panting, clearly exhausted, but I've never seen him this alert. "Forgive me," he says. "I shouldn't have sabotaged them."

I expect the roars, another voice . . .

I'm the only one here, though. He's not speaking like royalty. He sounds like a servant.

"Who did you sabotage?" I suspect he means his redesign of our stealth challenge, but I won't settle for anything less than actual confirmation.

"I shouldn't have treated them like that. Please forgive me."

"Okay, but who are you—"

"Let me take his place."

The cold returns. I'm a few inches off the ground, then one foot, two feet . . .

My temples burst with pain as I pull myself back down. The staff sinks deeper; I can almost graze the sand. Grunts and gargled noises rain on me—Real Feyn is in the middle of a meltdown outside. His dream counterpart just said something I didn't have clearance to know.

"Who's . . . place . . ." I'm shaking, but my boots are closer to the sand. "And for *what*?"

"Let me take his place."

"Who are you talking about, Feyn?"

"You will never save her. She belongs to us now."

The children are awake. They speak as one voice this time. They watch me without eyes, but I can feel them peering into my soul.

Real Feyn's noises, the explosions, the children's unnerving threat—none of it matters. I need to talk to Dream Feyn. *He* holds the key to whatever is happening. I pour the last drop of energy into pulling myself down. My fingers curl tighter around the weapon I've made, slipping and sliding every once in a while, but I don't let go. I just pull, pull, pull.

Until I'm standing tall again.

"You will never save her. She belongs to us now." The children form a circle around me.

They're closing in.

"Feyn! Who's place do you wish to take? Tell me what's going on!"

He shakes his head as the dead elves walk past him. "I don't want this for him. Please. Choose me instead."

This is pointless. He won't give me new information—he's reenacting the past. And the longer I think of ways to pry clues out of him, the closer the children's clammy hands are.

The little boy I first tripped over grabs me. Then another boy. And a girl.

"You will never save her. She belongs to us now."

"Get back!"

I can strike them. Their small, innocent faces won't stop me.

But they're *so* strong. They're fast, too, seizing me one after the other. All I feel are chilled palms on my skin. They don't go for my staff—they just hold on to me like thirsty leeches.

"Feyn! Answer me!"

The monster's roars rattle the cliff walls, the trees. It's behind me. And it's much angrier.

Dream Feyn is a trembling mess. He's crying.

"Let me take his place," he says through sobs. "*Please.*"

Tiny hands cover my face. The world is darkness . . . nails scratching at my eyelids . . . digging into the sockets and feeling for what's inside . . .

"FEYN!"

I lay in bed.

The real prince stands over me. He's holding his side and breathing as if he's in labor. As if the effort it's taking him to even be here right now is astronomical.

I touch his chest.

His shirt is too thick for warm weather. Too thick to search for claw marks.

But he's screaming.

He shoves me against the mattress. I hit my head against pillows, which soften the impact, but it still gives me whiplash.

I'm rushed out of the chamber. Feyn doesn't even have to give the order. Ciel knows how to help me down and lead me into the corridor. How to put me as far away as possible from the prince, whose screams follow me down the path to the lodge. When I pushed Aro, I confirmed he was injured, but even after my final dream session, I still don't know enough.

One thing has made itself abundantly clear—Feyn's injuries are *real*.

So is the monster.

THIRTY-THREE

L AST NIGHT, FEYN RESCINDED MY INVITATION to dinner.
    I watched fireworks from the living room windows. It was a dull evening at home with more guards stationed outside than ever before, including a sullen Raff. It's the next morning—officially Day Five in this hell of a retreat—and they haven't left yet.

My friends never came back. I need their ideas to make sense of mine. They might not believe my theory that a monster roams Eterna, Vieques, or anywhere in the vicinity. But together maybe we can figure something out. Is that why Feyn hasn't let them return?

No, not him . . .

The monster.

I WRITE DOWN EVERYTHING IN my nightmare as it appeared.

Beach. Explosions. Bodies. Roars. Feyn.

The prince begged for a specific request. Could it be tied to Aro? That's the only elf he'd beg for, and it's the only other elf that's clearly injured. Have they defied the monster together?

More important, is anything in that nightmare tied to Mami's kidnapping? The way those dead kids spoke about her . . . What would elf children have to do with my mother? She's never interacted with one in her life, but I'm sure she'd want to keep them safe from whatever killed them. Where are their bodies anyway? Is there a specific meaning behind their missing eyes?

And if my nightmare is a result of these gruesome magical challenges, why would Feyn not want me seeing something his *own actions* keep provoking? He's in charge of the Exchange this year! Can't he change it back to the tamer activities his parents once hosted? That would guarantee my subconscious focusing on more pleasant thoughts right before sleeping. Why were Jason, Ryujin, and I specifically chosen to experience such atrocious tests? Or were these new challenges always a part of whatever Feyn's plan is? Why change them at all?

Was he really the one who made the decision?

Beach. Explosions. Bodies. Roars. Feyn.

I don't know what connects them other than my nightmare, the elves, and Vieques.

I can't understand my own mind.

But I can dig deeper into my father's hometown.

———— ℓℓ ————

ACCORDING TO THE UNITED STATES Environmental Protection Agency, the damage caused to the Vieques Superfund Site is largely incalculable.

The EPA's website is a dead end for new information. I scroll down the same names I've already heard about on a handful of news outlets. Uranium, mercury, copper, lithium, and napalm are featured prominently. If this monster predates the very first elf, it must've come from a natural source, right? Maybe even the sea; I was almost drowned in my first nightmare.

I can't stop thinking about the children's eyes, either. I click on link after link in conspiracy theory forums. I make sure to dive into elf body parts—specifically, eyes—and reasons why they'd be stolen besides money. There are some posts on rituals for manifesting soulmates, getting your ex back, and spying on those who've wronged you. One post starts with a content warning for cannibalism. I immediately click out. I lose count of the pages and sites I've visited. My vision blurs from reading so much, so fast.

I'm starving. But I don't stop. Even if there's nothing relevant to my theory, I can't rely on anything other than myself right now.

An hour later, I'm clicking on every available website in a frantic attempt at finding *anything* useful. I stumble upon one that focuses on minerals in Vieques. Since I don't know much about the subject, I dive right in. Pinpointing natural resources becomes difficult when considering weather, organisms, microorganisms, and pollution. Limestone, quartz, and granite are the most discussed findings on the island. Each post repeats the same information as the last. It's like no one really understands what belongs to our soil and what was removed.

Just like what I see in my nightmare. None of it is my experience.

Somehow it still belongs with me.

I glance at the bed. What if waiting for the sleep sessions is making me waste precious time? Could I have the nightmare *outside* of the chamber? Since I usually can't remember what goes through my mind during sleep, I don't know if I've dreamed anything in this room. If it only works when Ciel puts me under. She's not here to help me lose consciousness, though.

Feyn's not here to force me awake.

I find a loop of nature sounds to help listeners fall asleep. I play the soothing tracks as I settle in bed, breathing in and out, in and out. This is the first time I've tried using music, but if it works for millions of people, it can work for me, too.

Seven rushing rivers and bird calls later, I'm still awake.

Moving from nature sounds to instrumentals—specifically those heavy on the piano—is much better. I put Frédéric Chopin's *Nocturne in E-flat Major, No. 2, Op. 9* on repeat and close my eyes. One moment I'm inhaling and exhaling slowly, hooked on every note, then darkness cloaks me.

The music keeps playing loud, clear.

But when I open my eyes, I'm not in my room.

I'm in Feyn's library.

His elixir fountain is missing. I sit in front of a desk where it's supposed to be. Watermelon juice drips from my fingers; I'm holding a thick slice inches away from my mouth.

"Careful there. You don't want to ruin your robes again," a woman says.

Queen Relynn walks into the office. Four guards enter alongside her. She smiles at me, then reads a wrinkled papyrus scroll. She's much taller than she seemed on television. Feyn could be her twin—the silver glitter around their eyes, the creamy shadow in metallic tones, and the slow, almost contained movements. I can't even *hear* her approaching. Then I remember she's Eterna's stealth master. It's not enough to never cast shadows. Her footsteps are silent, too.

"Su Majestad," I speak in my own voice, but the words aren't mine at all. I haven't tried opening my mouth in the first place. "Forgive me for eating in the office. I craved a snack."

"Está bien. *I* should apologize for barging in unannounced. But I wanted to be the first to share the news." Queen Relynn raises her scroll. "Your plan is officially approved!"

I set the watermelon slice on a plate. "It is?" I whisper.

"Sí. Arón will be meeting with you to discuss logistics bright and early. He's supposed to return from Vieques by midnight. But let me be the first to congratulate you on another job well done." Queen Relynn claps, but I can't hear a thing. "The Exchange is your best idea yet."

Wait. Did she just say—

"¡Muchísimas gracias, Su Majestad! I know it's a risk to invite humans here, especially after what we've survived, but our illusions *will* grow stronger if they help us. I've studied the human mind and dreams for far too long. Their potency when it comes to altering reality is unmatched. This will definitely take our magic to new heights."

It's still my voice. My lips. But none of the words make sense. Why am I dreaming about being the true source of the Exchange's origin? What does this conversation have to do with the horrors in my nightmare? And who the hell am I supposed to be in *this* dream?

Queen Relynn nods. "I was skeptical at first. So was Arón. We were both fools clinging to the past. That we could simply run away and live in peace. But this is the best way to protect our kind against the enemies across the sea. Their artillery will be no match for our magic."

"Yes, it will. I promise to—"

Gunshots ring outside.

There are three detonations in a row.

"Queen Relynn! Show yourself!" a man shouts. "We have the king!"

I slap both hands to my gasping mouth.

"Keep my sons in the cottage. Do *not* let them out," the queen orders her guards. Then she tosses the scroll to me. "Destroy it. We can't let the government find out about the Exchange yet, and that scroll has all our discussions on challenges. Once you're finished, follow me."

I tap the scroll and it bursts into flames. The ashes fall right on my palms, then disappear.

By the time I exit the office, the queen is already sprinting down the corridor, gripping her iron staff tightly. I'm running and panting all the way out of the cottage. But I don't step onto the path that leads to the garden.

Everything blurs into white-hot light.

Then I'm standing near Aro's beach house.

There are ten humans and one elf by the shore. All the humans are navy soldiers. King Arón kneels before them. Nine are aiming their guns at him. But the king winces as he leans away from the lone unarmed soldier. The man is holding something in King Arón's direction. It's a small, pale stone . . . and it looks familiar.

Ivory.

"Stay away from my kind." The king is pouring sweat. One of his ears starts bleeding. He keeps wincing and glaring at the stone. "I'll give you whatever you want. Just leave us *alone*."

As Eterna's strength master, King Arón should've easily defeated these humans by now. Is the ivory making him suffer? Does it work like some sort of poison that weakens elves? Has Aro been growing ill because of it?

Feyn doesn't have a ring. No other elf does. And even before this year's Exchange, I don't remember Aro wearing it, either. I would've noticed such a unique piece of jewelry. It's like he randomly put it on one day and I always associated it with him. Like it's an unchallenged fact that he's worn it all this time. But when did he actually start wearing it? And if the ring is poisonous, why would he even have it?

Queen Relynn and her bodyguards retreat, patting their bleeding ears dry. That stone is a greater threat than I could've imagined.

"Release him!" the queen commands.

"Our pact was clear. You're supposed to stay on this island forever, and we let you be," says the soldier holding the ivory. "Your husband and his guards were caught trying to destroy one of our armories. Does that sound like peaceful retreat to you?"

"It won't happen again! We're staying in Eterna! You can have our former lands and anything else you wish for. I promise. Please let Arón go."

"He broke our pact. Besides, a strength master would be quite useful," says the soldier. "Unless you have a better offer."

Queen Relynn is crying. Her ears are still bleeding, but she doesn't seem to care. All she can focus on is the elf king moaning in pain.

I take a step forward. Warm liquid drips down my cheeks—I must be bleeding, too. Other than the vague sensation of waves crashing against my stomach, I don't feel pain, but I'm sure that will change if I get any closer to that stone.

"Take me instead," I say. "Our king deserves to be with his family and his island. I'll proudly replace him for whatever you need me to do. His Majesty's strength is greater than mine, but my stealth and illusions outshine his. I can prove more useful to you than he ever could."

"No," says the queen. "Why are you doing this?"

"The boys need their father. I have no children to raise or loved ones to come home to." I nod to the queen. "Let me do this for you, Su Majestad. It's my duty to serve you, after all. I can manage whatever they're hoping to inflict upon me."

I spread my arms to request a hug.

When she nods, I pull her close and whisper, "King Arón is too impulsive. He left for their armory without a concrete plan. But I'm much more calculated. I don't know how to defeat them yet, but I'll find a way to dismantle their operation from within. Vieques will be ours again. All I ask is that you're ready whenever I call."

"We'll be ready," she whispers. "And we'll get you out soon. I won't let them hurt you. That's a promise."

"It's all right, Su Majestad."

"No, listen to me. You're not staying with these monsters. You're not dying. I *swear* it."

I sigh in relief, as if I've dreamed to be this cared for. "Sí, Su Majestad. Gracias."

I walk toward the soldiers, flinching and bleeding even more. My stomach feels like crashing waves, but I push through the nausea and keep going. King Arón stands and hugs me, too. He's squeezing me like he's never been happier to be in my presence. But the soldiers snatch me away. They put a bag over my head and cuffs around my wrists, which burn deep into my bones. They must be made of ivory, too. I'm dragged across sand and sea until I'm picked up and tossed into something hard. Probably a boat.

White-hot light flashes around me again.

Chopin's piano plays loudly as my eyes fly open.

I'm back in my room. I pat my ears—they're not bleeding. And I don't feel like vomiting.

But there's someone sitting next to me.

"¿Mi amor?" says Mami.

THIRTY-FOUR

"Mi amor," she repeats. "Where are we? What's going on?"

It's *her voice.*

I don't see wounds, scars, or blood. How is she okay? How the hell did she get here?

This could also be a trick. The monster would want me to believe this is my real mother. She's appeared just when I'm dreaming about a key moment in Eterna's past. I've discovered King Arón's mission to destroy part of the navy's base—something I would've *never* expected him to attempt. I know what ivory does to elves. What if this is Fake Aro distracting me? He doesn't want me to search for more answers about whose eyes I was looking through in the dream. But based on Ciel's cageyness relative to discussing her mentor, could this have been the former royal advisor? It has to be someone the royals trusted with their lives—literally.

"Sevim? Are you okay?"

Fuck, her voice is so convincing.

But so was Aro's at the parking lot and beach house.

I get off the bed, never taking my eyes off the woman who looks like Mami. The trickster *knows* she's the one person who can pull me away from seeking answers. I've already been fooled into thinking I was speaking to Aro. I won't be fooled again. Besides, why would I easily receive the very reward I'm here to fight for? And if she's real, have I completed the Exchange?

"Soy yo, Sevim," she says. "Soy yo."

She's bawling.

She sounds like the same woman who sobbed next to Papi's body.

I take her face in my hands. Her lips are chapped; she's frighteningly cold.

Part of me doesn't want to ask what Mami has been through. Reliving it could cause more harm than good. But if this is my mother, she'll know me better than I know myself—much better than her kidnapper. Asking surface things such as my school, hobbies, and struggles won't be enough. I have to ask her something only she could know.

"When I was a little girl, you loved to recite a specific poem. You changed the pronouns so it would suit you. This was after Papi's murder. Whose poem was it? What's it called?"

Mami smiles. "You remember that?"

"Yes. Whose poem was it and what was it called?"

"Oscar Wilde. 'Requiescat.'"

She doesn't miss a beat.

"Why did you love it so much?" I ask.

"All of my favorite poems are elegies. They focus on grief and end in hope. But Wilde speaks of daisies. He uses one of my favorite flowers to mourn the dead." Mami's sobs grow louder, wiping the smile off her face. "Your father was hope incarnate. Reading this poem made me feel closer to seeing him again."

A lump forms in my throat.

This is my mother.

This is the sweet woman I would've done unspeakable things for. The woman I would've burned this entire island down to save.

I lift her up. Then I crush her to my chest, our hearts rapidly beating against each other. We're both shaking, crying.

"You're safe now. Do you hear me?" I tell her. "You're *safe*."

"Sí . . . Te amo . . ."

"Te amo. Please tell me everything you remember, Mami. How did you get in here?"

"I don't know. I just woke up and there you were sleeping. I thought you were having a nightmare because you kept wincing and biting down in pain. Are you sure you're okay?"

We break apart, but only enough to look into each other's eyes. "Forget about me. What's the last thing you remember?"

"You'd told me we were visiting El Jardín Botánico. I went to shower while you put my red rose in water." Mami squints as she looks around the room. "After I left the bathroom, everything went dark. I shouted for hours. It felt like *days*. But nobody heard me."

How do I break it to her that she *was* stuck in the dark for days? Where do I even begin to explain whatever is happening on this island? That even though she's somehow here with me right now, we won't know peace until we leave. Maybe not even then.

"Nobody ever came for you?" I ask.

"No. I was always alone. And I couldn't see anything."

"Do you recall anything else that could be helpful at all?"

The door swings open.

Guards rip Mami out of my arms.

I lunge, but Raff locks me in his.

"Unknown human presence detected," says a female guard. "You may enter, Su Alteza."

Aro walks inside.

THIRTY-FIVE

"**W**HO ARE YOU?" HE ASKS MAMI.

I don't know if I should be grateful he's unarmed. He could still summon his staff or drag Mami away. As expected, he looks all the worse for wear—darker circles under his eyes, sallow cheeks, messy hair, and an obvious limp.

This could be the trickster. Fake Aro might be trying to steal back his hostage.

Real or not, this Aro is also wearing the ivory ring.

I don't know why I saw what I saw in that Eterna dream. But now I have another piece of the puzzle. I can't let it slip from my fingers. Not after learning there's kryptonite for elves and how the navy has used it against them. Did they bring ivory to Vieques knowing what it could do? Or did they discover its effects after their arrival? Whether it's just a stone or it's laced with some other form of magical poison, that ring could hold all the answers.

I just have to steal it.

"Natalia Ruiz," says Mami.

Aro offers her the cold glance his brother is known for. A glance that spells certain doom.

"She's my mom." I say. "Tell your guards to stand down. She's not the enemy."

"Where do you live?" Aro speaks louder.

Is he serious? He's just going to pretend I'm not here? I can understand he's mad at me, but this is on another level of immature.

Mami's tears are subsiding. "Carolina," she says.

"How old are you?"

"I'm forty-eight." Mami looks at his ears. "Am I in Eterna? Is this your island?"

"Yes. What's the last thing you remember?"

"Shouldn't she sit? She looks exhausted," I say.

"We'll take her in for questioning soon. This is a preliminary interview to check for brain trauma." Aro doesn't break eye contact with Mami. He's making it very obvious he's hurt. Not just physically—he can't hide that I've broken his heart. Fake Aro acted like I was using him this entire time, but he wasn't exactly mean. This time, though, it feels like he's still sad . . . and angry.

You shoved him and refused to speak to him. What more do you expect?

If this is Real Aro, I need to gain his trust again. I want him to let me in.

And I have to get close enough to steal that ring.

"What's the last thing you remember? You never answered," Aro asks Mami.

"I was at home. Getting dressed. Then . . . nothing."

"You didn't see who took you?"

"No. It's like I've been asleep for a long, long time."

Aro walks briskly to the door. "Guards."

"Wait! You're taking us both, right? We're going together."

Aro stops. "We must prove this intruder is who she says she is."

I yank myself free from Raff and storm toward Aro.

The guards lift their staffs, but none strike. I block their master's path. A master who nervously drops his gaze, keeping up the facade that he can't see me.

"Look at me, Aro."

He doesn't.

"Don't take her out right now. Don't keep me away from my mother any longer." I exhale close enough for him to feel the warmth of my breath on his chin. He still doesn't react. "No one knows her better than me. I can help you prove she's really my mother. And I'm sorry for how I behaved in the garden. I'm sorry for *everything*. You've had to put up with me for far too long, and I've been so disrespectful this entire time."

I choke up, realizing my apology is genuine. My regrets are as vast as an ocean.

"The ensueño challenge is postponed until we confirm the intruder's identity," says Aro. "Feyn will decide how to proceed upon confirmation. Wait for further instructions."

"But I can—"

"Sev!"

I feel their arms around me before I even see their faces.

Jason and Ryujin hug me while the guards walk past us.

They're taking Mami like she's a common criminal. All that's missing are shackles.

"Wait!" I yell.

"Stay here," Aro repeats.

"I can *help*!"

"We don't need you, Sevim. It's laughable you ever thought we did."

Aro signs to Raff: *Hurry up.*

They exit together.

THIRTY-SIX

SPEND THE REST OF THE HOUR confessing to Jason and Ryujin.

Well, everything except the Eterna dream. I don't want to invite them into that specific conversation until I know what's happening with the ivory ring, the navy's pact with the royals, whichever fate befell the elf that traded their life, and what it has to do with the monster. What it has to do with *me*, since I'm apparently tied to this mess, too. It's a lot to take in, even for an elf history buff like Jason. How could I possibly explain dreaming about two separate events I was never part of? Sticking with one will ease them into the chaos better.

Jason and Ryujin help me sit back in bed, hanging on to every treacherous word. I start with Mami's kidnapping and move to the murky waters of Aro's double. Ryujin squeezes my hand each time I mention Mami or the monster. But when I share what

Dream Feyn said, how I'm convinced the mysterious beast is real, her grip loosens.

"Did you see what it looks like?" she asks.

"No. I only hear the roars."

"There's never been any record of monstrous creatures in Eterna," says Jason. "Can you compare how it sounds to another living animal?"

"It doesn't sound familiar. But if hell had a voice, it would sound like that."

Silence falls as my friends glance nervously at each other.

"And those kids . . . were they . . . real?" Ryujin asks.

"I hope to God they're not," Jason replies. "That provides some context for why there aren't children in Eterna, but murdering such young elves . . . How despicable can the rebels get?"

"I don't know if the rebels are to blame," I say. "I think the monster is far more relevant to those murders than I fear. Dream Feyn was terrified, but I doubt he'd ever beg the rebels in such a pathetic way, especially after killing their leader, right? And my mom doesn't remember what happened after her kidnapping."

"So all we have is your nightmare." Jason sighs.

We also have the fact that Aro can dream. What if he's not actually dreaming, though? What if the ivory is making him hallucinate instead? Would that be one of its poisonous side effects? Or is the monster invading his thoughts just like it's invading mine?

"Do you remember if Aro has worn his ring before this year's Exchange?" I ask Jason.

"He . . . He didn't, no."

"Did his parents? Lexen?"

"I can't remember." Jason rubs his eyes really fast. "I'm having a hard time concentrating, to be honest. This is way more than I was ready to digest."

Tell me about it.

"Why is that important?" Ryujin turns to me. "There's no ivory in Eterna, is there?"

"Not that I know of. I'm sure the elves could've either stolen or purchased ivory from elsewhere." I save my kryptonite theory for later. My friends don't seem keen to jump down more conspiracy rabbit holes. They keep sharing uncomfortable glances, exhausted sighs.

Most of my attention is on Mami anyway.

Have they returned her to the monster? Did the elves not know she was its prisoner? Feyn seemed oblivious to my crimes, but he *must* know that beast is the reason my mother is here.

"Sev? You there?"

"Yes. I'm sorry for bringing you into this."

"You have nothing to apologize for. I'm surprised you kept it to yourself this long." Jason rubs his chin. "I'm trying to think about that ring on other royals, but I don't recall them wearing it. Robbing their graves would be too extreme, huh?" He laughs.

"Their graves aren't where they told us," I say.

He stops laughing. "What?"

"I've been to the other side of the island. Their graves aren't there."

"What were you doing all the way over—" Jason's eyebrows rise.

I stare at the floor. "I was . . . investigating . . ."

"And was Aro's beach house part of your investigation?" I can actually *hear* the playful smile in Jason's tone. "Specifically, his bedroom?"

"Jason!" Ryujin slaps his shoulder. "That's none of our business!"

"I'm just trying to understand why she was over there! Hooking up with Aro sounds like the most logical answer. And honestly, I respect that."

"What *matters* are the missing graves," Ryujin speaks even louder, as if she can cancel out Jason's curiosity with sheer volume alone. "Why would they hide those bodies?"

I consider her for a long, long moment. Neither Jason nor I speak; we're conjuring webs and more theories.

Then he says, "You said the rebels probably didn't kill the children in your nightmare. What if the rebels didn't kill the royals, either?"

I gasp. Of *course* they'd blame their enemies. Despite this ongoing war and that bizarre trade between navy and elves in my dream, Aro and Feyn have kept their island relatively safe. I've only captured rebel corpses. If they're so dangerous, why are they dying more often? Would they be capable of killing so many royals?

"I need that ring," I whisper. "It might not get me anywhere, but I have to try."

"Wait. *Aro's* ring? Why do you need it?" Jason asks.

Fuck.

"It's a working theory. I'll explain as soon as I can confirm it."

"Stealing corpses is one thing. Taking something off a living body is different," Jason warns. "Aro is pissed at you. How are you getting that ring if he won't let you too close? Do you understand how risky that is? You're already on Feyn's shit list. They have your *mom*. I don't want you putting her—or yourself—in greater danger."

Ryujin nods. "You just reunited with your mother. She must've been so scared. And we don't even know what she went through.

Let's wait until the interrogation is over so we can understand what's really going on and find out if she has any answers."

"Exactly. I'm always down for solving mysteries, but we shouldn't be reckless."

I want to promise them I won't ruin this. I'll formulate a fail-proof plan this time. They can even help me figure out each detail. Three minds are better than one.

But they stare at me like I'm a wounded baby bird. Maybe Jason and Ryujin might listen to me, but who knows how far they're actually willing to go to help me? Any other day, my first reaction would be rage—I have to do whatever it takes to get Mami away from these elves.

Then I remember only my mom has ever worried about me this much.

Being loved by someone whose main purpose is to love you is one thing. Winning over the affection of strangers . . . I'm not used to it . . . but I definitely could be.

I guess this is what having friends feels like.

"Sevim Burgos, come outside right now." Feyn's voice booms across the house.

I run.

———ℓℓ———

MY MOTHER IS WAITING FOR me.

She's a few feet ahead of Feyn, Aro, Ciel, and Raff. Mami sighs in relief once she sees me. But she doesn't approach—it's like she's tethered to an invisible string in Feyn's grasp. I search for fresh cuts, bruises, anything strange. Her hair has been combed; her dress is free of wrinkles. I wonder if I should go to her. Hug her close. See if this woman is really my mother.

"Is everything okay?" I ask.

"We're pleased to confirm your mother's identity," says Ciel. "This is Natalia Ruiz."

An elf's word is the last thing I should trust. But Mami knew about Wilde's "Requiescat." Besides, if there's anything fishy, I'll catch it when speaking with her in private.

I nod. "Like I said."

"Since she's not invited to the Exchange," Feyn says as he steps forward, "she can't stay here. I've agreed to let her board *Tesoro del Mar* so that she may return home immediately."

Wow. Talk about haste.

"So . . . can I have a word with her before she leaves?" I ask.

"No need. You're leaving together."

THIRTY-SEVEN

"YOU'LL BE STRIPPED OF YOUR MAGIC before boarding *Tesoro del Mar*. A replacement will be arriving from the mainland shortly—a much better fit for this retreat. Say your goodbyes to Jason and Ryujin. Take as many souvenirs as you wish. Your time in Eterna is over."

Five days. I can't even believe it.

I never wanted to come. I'm only here to save Mami. Now she's safe. Getting her home is crucial—I won't rest until she's out of this island forever.

But there's *so much* left to uncover. So much left to understand.

The monster captured the last family member I have. It toyed with me. It's been hurting Aro for God knows how long. It could hurt other humans in the future; I can't be the *only* person to anger it. How am I supposed to leave Jason and Ryujin on an island with a roaring beast hiding somewhere? Even if they're not as invested in figuring this mystery out as I am, their lives could very well still be in danger. My departure won't guarantee their safety. It won't end Aro's suffering, either. It's simply going to prolong it and make it worse.

Besides, I won't forget everything upon returning home. I'm carrying these memories until my dying breath. There's a saying in Spanish: "No puedes tapar el sol con una mano" (You can't cover the sun with one hand). Just because you can't see it doesn't mean it's not there. Feyn, the monster, whoever wants me gone . . . they can ask me to leave.

And I will. I'm getting on that boat to escort my mother home.

Then I'm turning right back—I have to save the prince and my friends.

"Mi amor, ¿estás bien?" Mami asks. "Do you need to sit down? You look really tired."

I can't look at her. It'll make me second-guess myself. And I definitely don't glance back at Jason and Ryujin. Unlike Mami, they have magic. The last thing I need is to alert them to what I'm about to do. "Sí, Mami. Estoy muy bien."

The ring still sits comfortably around Aro's finger. If only I could get close enough to break into the stone . . . search for magic within . . . push any secrets into the light . . .

I need to get him alone.

"Will you be taking us to the mainland, Your Highness?" I ask Aro.

He stares at me like I've dropped him on the side of the road and forced him to walk to his house in the middle of a rainstorm. "*Tesoro del Mar* is my brother's boat. *He's* taking you."

"Can't you join us?"

"No."

I flinch. Maybe a flying baseball to the knee would've hurt less. "I'm looking forward to joining my mother on the voyage back home, but I do have one request, Your Highness," I speak to Feyn. As absurd as it sounds, he'll probably be the most sensible prince in this conversation. "Once I'm certain she's inside the house, may I return to Eterna and complete the Exchange?"

But Feyn laughs cruelly. "You're no longer a ticket winner, Sevim. That means you can't return. There's nothing here for you to complete."

"And how did you come to that decision? How does it make sense for you to kick me out just because my mother has appeared on the island? You knew I stole elf corpses. You knew your brother was providing me with clues to win the challenges. You always stopped me from seeing what's in my recurring nightmare. Quite frankly, you've hated me since we met." I fold my arms as I step forward. "You still kept me around."

"Precisely. It's all added up now, and it's too much to keep dealing with. Hurry up with those goodbyes, Sevim. Your replacement is waiting," says Feyn.

He's not going to budge. Neither will Aro.

Let me try a different approach. Something that could potentially humiliate me, which is what Feyn lives for.

"Give me one last magical test, Your Highness. Not a formal Exchange mission—like you said, I'm not a ticket winner anymore. But ask for whatever you wish. Make it as outlandish as possible. Anything that seems too difficult for me to accomplish. If I fail, I head home with my mother. If I succeed, I escort her to the mainland and come right back."

"You have no authority over me. You have nothing to bargain with."

"I'm politely asking for one last chance."

"And you won't get one, so stop——"

"One last chance, Feyn," Aro interrupts. "We both know she won't succeed, so I think there's no harm done in letting her use magic before she leaves. This will be her goodbye." He cocks an eyebrow at me. "Forever."

You wish.

Feyn's sigh is as long as my list of questions about what's really going on. He throws me a nasty glare. "Aro's right. You won't succeed. But if this will get you to *shut up and go*, let's begin. Aro? Did you have something in mind?"

He nods. "Ensueños are the world as you wish to see it. They're mostly used to conceal, but you can craft the loveliest things from your deepest desires." Aro hides his hands behind his back. "For your final test, you'll need to picture something beautiful in your mind. It should be big enough to fit in the palm of your hand. Give it as much color and detail as you wish. Then try imagining it in our world. If you can focus hard enough, it will become real."

"So . . . it can be anything?"

"As long as it fits——"

"In the palm of my hand, yes."

"You already created a staff, which is much bigger, but it was actually easier to make. The adrenaline of being stuck in a burning forest helped you focus better. You were driven to create something *useful*, not aesthetically pleasing. Art cannot be rushed. Something that tiny and breathtaking takes more time and effort. Which is why you'll only have three minutes."

Damn you.

I try thinking of so many things that could fit in his palm. But only one makes the most sense. Only one strikes me as the beauty he's so ardently passionate for.

I have to make him a red rose.

Sometimes I dream of a rose garden, the trickster told me in Aro's room. *It's on a glass stage above the sea. Only I and whoever else I invite may enter.* What if I make a whole garden instead? I'd give the real Aro what he's asked for, but I'd also create a space where I can corner him and see what I can find from his ring.

"May I begin?" I ask.

"Sí."

I bow. "Thank you, Your Highness."

Then I close my eyes. Everything is red—first I see one petal, then another springs from its side, then another until the rose is in full bloom. I reach a hand out as I imagine more roses filling up the garden. Their stems grow taller. Dozens of flowers are piled tight in a perfect circle; the tips of their thorns touch as if they'll make a promise.

Water rises beneath the roses. Teal waves spin like the world's slowest carousel. They halt twenty feet off the ground. I let more roses loose around the garden, imagining tables and archways made of starlight silver. Each human and elf in attendance has their legs wrapped in petals. Slowly, the petals transform into their seats for the afternoon, complete with thick vines that bind their wrists, cover their screaming mouths . . .

I finish with the glimmering waterfall. It enfolds the rose circle like a curtain. No one can see through it. And thanks to the chains, no one can move.

My clothes stick to me as if I've sprinted into a storm.

My knees knock into each other as I gaze at the circle of roses and its surrounding waterfall. Most of our guests are seated beyond.

Aro and I are alone among his favorite flowers.

"What did you do?" he hisses. "How did you even make all of this?"

"You dream of a rose garden, so I made one. I pictured something beautiful in my head. I could only picture you."

Whatever Aro planned on saying is lost in the wind. His body relaxes and tenses in the span of a second, as if he wants and doesn't want to be complimented.

I place a rose on his hand. "Since you're already real, I settled for something you'd like."

He blushes fiercely. "Hmm . . . That's . . . wow . . ."

"Did I succeed, Your Highness? May I stay?"

Aro doesn't answer. He's lost staring at the rose, as if he still can't believe what I've done. Catching him speechless is a rarity and a gift. But I'd very much like to know my fate.

"May I stay?" I repeat.

"I'll . . . talk to Feyn and, uh . . . we'll deliberate."

"I thought you said—"

"We have to deliberate," he says louder. He's refusing to look at me. It's like he doesn't want me to see the lies swimming in his irises. The princes have nothing to deliberate. Aro might just be nervous about the monster getting pissed with me still being here. Chances are it's still kicking me out or maybe worse, especially if it learns how powerful my illusions have become.

I have to hurry.

"Aro?"

"Yes?"

I touch his ring.

The ivory stone splits open in my wild, racing thoughts.

Then it seals itself shut.

You're not hiding from me anymore.

I picture it opening wider, wider, spilling out its golden light. The stone quivers as if it's about to burst. I quiver, too.

"What are you doing?" Aro tries to pull his hand away.

I hang on to the ring that's fighting to keep its secrets and imagine its stone cracking at the edges. I continue breaking, breaking, breaking, and I only stop once the stone is in pieces.

"Sevim, stop! You have to—"

BOOM!

I'm at the beach now. The skies are still clear—more than in these past few days.

A golden ring of light circles over the island.

It hovers above the kneeling elves on the coastline.

The beach is overrun; it's like all the islanders have been summoned. But there are still no children. Everyone silently faces the water with bowed heads. Are they praying?

Or are they waiting?

THIRTY-EIGHT

RUN BEHIND A PALM TREE.

And I trip.

The fall is swift. Only the sand rustles as I hastily pull myself up again.

Nobody turns. My stealth magic must be silencing each step. Unless this is a dream. Or is it like my other visions? If memories can be accessed through Aro's ring, does this one belong to him?

He kneels between Ciel and Raff. Aro's head is bowed the lowest as he rocks side to side. His gloved hand is on top of the other. I can't see if he's wearing the ring.

The golden light keeps circling above. The elves remain motionless. Magic must hide them from prying eyes on neighboring islands. If there *had* been witnesses, we would've heard of such strange activity ages ago. The light glows brighter until most of the beach shimmers in golden hues.

Footsteps crunch the sand.

Feyn breaks away from the rest, his chin up. His eyes are red and barely open, though. He must've been crying most of the night. The prince walks to the very middle of the beach. With a long, deep breath, he faces the golden light above.

The light stops.

All of its glowing tendrils shrink into a ball of energy. It grows smaller and smaller until it's the size of a fist. Then it hovers over Feyn's head.

He shuts his eyes. Quietly breaks down.

"Please spare him!" Aro yells as he raises his hands.

He's not wearing his ring.

"Cállate la boca," Feyn says over his shoulder.

"No! Choose *me*! He doesn't deserve—"

"¡Te dije que te calles! Remember your place, Aro!"

"Stop telling me to shut up! This isn't fair!" Aro puts his hands in prayer form as he speaks to the light. "Please! Choose me instead! I'm begging you!"

"And how exactly would that make anything better? One of us would still be chosen! Our family . . . we would have to go through this . . . we'd have to go . . ." Feyn's cough is loud enough to scare off the pigeons on the tree beside mine. "Through this again . . ."

I hadn't even noticed Ciel's head against the sand. She's completely resigned to the prince's fate. Or perhaps she's avoiding it—her fiancé must've gone through this, too.

Something growls.

Then . . .

The monster's roars overwhelm the beach. Sand jumps with

each bloodcurdling note, as if it's hiding in the island's depths.

"Prince Feyn Herrera, master of combat."

The light is *speaking*.

It's a man's voice.

A man I've not heard in Eterna, my nightmare, anywhere.

"You were born for war. Such a strong, fearless fighter." There's a brief pause, then the loud, unmistakable sound of licking lips. "I have craved your talents for far too long."

Feyn nods. "I . . . I know . . ."

"King Arón and Prince Lexen were both masters of strength."

Ciel whimpers. I can't imagine what hearing her dead fiancé's name feels like, especially from a monster about to claim another royal.

"Your mother, Queen Relynn, mastered stealth." That cringeworthy sound of lips licking carries on. "As next in line to the throne, you will empower me even more."

Feyn's jaw twitches. He's biting down hard, as if fighting back insults, tears, or both.

"Next in line," I whisper. The way this light talks about the dead royals . . . almost like he claimed them, or rather, their abilities . . . like they were all . . .

Sacrifices.

I remember how there were no graves near Aro's beach house. Feyn told us he killed the rebel leader right after Lexen's murder. How he avenged his family's deaths. But he hasn't avenged anything—the murders are still happening. It's *his* turn to die.

"Please!" Aro digs his hands into the sand. He's shaking like he's about to burst. Like he has a million vicious words to launch at the light.

Feyn turns around. "I'm not going to say it again! Shut up and stay out of this!"

He faces the light once more.

"I'm ready," he says shakily. "I'm ready."

"Fate does not care if you are ready, Feyn. It waits for no one," the light says. "And yours has finally arrived."

BOOM!

A ray of light shoots down to Feyn.

Aro sprints.

A panicked Raff follows him.

But he's not as fast. None of the guards are—they all chase the reckless prince in vain. His despair has given him wings. He pins Feyn down, exposing his back to the light.

It hits Aro instead.

"NO! WHAT HAVE YOU DONE?!" Feyn tries pushing his brother off, but the light's powerful blast keeps them both down. "WHAT HAVE YOU FUCKING DONE?"

Screams fill the beach.

Aro's are the loudest. The light covers him whole; it creates a bright outline of his body.

This is where it all began. This is where the youngest prince knew his brother would be chosen for certain death . . . and took his place.

That's why Dream Feyn begged to replace him. It was always supposed to be the next in line. He couldn't stop Aro from saving him. Even if it's a short-term solution, even if Feyn will still have to die soon, Aro made sure his brother won't suffer before *he* does.

Aro isn't being tortured. He's not suffering injuries from constant battles against rebels.

He's *dying*.

Roars shake the earth.

The elves tremble along with it.

"You will regret this, young prince!" The light's voice echoes across the beach. It slowly returns skyward, leaving behind an unconscious Aro.

A golden string wraps itself around his finger. When the light disappears, all that's left is the ivory ring—the mark of his sacrifice.

Raff pulls Aro off Feyn's back. He's shaking his head as he cries.

"Por favor, no . . ." Feyn rips Aro away from Raff. He sobs into his little brother's chest. "Por favor . . . Aro . . . no me hagas esto . . ."

The roars continue as the light shoots off in different directions.

It sparks and buzzes across the whole beach.

GET BACK TO THE GARDEN!

The voice no longer sounds like it comes from the light.

Now it's in the sky, in the warm breeze sweeping past me, in the tree bark I'm gripping tight. It's in the rays of light circling me, heating my skin until I'm drenched in sweat. The voice is rightfully furious. I'm an uninvited guest to a memory I should've never seen.

Now I have to take a souvenir.

I clutch a ray of light. It burns ever so slightly, but I hold on. "What are you?"

Anguished screeches fill my ears. Colors swirl around me . . . hundreds of bombs are detonating . . . the elves vanish as if they were specters . . . the world becomes fire and fury . . . but I hang on. The light resists, pulls back . . .

I yank it closer. The harder I force the light toward me, the faster it morphs into a pale, porcelain-smooth hand—the monster's true form isn't monstrous at all.

LET ME GO!

Explosions, roars, screeches . . . it all morphs into one sound . . . I flinch and tear up and gag.

But I don't let go.

GET BACK TO THE GARDEN RIGHT NOW!

The palm of my hand is scorched to the bone. I won't have bone left if I hold on.

"No!" I say.

I yank the pale hand out of the light.

I fall on my back. The chaos on the beach is over—everything sinks into darkness.

Someone tumbles down with me.

THIRTY-NINE

L IGHT SHINES ON THE STRANGER.

Black hair falls to their feet—much blacker than mine. It covers the stranger's face. They wear gold robes made of the finest, shiniest silk, making their flesh seem whiter. Fantasy and horror films have conditioned me into thinking a roaring beast would be grotesque. It would have many limbs or none at all. Monsters have tails, wings, fangs, or anything else that makes it less human. But there's nothing inherently monstrous about whatever lies a few feet away.

I rise. My hands are up, even though my burned palm is bleeding. I bite down as I try closing it into a decent fist, but the pain is insufferable.

"What are you?" I ask.

The monster's movements are too fluid, too graceful, as if

their body is boneless. They sweep their hair back, revealing my enemy's true face.

"You insolent little devil," he says.

The deep rasp is gone. I've heard it countless times in his messy living room, where he first explained how to dab Feyn's elixir into my eyes, how to properly fit a dead body into the trunk of Mami's car. It's not the voice of a sad, desperate man with a vendetta against Eterna. The man who believed elves killed his childhood best friend.

He's not even a *man* anymore. His ears are elongated into sharp tips; his eyes are as gold as his robes. He's much taller, as well—almost seven feet.

"You . . ." I drop my hands. I don't have the energy to lift them again.

Not after seeing Doctor Ramírez as an elf.

"Things did not have to be this way, Sevim. You were never supposed to see that memory, but your stubbornness is your downfall."

"*You're* the one causing all this grief, Doc—" I let out a sigh. The man I knew is gone. I wish learning the truth was as easy as accepting it. "You haven't answered me. What are you?"

The elf smiles. Blood coats his teeth. He slowly licks each one, as if he's savoring their coppery taste. My thoughts transport me back to the parking lot conversation with Aro. He licked his blood-stained teeth, too. He's never licked them in front of me since.

"You've been pretending to be Aro, haven't you?"

"Ah, yes. I had a different name once. But we don't speak it anymore. It belongs to someone who no longer exists. You may call me Primero."

"The first? What are you the first of?"

He moans, as if contemplating what to say. "I do believe that name is also problematic. I'm not just the first—I'm the only one."

"Of *what*?"

Primero laughs. I never knew Doctor Ramírez could make such a joyous sound, and now that it's coming from such a cruel creature, I wish I'd never heard it.

"Not only have you invaded my memories, little devil. You also demand answers you are not prepared for. Defy me all you wish. You will never be ready to face the truth."

"Memories? Plural? What do you——"

Aro's sacrifice on the beach is only one of the things I wasn't supposed to see. The Vieques nightmare is unmistakably another. But there's one more secret I was never meant to discover. A pair of eyes I saw it all through. Someone who risked their life for the king and promised to dismantle the navy's base from within. If this is the same elf, wouldn't Aro have recognized him when he researched Doctor Ramírez? Unless he was disguising himself even in pictures or fooling Aro in some other way?

Ciel's heartbreak over her mentor's death . . . Feyn's hesitance to talk about him at the prison . . . Aro speaking about how complicated loyalty is after I woke up from the cobra bite . . . it's all sewing itself into a twisted tapestry in my head.

"You were the royal advisor. You offered yourself to save King Arón." My mouth runs dry despite how much I gulp. "The Exchange was your idea. Aro's parents made it look like it was theirs instead. And you failed to do what you promised in Vieques. The navy didn't leave because of you. The ivory kept you trapped there, didn't it? It kept you powerless?"

"Sevim," Primero says my name like a warning. Like I'm

pushing through doors that have been locked not to keep me out—but to keep me safe.

I don't care about safety. That's been out of the equation for way too long.

I want answers.

And I think I've had them all along.

"The fact that you're killing *royals* . . . you're so determined to punish them and steal their abilities . . . it seems personal. But how does someone go from sacrificing himself for King Arón, after devoting years of service to him, and wanting his entire bloodline dead?"

"Now, now, little devil. Careful what you wish for."

"If it's personal, then not only did you fail to uphold your promise, so did King Arón and Queen Relynn. They never saved you, did they? You were trapped in Vieques waiting for them to free you, but they didn't come? Is that why you hate them so much now?"

Another spine-tingling laugh escapes Primero. "Everything you say is true. The king and queen abandoned me. I was taken back to our ancestral home and left there to rot. They swore they had their reasons. Ivory is extremely poisonous for elves." Primero switches to a higher pitch, as if he's imitating the queen. "The navy could've created weapons with it and killed us. We were hoping to strengthen our magic through the Exchange before rescuing you."

Primero's golden eyes flash. "They preferred to use my plan for their own personal gain and glory." He's back to his normal voice. "To have the world beg for their magic and treat them like gods. After all I did for them and their children, abandoning me was how they repaid me."

I gape at him. This isn't the way he spoke in the memory. That elf had been compassionate, patient, and optimistic. "What exactly happened to you in Vieques? You sort of look like an elf, but you're still different. And you can do things no other elf can."

"Oh, you are indeed smart. The elf I once was died soon after my return to Vieques. My makers were committed to transforming me into the most powerful magical being alive. They poked and prodded and made me bleed out the old version of myself. They took many years to perfect what I am now."

"They were conducting experiments along with their war drills?" I hold my head as if it's about to fall off. It keeps thumping, spinning. Then Primero's last words strike me like a thunderstorm. "Wait. What was missing?"

"Magic. My makers obtained Feyn's elixir after joining forces with the rebels. They were promised weapons, tactical assistance, and other rewards they never received." He laughs again. "This was long before Feyn put the protective spell around his fountain, so stealing his elixir was rather easy. The hard part was taking the children."

I'm back at Playa Negra with the bodies. Those small, eyeless corpses were real, too.

"Children," I repeat. "They killed . . . *children* . . ."

"No. They took them alive. Their blood was my sustenance."

"Did it . . . make you more powerful?"

"My makers viewed children as an endless source of raw energy. They could cast spells and exert themselves for longer hours than adult elves. They also wanted to punish the king and queen for trying to break into their armories. Those kidnappings devastated my enemies." He grins. "I was only supposed to drink a little blood. But their eyes were so delicious."

Those kids must've suffered immensely. I can't imagine their heart-wrenching screams, their wasted efforts to fight back, to escape this fucking soulless beast.

He walks out of the chamber's illuminated section.

But wherever he moves, a sliver of light follows. I'm the only one shrouded in darkness.

"Soon I fed more. My makers tried limiting how much I consumed, but I was so, so hungry. I wanted stronger elves. Stronger *magic*. Then the soldiers started leaving Vieques. We stayed in hiding after most everyone had gone, so many years later, but our laboratory would be closing anyway. I was scheduled for relocation. I snuck out the night before and infiltrated Eterna. King Arón was sitting by the beach when I found him. His capture was the slowest—I was not as powerful as I am now. But I enjoyed hearing him scream."

"So the rebel leader Feyn killed didn't murder his father."

"There was never a rebel leader. He didn't kill Ryujin's mother. Feyn only said that to comfort her." He cocks his head back, smiling, as if he's reminiscing about better days. "The king died months after I captured him. My favorite part was his strength rushing through me. He had been powerful, but I was *invincible*. Feyn's elixir made the magic evolve tenfold.

"When I first broke into Eterna, the royal guards fought me in vain. Queen Relynn promised my death and failed to uphold it. A year after her husband's sacrifice, she went next. Her oldest son followed the year after. I have taken the blood of the mighty to become the mightiest. Eterna is mine. So are the gifts the royal family has hoarded all throughout their reign. I have two more heirs to claim, and after this week, only one will be left."

He's talking about the Exchange like it's a deadline.

Like Aro's death is *connected* to it.

"After . . . this week?" I ask.

"Yes," he says coolly.

"What does this week have to do with a prince's death?"

Primero is getting too close for comfort.

I slip deeper into the darkness. My steps are brisk, careless.

He trails after me. It's like being chased by a shark in the dead of night. "Three years ago, I transformed the Exchange's challenges from fun, harmless exercises into brutal ones without the past winners' knowledge. Their eyes only saw the pleasant illusions Aro designed upon my command. I tried something different this year. I had a theory that letting you witness the true terrors—letting you embrace your fears and deepest secrets— would make you even stronger. These new tests are forms of leveling up the skills needed for a ritual on the seventh sunrise."

The seventh sunrise is in two days—the same deadline I had to save Mami.

The day Aro is now scheduled to die.

"So the challenges are just . . . we've all been training to . . ." My throat tightens.

"My children are bound to me in many ways," Primero says with a nod. "As their ruler, they cannot resist my commands, rebel against my wishes, or put a hand on me."

"Oh my God . . . Feyn changed the stealth mission at the last minute and he—"

"Paid dearly for it."

That explains his injuries afterward. He risked Primero's wrath because he was mad at me.

"Speaking of Feyn," Primero continues, "his bloodline is the most powerful one in Eterna's history. It fuels me like none other, and I will not stop until its magic belongs to me. I must feed on royal blood every year, but my creators must provide the meal. This is the magical limitation I was cursed with. Humans made the best version of me. Therefore they preserve me."

Everything I am is pounding, burning, aching.

If Primero needs humans in Eterna, the Exchange is an excuse to invite them. Seven days of lending magical abilities that would serve a warrior well in battle. Seven days of making his so-called children watch three strangers master the art of fighting them.

Of *killing* them.

"The ticket winners . . . you chose us so we could kill Aro?" I press my burned hand against my chest, even though I wince from the sudden burst of pain. Nothing could ever hurt worse than realizing Aro has been sentenced to death. "We'd never agree to it!"

"Of course not. Winners do not know why they are brought here. But their purpose on this island is simple—make me the strongest creature alive."

"How can we fucking feed you if we refuse?"

Primero stops right in front of me. I want to punch him, push him away, but his golden eyes pierce what's left of my living carcass, rooting me to the spot.

"Aro's decaying body is part of his sacrifice. He defied me so his brother could live one more year to search for my weaknesses and *defeat me*. Normally, the royals do not suffer this much, but his rebellion cannot go unpunished. I have ensured he hurts much worse than all his relatives combined." I'm about to say something, but Primero interrupts me. "Winners must finish what they started, and the Exchange has not ended yet."

I remember the scheduled activities we were given upon arrival.

"The farewell ceremony. Is that when he dies?"

"No one will leave Eterna until the sacrifice is complete. Everything would have gone perfectly had you not failed me."

"I'll fail you as many times as I need to. I'm *not* killing Aro. You won't—"

Primero's laugh booms across the darkness. It envelops me like a hug from someone you loathe; it's such a gross, suffocating horror. "You were made to break him long before his death. *You* are Prince Aro's punishment."

My urge to knock him unconscious grows. "What?"

"Aro is this year's sacrifice, but he was not chosen. I promised to make him pay. It took me a while to find his perfect foil— something he would desire against his better judgment. I wanted to shatter his heart into a million pieces many times. *You* were the answer. The girl of his dreams and nightmares all rolled into one vessel." Primero's teeth are bleeding again. As he licks them, his smile widens. "My greatest creation."

The way he calls me that . . . it runs a sharp, cold nail down my spine . . .

"Why do you say that?" I barely whisper.

"Because you are, Sevim. You were born out of Aro's deepest desires. Created to make him suffer through rejection and cruelty," says Primero. "You, little devil, are an ensueño."

FORTY

A STORYBOOK FLIPS OPEN INSIDE MY THOUGHTS. Roses and skulls are drawn on its pages.

The slanted handwriting isn't mine.

But the tale is about me.

Eight months ago, a woman watered daisies in her garden.

She was used to the silence. Natalia Ruiz was a widow. Her husband, Eduardo Burgos, had been killed by a rebel elf. She found his body outside the restaurant where they celebrated their tenth marriage anniversary. She sobbed into his bloodied shirt as police arrived.

Natalia mourned her husband in small ways. Reading poetry that reminded her of him. Cooking his favorite meals on his birthday. Driving by the school where he taught algebra and became a beloved teacher in their community.

Gardening brought her peace, too. She didn't have all the flowers she wanted yet. Her small house in Carolina couldn't accommodate them, but she was also struggling to stay employed. Despairing over her next paycheck took up most of her time.

She was lucky, though.

She didn't have children.

———— e e ————

Eight months ago, a girl opened her eyes for the very first time.

She didn't know where she was. The room she woke up in was clean and cozy, but she wondered whose bed she was sleeping on.

The girl's reflection made her pause. She looked much older than she felt—a teenager without memories or the slightest understanding of what she was. She had brown skin and short black hair. Her knee-length dress was black. So were her fishnets and leather miniskirt. She could've sworn her eyes had a golden glow, but the longer she stared, the less she noticed it.

"I dream of a rose garden," a boy spoke in her mind. "I dream of sharing it with someone special—someone I can fall in love with."

"Who are you?" the girl asked.

The boy didn't respond.

"Hello? Is anyone there?" she said.

But no one spoke.

So she quietly opened the bedroom door, careful not to startle whoever else was in the house. She walked down the corridor and into the kitchen. The girl didn't know the names of anything in the house—she didn't even know her own name—but she kept going.

When the girl reached the living room, a woman entered through the front door.

They glanced at each other, gasping in surprise.

And so the spell was cast.

———— ℓℓℯ ————

Eight months ago, Primero kept his promise to Prince Aro.

He snuck into the elf's dreams and saw the girl who lived in them.

A girl shrouded in shadows. Her face was obscured. Her voice was scrambled. The only thing Aro knew was that his heart called to her. Whenever he dreamed of the girl, he also dreamed of roses. He built a garden over the sea just for them. Aro escaped to his hideout every night, hoping to dance with his mystery lover. Hoping that one night, he could see her face.

But Primero took her. He molded her from shadows, darkness, and Feyn's elixir. He turned her into flesh, bone, beating heart . . .

Then dropped her into Natalia Ruiz's home.

His enchantment activated once the strangers locked eyes. The widow would see a girl in her house and believe it was her only child—a daughter of seventeen years.

The girl would see the widow and believe it was her mother. A single parent who loved poetry and flowers. A woman who couldn't keep a job.

With one look, the girl finally knew her name. Sevim Burgos.

She knew a rebel elf killed her father. Even though she hadn't been there, she had memories of discovering his dead body, and later of finding his killer. She remembered how watching her mother cry would rip her chest wide open. How she wished for the pain to end. For her father's murder to be avenged.

Sevim's mind flashed with images of stealing the elf's body and stuffing it into her mother's car. She saw herself searching for the highest bidder online. Then choosing to trust Doctor Alberto Ramírez instead. Handing over the corpse in exchange for a thousand dollars in cash. She brought him more bodies so he would keep paying her. That's how she helped her mother keep food on the table. Being a thief helped them survive, but Sevim was enjoying it too much.

The girl's love for her mother, her hatred for elves . . . everything began with a lie.

She was the greatest lie of all.

FORTY-ONE

'M NOT AN ENSUEÑO. I *CAN'T* be.

How have I only been alive for eight months? How am I supposed to believe that an elf prince's dreams are my real home? As powerful as Primero is, could he truly cast an ensueño in human form? He's manipulated me before. This could be another attempt.

Primero said there was never a rebel leader, but Ryujin's mother was still murdered . . .

"Did you kill Ryujin's mom?" I say.

"It was necessary. Unraveling her mind helped me create you. I entered her thoughts long before I entered Aro's, poking and prodding until she could not resist my presence any longer. It was exhausting. But without pushing my magic to new heights, I would not have been capable of casting the complex spell that made you real. A spell no one else has ever cast. You are the first of your kind, Sevim. How lovely is that?"

An innocent woman died so I could live.

Primero drove her toward suicide, but he's still her killer. He wiped the world clean of her existence. And if a person can be vanquished, they could also be created, especially with the help of Feyn's elixir. Doctor Ramírez never gave me the golden liquid. It's already part of me.

Just like the nightmare and memories.

I wasn't seeing something that belonged to my subconscious alone. It was Primero's.

It was ours.

No. Don't let him fool you again.

"If I'm not real, why do I have free will? You kidnapped my mother to punish me. I must've been doing things wrong for you to intervene."

"You do have free will. But you were also behaving exactly how I desired."

"That literally makes no sense."

"It does. Take Ryujin's mother, for example. She was loyal until the end. But I grew weary of her. Humans can only be entertaining for so long. You, on the other hand, were challenging. I molded you into what Aro most desired in a romantic partner. I also gave you the cruel heart that would poke holes in his ego. Yet you simply ignored it."

My chin quivers. I can feel the tears springing forth, but I close my eyes to thwart their release. "You killed that poor woman. She had a whole life. A family. You took it all away."

"Indeed. *She* was once real. But you have never existed. Not in the way the other winners exist. They have families, memories.

You have what I gave you." He presses his hands against his chest like he's just seen his child speak her very first words. There's pride in his eyes—and I never want to see it again. "What is it that the mourners request from the Garden Witch?"

Mami hasn't even read those pages yet, but this asshole knows all about them. He's acting like he put them there. Like I'm not the one crafting the tale, leading the characters and plot along, choosing anything based on my style and preferences.

"They want to bring back the dead based on what they remember," I whisper.

"Yes," says Primero. "They want the Garden Witch to pluck loved ones from their minds and grant them real, living bodies. That is what I did with you, Sevim. You only write about such magic because it is your very origin. Those words are your truth."

"Don't make it sound like I don't have a choice! You kidnapped my mother so I could come to this island. Why not just command me to do whatever you wished? Why lead me here as if I ever had a say in the matter?"

"Humans live on the mainland. I needed one to meet Aro there."

"Yes, but why *make me* believe I'm real? You could've let me know I was created to break Aro's heart. I didn't have to wake up every morning thinking my name is Sevim Burgos!"

"That *is* your name. I gave it to you."

"No, you didn't! My parents gave it to me. They met in Istanbul and—"

"Their love story is real, but they never had children. They never even wanted them. Once your mother laid eyes on you, my spell made her forget. She loved you as if she'd brought you into the world. I was proud of how strong my magic had become.

"And I was very proud of you at first. You were fighting your attraction toward Aro, and in turn, your coldness accelerated his physical, mental, and emotional deterioration. Your efforts to understand the nightmare did not worry me. But when you refused to leave Eterna, I knew my plan had failed. You were supposed to choose your mother over Aro. To choose yourself."

"I *did* choose my mother!"

"Then you begged to return for Aro. That, little devil, was not part of your story."

Primero reaches for my face.

I flinch, and he stops just before making contact.

He snaps his fingers.

I'm in my house.

Mami isn't here. I miss her dancing in front of the stove. How she inquired about my time at the coffee shop, where she thought I designed art prints for an imaginary online store. Everything from that morning is so vivid—seeing her car in perfect condition, chasing after the ensueño's trail, finding Aro in the parking lot. That was supposed to be the morning I disappointed her with a damaged car. It was the beginning of something worse.

"The greater the lie, the stronger the belief," says Primero. "I had to cast an ensueño that even the ensueño master himself would not be capable of detecting. You needed to be as human as possible. That included providing you with desires, fears, prejudices, and love. A bond like the one you share with the stranger you call your mother is exactly what Aro wants in a partner. He loved *his* mother very much. Shaping you into a loyal, brave daughter who was willing to go up against all odds for her would make you irresistible to him.

"There were other things to consider, such as your beauty and your dark taste in fashion, but what most attracts Aro is a girl made of opposites. You needed to be intrigued by elves yet disgusted with their privilege. They had to be your enemies before you met them. My children are not used to being hated by humans, especially Aro. And being hated by a girl who looks like his dream come true was supposed to rip him apart. You grew more hateful toward *me* instead of the prince who kept secrets."

"You used me to seduce and abandon Aro."

"Yes. And you failed."

I'm shaking so hard from the anger burning deep within. Not only did this beast conjure me to fulfill an elf's fantasy, but he's also furious because I had the audacity to forge my own path.

How can you plant a rose and not expect its thorns?

I won't let him destroy—or use—what's left of me. I'm definitely not letting him hurt anyone else. Prince Aro of Eterna won't be killed in two days. Jason and Ryujin won't be used to kill him, either. They're not pawns or tools. They're my *friends* and I'm saving them.

Mami is still on that godforsaken island, too. What good was it to reunite with her earlier? She's already been through hell. I won't let her go through more.

"How will they do it? What elaborate bullshit is in store so the winners can commit murder?"

"That does not concern you anymore. Your replacement has already been chosen."

Primero snaps his fingers again.

He's gone.

The burn on my palm bleeds golden. This is what my blood really looks like. What I've been hiding under skin that was never mine.

Light bursts out of my chest. It pierces holes through it. There's no stabbing or pricking sensation. It's not singeing me further. But the holes grow bigger, bigger, bigger.

I'm disappearing.

FORTY-TWO

MY BURNED HAND VANISHES FIRST.

The rest of my arm follows.

The holes spread down in swift blasts. My legs are incandescent, but there's still no pain, no discomfort. I'm merely a spell that's being un-cast.

"NO!"

I lie on my back. Once my legs disappear, I won't be able to stand.

But I won't go down without fighting Primero's magic. How do I keep myself whole if I'm not real? How can I force my body, my entire existence, to resist its inevitable fate?

I had to cast an ensueño that even the ensueño master himself would not be capable of detecting, Primero had said. If I'm strong enough to fool Aro, am I stronger than him overall?

He seemed taken aback when I conjured the rose garden—I brought his dreams to life, too. I went against Primero's plans and *chose* my fate. I decided to help the elf prince he sent me to destroy.

I'm so much more than a spell. My true magic comes from my choices.

And I choose to live.

Light beams shoot through my stomach. The holes are rising now, taking over my torso.

"No . . ."

I close my eyes. When I conjured the rose garden, I imagined every stem, every thorn, until they became real. So I picture myself standing in the middle of the living room, flesh and bone and fully healed. My combat boots are strapped on tight; my short dress and fishnets are as black as the chamber Primero revealed himself in. The choker is tied around my neck. Both fists are clenched and ready to connect with Primero's face.

More holes burst through my chest. Then my neck is blasted apart. Everything lower than that is a luminous ball—I only have seconds left.

Why isn't it working?

I can't die like this. Not when Aro is two days away from being murdered. Not when my friends will be manipulated into feeding a monster's revenge. Not when my mother remains a hostage despite being freed mere moments earlier. Not when everything in my life was a lie. Primero doesn't get to tell me who I am. What I'm good for. No one should have that power.

The beast of Eterna molded me into a destroyer.

I've finally found what to destroy.

There's another Sevim in the living room. We wear the same

clothes, have the same hair and face and rage-filled expression, but she's fully healed.

She dreams of ripping the beast apart, too. Tearing limb after limb and tossing it all into the ocean. She sees a beach of dancing elves, celebrating their newfound freedom, and thanking their human guests with endless food and drink. The girl sweeps the youngest elf prince into her arms, and he lets her. They hold on as if their hearts are tethered to each other.

The girl misses her mother. She misses the friends she made in Eterna. Jason and Ryujin don't know they've been chosen to kill a prince. She wants to stop them from hurting Aro, but she's also desperate to get them off the island. The elves can't rebel against Primero. They can kill my friends if he commands it, though. Or he can just finish them off after the ritual. Once Aro and Feyn are dead, Primero won't have more royal elves to claim. He'll abandon Eterna to fend for itself against endless questions, attempts to figure out what happened to the missing teenagers . . .

The girl says, "Now."

I unleash a gut-wrenching scream.

I'm pouring sweat as holes appear on my face. Half of my right eye is gone, but the louder I scream, and the angrier I become, the more the light recedes. Each gaping hole fills up with the body part that was blasted away. Seeing my brown skin has never made me this emotional. This is what Primero thought he could erase. But I'm stitching myself back together like a tapestry of wrath and willpower. Soon all the gaps are closed up, my dress and fishnets covering me again.

When the last beam vanishes, the healed Sevim in the living room flies toward me.

We crash into one another.

I collapse.

———— ℓℓ ————

I SIT UPRIGHT.

I'm still alone in a house I never grew up in.

The sun rises out the window. I reach out for the television and turn it on with my magic.

A female news anchor appears on-screen. There's an aerial shot of Eterna behind her.

"Thank you so much for that weather forecast, Diana. Looks like we'll have clear skies to receive our winners after an exciting week in Eterna. Remember to tune in this afternoon for our live coverage from Ceiba as we greet the winners back to the mainland. But for now, let's leave them to enjoy the farewell ceremony."

"What . . ." I wait for more updates, but the screen shows a traffic jam in San Juan.

I read the date and time. I've woken up on the Exchange's seventh day.

The last sunrise in Eterna.

Aro's murder has begun.

FORTY-THREE

AMI'S CAR IS STILL AT THE Burger King, but I need something *faster.*

The yellow Mustang four houses down looks tempting. It's not mine, though. Besides, Primero wanted me to steal, and I'm not his ensueño anymore. I should start acting like it.

An ensueño . . .

I can use magic to conjure exactly what I need. I think of Raff and the bodyguards racing around the mainland. Their ensueños leave golden tendrils of light behind. Could I shape them into something I can drive? Maybe they can transport me all by themselves.

Like a . . .

Portal.

I can get you to the garden faster! I've been testing a new spell.

You walk through a golden archway and arrive to your destination. Primero said this at the beach house. Did he want me to try the spell, too? Or did he mention it because it's impossible for me?

I've never heard of elves creating portals. Surely they've tried. But can I get *into* Eterna using one? Primero could've cast a shield around the island while Aro's execution takes place.

"He's not going to die," I say as I pull myself up. My balance is sturdier now; this real body feels strong and ready to fight. "Let's cast this fucking portal."

I think of the golden lights.

Then I picture them as an archway. I trace every nook and cranny like a sketch. When I reach the arch at the top, I'm sweating and grinding my teeth. The shape proves difficult for a novice. I smooth down the metal until it's the closest thing to an arch, its corners slightly crooked, then straighten its right side. The leg hits the floor with a loud thud, then the other.

Soon the entire structure sits in my living room. There's nothing past the arch; I can still see the TV and the cracked paint on the wall. My creation glows as gold as my blood.

"Please let this work," I say.

I sprint through the archway.

———— *ℓℓ* ————

MY HANDS BREAK MY FALL against cement.

Humans stare at me like I'm an apparition. They gasp and jump back.

When I look around, I can definitely see Eterna . . .

Miles away.

I'm on the crowded port in Ceiba.

"Isn't that the girl who arrived last?" a woman asks.

"Yes!" says another.

"Oh my God, it's the last girl on the boat!" a guy says. "What is she doing off the island?"

Phones are in my face. Flashes go off in a blur. Reporters and camera crews are running toward me. Cops yell at bystanders to retreat; only a handful listen.

How am I supposed to reach Eterna? No boats are headed there right now. Clearly I need to work harder on the archway spell. If I don't slip away from this crowd soon, I'll be dragged into the back of a news channel's van. I have to cast something easier than magically moving myself through time and space. Something that can get me to Eterna's shores quickly and in one piece.

What about a bridge?

"Back up, everybody!" a cop says.

I'm hauled off the floor—people are dragging me toward them.

"TELL US EVERYTHING!" a teen boy shrieks. "EVERY-THING!"

"Hey! Let her go!" More cops are coming.

And more fans push against me.

"HAVE YOU BEEN BANISHED? IS THAT WHY YOU'RE HERE FIRST? WHAT DID YOU DO TO PISS OFF THE ELVES?"

I shove him.

He slams into a wall. When he slides down, he reveals a human-shaped dent behind him.

"OH MY GOD! DID YOU RECORD THAT?"

I stomp the ground. Fans, cops, and journalists alike bounce ten feet away. They're disheveled, taking their sweet time to collect themselves.

Now!

I thrust my hands toward Feyn's preferred parking spot. Tesoro del Mar might not be here, but I can still follow its same route. I stand there awkwardly, waiting for my daydream of an endless golden bridge to come true. It doesn't matter how many times I slap the air or groan in desperation. My magic isn't working.

All the cops aim their guns at me.

"Stay right where you are, young lady!" I hear one yelling.

They're closing in. Forget about the news van. Soon I'll be cuffed in the back of a cruiser.

"Come . . . on . . . ." I'm showered in sweat again, shaking, losing strength in my legs.

"Keep your hands up!" another cop says. "We just want to——"

BOOM!

Gold bricks spring from thin air.

They stack against each other, lengthening across the Caribbean Sea. A bridge appears as if invisible construction workers were moving at ten times their regular speed. It traces Tesoro del Mar's entire journey back to Eterna. The bridge's opposite end stops right on the black sand.

"I fucking did it . . ."

Applause breaks out.

And people start running to the bridge.

"No!"

Blistering energy surges through me. My fists are cradled in light. I punch the air. Each beam ricochets against the golden bricks.

When people set foot onto them, they're sent flying every which way. The port is overrun with the constant sound of splashing water—some are falling into its depths.

I sprint past the cops.

Their bullets miss me. As more bystanders rush the bridge, I will my magic to repel them, shooting them back into the port. My boots avoid stepping on hands and arms, but after a while, it becomes inevitable. With one last jump, I soar over the same male fan that dragged me earlier.

I land in a crouch on the bridge.

Then I bolt.

I ignore the cops' pleas for me to double back. My calves burn every time I pound these boots against bricks. I'm out of breath, out of shape, and it's taking forever just to make decent headway. Soon I'll be crawling across the rest of this magical platform. But when I think about Aro being killed and my friends being in danger, I can push past the pain.

Behind me, a motorcycle engine revs loudly.

Then another . . . another . . . I count five golden bikes.

"Stop her! She's the getaway driver from the other night!"

"We kill the girl first, then head to the island!"

"Ride fast!"

Rebel elves chase me down the bridge.

FORTY-FOUR

*J*UST WHAT *I* FUCKING NEEDED.

I dodge their lightning bolts and blasts, but I'm much slower than their bikes. Soon they're at my sides, swinging their staffs at me.

I duck, but another hits me in the shoulder.

I'm down on my side. Three more staffs are coming in hot toward my face. I roll over, shuddering at the sound of metal clanging against brick. I stand, but my legs are swept from underneath me. I land on my hip this time. Sharp pain explodes across the bone. I cry out and drag myself away as fast as possible. I can't outrun them. My only choice is to fight.

Summon your weapon!

One grabs me by the hair. He's yanking me up.

I drive my fist into his groin.

When he doubles over, I punch him right in the face. He falls into a limp sack of limbs.

I cast gold light over my scorched flesh. It heals immediately.

Then I picture myself holding the black staff.

A lightning bolt hits my calf.

Fresh blood splatters onto the bricks. It hurts like hell, but I keep running as I cast gold light around the wound. I'm shaking too much; the light bounces erratically on either side of my leg instead of touching the injury.

I'm shoved down. The light disappears, and I can feel the blood dripping into my shoes.

Rebels surround me.

"You helped the prince escape," one says. "Do you see him returning the favor now?"

"Kill her," says another.

They swing their staffs down hard.

And clash against mine.

No matter how much I push, there are still five elves pinning me. They're trying to break my weapon and crack my skull. I'm bleeding and throbbing and screaming. I won't defeat them in hand-to-hand combat—Feyn never taught me fighting tricks or techniques. His challenge was about self-preservation; Pasiphae's illusion helped her get what she wanted.

Illusions . . .

If I can't win fair and square, I'll have to cheat. These rebels use lightning bolts. Could they have trained themselves to withstand the pain? What about other threats like . . .

Cobras.

Even if these elves don't fear snakes, they're still a good distraction.

I'm kicked on the side.

"Ugh!" As I fall, my staff rolls away.

The rebels try striking me again.

I lunge toward my staff, then swing it in the air, remembering the pit of cobras I waded through, the crimson pool I almost drowned in, the chains binding me to an electric chair, the detonations on an island I've never visited . . . it's all clear, loud, *real* in my head.

BOOM!

Dozens of cobras shoot through the air like fanged arrows. Their teeth find flesh—necks, specifically—and latch on. For a moment, the rebels forget they have magic, too, screaming and flailing and spinning in circles. One makes the mistake of yanking the cobra off. A large chunk of his skin goes along with it. Blood splatters the elf beside him.

Lightning bolts come next. Once they hit their targets, they morph into metal chains, locking the rebels' arms. The bolts zap them mercilessly; smoke trails off their clothes as the cobras keep biting. None of the rebels break free. They shake and bleed out.

But they don't die.

They could set themselves free and chase me again. Or worse, run back to the mainland and continue their senseless murders. I've never taken a life, and I certainly don't want to. I'll have nightmares about shattered bones and torn flesh. Besides, the princes currently have one rebel detained after that dinner ambush. Maybe he'd like some company? And Jason could use more elves to interview for his book, especially since he doesn't remember his deal with the rebels.

I turn to the island's shores, my staff gripped tightly. I heal my injured calf and walk a few paces. It doesn't bother me anymore. The bleeding has finally stopped, too.

I follow the bridge to Eterna.

FORTY-FIUE

THERE ARE NO DRUMS TO GREET my arrival.

The elves have shut their doors, their windows. Either they've locked themselves in, or they're all at the farewell ceremony. It could be *anywhere*, but I'll start with the royal garden.

I sprint across the black sand. My weapon is raised high. The weather becomes muggier, as if I'm swimming from one steaming bowl of broth into the next. Cotorras joyfully squeak in the treetops; lagartos scurry away at my approach. They're my only reminder I'm not alone.

But if they can see me, so will Primero.

I focus on my stealth magic. I remove my shadow, the loudness in my steps, and now I strive for complete invisibility. As I run down the sandy path, I wish for skin that blends into my surroundings, for a voice that can never be heard. A cold, tingling sensation courses through me. It lasts a few seconds, but it's so refreshing against this abominable heat.

When I look down, I can't see myself anymore.

My invisibility makes it easy to sneak through the crowd ahead. Every elf has indeed been summoned to the royal garden. Nobody bristles as I slip past. I can't find Aro anywhere, but I do see Feyn, Ciel, Raff. Jason and Ryujin are in the middle of the garden.

With my mother.

She's repeatedly blasting golden beams of light alongside my friends. She has a staff, too, but it's made of regular iron. I don't want to know what she went through to obtain magic on such short notice. The fact that she's still even here . . . Primero threatened her. Why else would she agree to participate in the Exchange, especially when she's supposedly too old for it?

The statue she's blasting is as golden as her light. It's a giant structure in the middle of the garden. News helicopters would see this from miles away. I hadn't seen anything until I arrived, though. Primero must be hiding the garden under a magical veil right now.

I look at the statue more carefully. Parts have been blown away—mostly the torso, chin, and nose—but the upper half of its face . . . those eyes . . .

This is a statue of Aro.

"It's almost down! Keep going!" Jason tells Mami and Ryujin.

Cracks appear along the statue's forehead and ankles. They widen with each powerful blow. Big pieces fall off—it's coming undone. In less than a minute, there will be nothing left.

"STOP!"

With a wave of my hand, I lift the invisibility spell and run to the winners.

They immediately turn around.

Mami startles as if she's seen the dead rise at a wake. "Sevim!"

"Stop hitting the statue! You have to—"

I'm pulled into arms that barely let me breathe.

"Stand down. You're not part of this anymore." Feyn says as he squeezes the shit out of me. "How did you even get back on the island?"

"We can discuss that later. I know this is an execution, Feyn. I know about Primero."

Raff and Ciel share a terrified glance. Then they look at Feyn.

"Where did you learn that name?" he asks in a strained whisper.

"*He* told me everything. And he tried to kill me afterward. I know none of you can disobey him, but if you just let me stop Mami, Jason, and Ryujin, I can save them along with your brother." I wriggle as hard as I can, but Feyn doesn't loosen his grip. "You have to help me save them, Feyn. Help me save *you*, too."

"Let her go!" Mami yells.

"No, stay back! I can handle this! Just keep your magic away from that statue, okay?"

"What's wrong with it?" Jason asks. "And what are you even doing here? We thought you disappeared to the mainland! You left us in that rose garden and bolted, Sevim!"

I want to keep them talking to give Aro more time and figure out my next move, but confessing about Primero is the real advantage. I need Mami, Jason, and Ryujin to be on my same page. Together we can stop him from hurting them or anyone else on this island.

"Remember what I said back at the lodge last time we were there? Well, my theory is true, guys. I didn't want it to be, but it is. And I need you to stop hitting that statue until I can fully explain. This mission isn't what you were told it is. Nothing we've done this past week is."

"Stop talking right now," says Feyn.

I understand his warning. The elves can't resist or revolt against Primero. They can't physically stop the execution. But sharing Aro's location isn't betrayal.

Not if it's given in code.

"Where does your brother sleep?" I whisper to Feyn.

His heart pounds against my shoulders blades. At first, I suspect he's too scared to risk an answer. Or maybe he's thinking about how to disguise the truth?

Then he says, "He sleeps where pieces remain."

If I understand him correctly, Aro is *inside* the golden statue.

It's not meant to represent him or his likeness. The winners aren't destroying an object that's magically bound to him— they're literally beating him to death.

"I have to get him out," I say.

Feyn is still holding me. "Primero will come for you."

This is the first time he's shown concern for me. As flattered as I am, I know he's mostly worried about his brother.

"What are this challenge's rules?" I ask.

"Break the statue using only ensueños."

"Then that's what I'll do."

Feyn squeezes me just a little bit more. "Hurry," he says.

Then releases me.

I scramble toward Mami and my friends. I want to take turns hugging each, but there's no time. "Let's remove each piece instead of blasting the statue apart! We can pick it apart without using force! Trust me, it's a much better strategy."

"Those aren't the rules," says Ryujin. "And you didn't answer Jason's question."

"Yeah. What are you doing here, Sev?"

"Aro told me he would kill you if I didn't take your place," says Mami. She's grabbing my shoulders like she needs them for support. "He said you'd die."

Jason raises his hands. "Wait, what? You didn't tell us that!"

"That wasn't the real prince," I reassure. "And why are you even participating in the Exchange, Mami? It's supposed to be three teenagers. Wasn't there a replacement for me?"

"She couldn't handle so much magic in such a short amount of time," she says sullenly. "She was also an insomniac. The girl tricked the elves into thinking she could dream and evolve her magic. But their abilities overwhelmed her body. It was . . . painful to watch. Aro said he'd use me if she failed—a woman my age would fare better under grueling circumstances. When the girl lost, she was sent home and I was chosen. If I refused, you would be killed."

"Like I said, that wasn't the real prince, Mami. In order to get off this island safely, all three of you need to help me open that statue without hitting it. Okay?"

Nobody moves.

Then Ryujin says, "What do you mean that wasn't really Aro?" She looks to the other elves. "Is she telling the truth? You can impersonate each other?"

I can't wait for them any longer.

I charge at the statue and trace lines on it with my staff's thorns. They cut a large square into the stone—big enough to fit a body. When the square is fully formed, I pull it out and toss it.

Aro lies unconscious at the base. His left eye is black, too swollen to open. Blood and spit run down his ripped shirt. Most of his skin is yellowish blue and bleeding from multiple gashes. His right elbow and knees are bent at odd angles. Fractures. It's like he's been attacked for *days*.

Like he's never waking up again.

"You're still alive. I know you are."

I start crying as I pick him up. He weighs nothing, but even if I didn't possess magical strength, I'd endure anything to carry this dying elf to safety. His head rests against mine. The faint beating in his chest confirms I've arrived in time, but it's not enough to remain hopeful. I wish I could sneak into his dreams and tell him I've got him now—that I'm not letting go.

"Oh my God! Is that the prince?" Mami says as I run to her.

The earth rumbles—Primero's roars are coming from underground.

The ground splits in half.

A monster erupts from the depths.

FORTY-SIX

DUST AND SMOKE CLOUD MY VISION. I cough; heat pricks at my eyes, making them swell and tear up. Toppling bricks, glass, wood—crackling flames in the distance—rushed footsteps and screams . . . my ears catch it all, but the smoke thickens.

The ground is still again.

I hold Aro tight and face my enemy.

There's a bald creature towering over the trees. It's standing between the winner's lodge and the royal cottages—right behind Aro's statue. The monster of Eterna has Primero's face, elf ears, and golden eyes, but its pale arms and legs are gigantic. It must be forty feet tall, maybe a little more. The robes Primero wore are ripped and dangling in patches on its lower body.

Its entrails are hanging out.

Pieces of iron stick out of its rotting ivory flesh. Its bulging muscles look like balls of pus. The beast's eyes are larger, rounder, and glaring much harder than the last time I gazed upon them. Gone are Primero's beauty and poise. I don't know why this is the form that reflects his decaying soul, but I hope it's his punishment for killing elf children and betraying his kind.

He shoots a fist at me.

I jump out of the way. Aro's body lands on top of mine.

"SEVIM!" Mami drags herself toward me. She's not even glancing at her captor; she probably doesn't recognize Primero in his true form.

"Is this part of the challenge?!" Jason yells. "How do we stop the beast?"

"The mission is to destroy the statue!" says Ryujin.

"Forget about the statue!" I plead.

But the order means nothing coming from *me*.

Feyn is on his knees. There's a thick slash across his forehead—something must've cut him when Primero burst from the earth. He's staring up at the monster, eyes drowning in tears, lost in whatever pain he's reliving in his mind. All the elves are kneeling, too. Their heads are bent low in reverence. Only Feyn dares to look. He's turning red. The veins on his temples are popping. So is his jawline. It's like he's at war with himself.

"Tell them to leave the statue alone!" I tell him.

Feyn cries in silence. He's shaking as if his entire body is resisting Primero's magic. He's not even strong enough to speak in code again.

"Is he breathing?" Mami asks as she checks Aro's pulse. "He's barely here . . ."

"We need to get everyone out of this garden. Nobody should touch that statue again, and I have to figure out how to defeat the monster."

Primero throws another punch.

"Ugh!" I throw a wall of golden bricks at his fist.

He smashes it. The bricks strike his face. With a screech, he swats them away. I send more bricks, and this time, I add some lightning. Primero keeps edging farther and farther. He's desperately trying to shield himself, but can't he move fast enough?

"Take Aro!" I tell Mami. She immediately pulls him into her arms. "Let me handle it! Just keep the prince away from him!"

"But what is that thing? Is Jason right? Is this part of the challenge?"

"No! He's the one who kidnapped you and threatened to kill me!"

I rise as Primero dodges my last set of bolts. He growls, leaning forward with his bleeding, rotten teeth on full display.

The beast lunges.

I slam my staff against his chin. It stops him for about three seconds.

"Sevim?" Mami's voice is too close—what is she *still* doing here?

"We can't talk right now, Mami! Just run!"

"Sevim!" she says louder.

Aro remains unconscious.

But he's convulsing. Blood and spit fall from his chapped lips again. His black-and-blue bruises deepen, widen, spread . . .

Jason and Ryujin shoot golden light toward the statue.

"Don't worry, Sev! We're going to get this monster away from you! Hang tight!" Jason smiles like he's actually doing me a favor. "The statue's almost gone!"

"JASON, STOP!"

Primero's hand flies past me.

He snatches Aro out of Mami's arms.

I blast Primero with fireballs. They barely make him retreat, let alone knock him down. But they're good enough to distract him—I shield myself in invisibility again. As he searches for me, I run toward his grimy legs, then slam my staff against them in fierce strikes.

He doesn't flinch.

I evade his kicks. I combine my strikes and fireballs, alternating at breakneck speed. He *has* to fall. I need to retrieve Aro, but I have to get closer first. I just can't stay invisible and keep up this hectic pace. It doesn't matter how much magic I carry. This abomination is stronger.

I conjure another bridge.

This time, it's in the shape of a winding wave leading up to Primero's hand.

I race all the way up, shooting bolts and sharpened daggers. They sink deep into his disgusting skin. He doesn't bleed. He's not even defending himself. I keep attacking as I approach Aro. He hasn't woken up. But his chest rises and falls—the prince still lives.

I swing my staff down on Primero's wrist. The thorns bury themselves into him, but he's perfectly still. With a roar, he punches through the bridge's base.

The whole thing disintegrates.

My arms flail as I plummet. But I cast a new bridge seconds before hitting the ground. Yet again, it's a wave that soars toward Aro. I run the length of the bridge at full speed. Primero smashes his fist through it again, launching me several feet in the air, but I'm casting a third platform toward the elf prince. I conjure dozens of metal spikes. They spring from the earth and right through Primero's body. They hold him in place like a grotesque monument.

He crushes them into smithereens.

Golden dust rains all around. Primero shrieks in high-pitched, almost demonic noises, stomping and swatting at the particles. Then he breaks through another brick wave. He tosses me side to side. I barely hang on, still shooting bolts and daggers at his face, but now they're bouncing off like there's a shield over him.

He throws his whole body against the wave.

I fly high, then plunge in a straight line.

The bridge is dust, too.

"Winners, you're wasting time! Destroy the statue to save him!" His voice is a gurgle and a shriek at the same time—the closest thing to a demon tongue I've heard.

"He's lying! If you break it, Aro dies!"

"SILENCE!"

"You have to help me beat him! Only humans can kill him! He wants you all to murder Aro so he can feed on his blood and become an ensueño master!"

"Feed on him?" a baffled Ryujin repeats. "To . . . steal his magic?"

"It already looks pretty powerful to me," says Jason.

"Nothing you're saying makes sense," says Ryujin.

"None of it," Jason says.

More shrieks pierce my ears; they pulse as if Primero is stabbing them. Could this be a spell, too? A magical way to pit my friends against me? Why are they so intent on doubting everything I say?

You left them. They don't trust you like before.

But you're not the only one who knows the truth.

I point to the elves, shouting over Primero's unbearable noise. "Why are they scared right now? Does it seem to you like Feyn's still in charge?"

Only Jason turns.

Once his gaze meets Feyn's, the prince cries harder. He looks away as if he's embarrassed, but Jason keeps staring, his brow furrowed.

"Feyn?" he calls.

This is the first time he's addressed him by name.

The prince unravels into sobs. He's lost what little composure he had left.

Ciel doesn't look up at him, but her shoulders shake as if she's crying, too. She places a hand on top of his.

"Feyn."

Jason runs.

He kneels in front of the prince. "I won't tell you not to cry, but can you please try to get up? Your brother needs you. The entire island needs you. Act like a prince for once. I know you've got it in you *somewhere*." Jason offers him a hand. "Here. Let me help you."

The prince doesn't slap his hand away. He's not grabbing it, either.

"Feyn? Your hand?"

"You're fucking intolerable, Jason Baxter," the prince says.

"Likewise. Now take my—"

Feyn clutches Jason's hand. The moment he's up, he pulls Jason close enough to whisper his message. My friend's expression shifts from concern to understanding. I know the prince can't reveal much, but whatever he's confessing has Jason in complete shock.

Excellent.

"What's wrong with him?" Ryujin asks. "Why is he suddenly so emotional?"

"They're prisoners on their own island. That thing—Primero—invaded Eterna three years ago. Since then, he's been their ruler. But he doesn't rule us. And he's . . ."

Ryujin isn't even looking at me. I don't know if she's caught a word I've said.

"Listen to me, Ryujin! *He* killed your mom!"

She finally notices me. Something flashes in her eyes—they seem darker, as if shadows have taken up residence. And they're watering. But she's not *doing anything*.

"My mother . . ." she says. "She . . . was killed?"

She makes it sound like I've planted the seed of doubt in her mind. I have to make her fully remember the memory she sacrificed—it's the only way she'll fight Primero.

"Your mother abandoned you because he forced her. She tried coming back to you. She loved you very much and wanted her life back, but his magic wouldn't grant her peace. He tortured her mind and pushed her to the edge. Then he erased her from—"

Pain bursts on the side of my face.

I tumble and roll away.

The taste of warm copper takes over all my other senses. I spit out gold blood, then touch where the pain is coming from—there's a gash in my skull.

Mami is down, too. Somehow I've landed right next to her.

Primero's foot is inches away from crushing us.

A golden beam slices it in half.

It lands in front of Ryujin.

Her hand shimmers from her offensive spell.

FORTY-SEVEN

A s Ryujin advances on Primero, I heal my head injury. It takes me a minute to stop the blood, to seal the open wound. I can't keep my eyes off Aro. Every time Primero swings at Ryujin, he flings his hostage side to side.

"Are you okay?" Jason helps me stand. "Do you know your name? How old are you?"

"I'm not concussed! We need to bring Primero down!"

"*That's* what it's called?"

"I'll give you all the details later!" I pull Mami up. "Are you okay?"

"Sí, mi amor . . . but the prince . . ."

"I'm on it!" Jason runs toward Primero. He throws his staff at the monster's eye like a javelin. It sends Primero backward. When the staff returns to Jason, he casts the same bridges I once made, but his wave soars higher, faster. Ryujin creates another wave under his. They're attacking Primero on both his upper and lower body.

I've never seen anything more beautiful.

But Aro is still in the monster's grasp.

Cut off his hand.

"Mami, can you make sure Aro doesn't fall? I'm going to slice Primero's hand off, and once it's loose, I don't want him to hit the ground."

My mother breathes heavily. She's starting to sweat. "Um . . . yes. Let's . . . let's try it."

"Not the confidence I was looking for."

"I'm sorry! This is all so stressful! And I don't want to hurt anyone!"

"You won't hurt Aro, Mami. You can do this. I'll aim for the monster's wrist. You just focus on getting the prince over here."

Mami sighs. "Okay, I'll try."

"No. You'll *do* it, and it'll be amazing."

I don't know what's running through her mind, but thankfully, she doesn't contradict me.

She smiles at the girl who was never her real daughter.

The girl who'll never stop showing how much she loves her.

Our shoulders touch as we face Primero. Ryujin slams the hell out of him with her staff. She's at the top while Jason attacks Primero's wobbling legs. The monster's shrieks are too piercing for me to concentrate, but I push through the ruckus and pour all of my energy into creating a sharp, fiery boomerang. Then I launch it at Primero's wrist.

It scorches through bone.

"Oh my God! You did it!" Mami says proudly.

Primero's anguished cries drown out whatever else she's yelling. Luckily, she's quick enough to guide the severed hand toward us, keeping its pace steady. Once I'm close enough to touch Aro, I unclench Primero's fist and drag him into my arms.

"Aro? Can you hear me?" I say into his ear. He still has a pulse. But seeing his blood-soaked clothes, his black-and-blue face . . . knowing he *chose* this to save his brother . . . it makes me want to bury him in kisses that heal, restore his faith in good things.

His ring keeps glowing. I try ripping it off, but the damn thing won't come off. It's stuck.

"Primero has bound him to the ring," says Feyn.

He, Ciel, and Raff run up to me. I let Feyn hug his brother. Raff pats his back as he pushes Aro's hair out of his eyes.

"Stay with him. I have a monster to kill."

I race to Jason and Ryujin.

They're beating Primero bloody. He's screeching and squealing like a feral animal.

Then he sees me.

"You leave me no choice!" he says.

WHOOM!

The island rumbles like a thousand earthquakes are being unleashed at the same time.

A sweeping breeze hurtles overhead. Palm trees, fountains, hedges, rose bushes—everything it touches becomes light. Large piles of ashes remain in its wake. The island is unraveling just like Primero tried unraveling *me*.

He's destroying Eterna.

FORTY-EIGHT

CLOUDS OF DUST FILL THE AIR. The royal cottages and the winners' lodge explode into golden particles. I can't see most of the destruction.

But I hear cotorras squawking in pain seconds before turning to ashes and raining down on me. I hear the waves crashing ever closer, as if they're desperately gulping the sand and soil. Wooden trunks snapping . . . concrete and stone exploding. I'm at the heart of the end of the world.

Primero howls as the wind carries away everything he's stolen. Then he shakes as if lightning fries him from within. The elves are shaking, too. They fall on their sides, deathly still.

I never thought Eterna would disappear.

I never thought it *could*. The island's name implies permanence. Forever.

When the very first elf opened his eyes, I doubt it ever pictured this fate. But the end is here, happening right now, and I'm unfortunate enough to bear witness.

I never thought Eterna would disappear.

Most of all, I never thought I'd want to save it. Before Primero tried to kill me, he told me I wasn't real. He needed me to feel less. Then he unraveled me piece by piece.

The royal advisor to the Crown is dead. Doctor Alberto Ramírez never existed. Primero was altered in a lab. He was supposed to follow orders—to be less. He chose his powers. His reign of terror. He only knows fear as a weapon.

Jason and Ryujin are somewhere inside those dust clouds. They can't stop the monster from shrinking into his smaller body—one that's easier to hide in the chaos. He still has all his limbs, but he bleeds from top to bottom.

His robes swish as he sprints.

I hold out a hand. I picture myself erasing the monster that tried erasing me. I will be the last ensueño he'll ever cast. I will be his greatest regret.

A golden halo covers me whole. I'm lit up like the sun, my throat hoarse and aching.

Primero floats over the largest dust cloud. He's kicking, bleeding, swatting at the air.

A hand covers mine. Then two more wrap themselves on top. Jason. Ryujin. Mami.

"What do you need?" my mother asks.

"Imagine he's coming undone from inside. His very core needs to be unraveled. He was born from the darkest parts of human nature. Just like our missions. Take your rage, heartbreaks, fears, shames, secrets, nightmares, *all* of it, and pull at his threads until there's nothing left!"

They nod.

Then the four of us channel everything that's ever hurt into the same spell. I'm cradled in pain that's never belonged to me. Jason might not remember what he did with the rebels, but there were other moments where he felt lost, sad, hopeless . . . There was love, too—his parents, little sister, grandmother, friends—but they were never as loud in Jason's head. They couldn't get him to see the bright, successful future he deserves.

I wobble along with Ryujin on the bar during her gymnastics competition. All those expectant eyes on her . . . all those disappointed stares . . . how she cried herself to sleep after her mother's death . . . The memory is hers again, and she's reeling it back in. She's holding all of her love and pain for her mother—fully embracing it.

Mami's pain is more familiar. I can smell the blood on my father's shirt and her fruity perfume mixing with it when she hugs him. I see her dancing in the kitchen and reading poetry aloud and forcing books into my hands. I hear her sobbing while the shower runs, and see her scrolling through Papi's old text messages. I see a woman who was never really my mother. How hard she mourned the man who was never really my father.

And I love them.

They *are* my family.

THE BEST DREAMS DON'T HAVE monsters pulling the strings or ripping them apart.

They have monsters fading into a ball of light—large enough to be seen from across the Caribbean Sea.

They have elves reawakening, rising.

The ivory ring exploding.

And the youngest elf prince cracking one eye open.

FORTY-NINE

"**S**EVIM."

Aro speaks my name like an oath—a serious, purposeful statement. It sounds even more real coming from his lips. Even though his clothes are blood-soaked, his injuries are starting to heal. He touches his face, chest, and stomach without wincing.

"Sevim," he repeats, "are you hurt?"

I don't answer him.

We both run, our arms open, then embrace each other.

"You're going to be fine," I tell him. "Primero is gone. He can't make you suffer again."

Aro's warm breath caresses my ear. "You saved me."

"I—"

Feyn knocks him out of my arms.

They sway with matching claps on their backs.

"You're okay," says Feyn. "You're okay now."

"*We* are. I'll never let anything happen to you."

"That's my job, cabrón. *Mine.* You're just supposed to be taken care of."

"Cállate, ridículo."

The princes keep bantering and crying tears of joy. Their relief is bittersweet—pain and sadness follow these two even in such a heartwarming moment. They could confess to the world what their family went through—how their parents and older brother were *really* killed—and no one would quite understand their pain. No one can comfort them like they can. As much as I despise Primero for robbing them of their loved ones, I'm happy they still have one another.

"Gracias." Ciel appears next to me. She's pressing her hands against her chest, as if she's afraid her heart will beat out of it. "You avenged them. You *freed* us. Gracias, Sevim." She turns to Mami and my friends. "Gracias a ustedes también."

Raff quickly signs to me: *Thank you.*

Eterna is a wreck, though. Vieques is still dealing with the effects of Primero's makers, too—and God knows what else. There's no wondrous sense of victory. No celebratory soundtracks playing in my head. There's only the certainty that Primero can't hurt anyone again, but I still suffered. So did other people, the elves . . .

But some of us survived. We'll live to regroup and rebuild. Eventually, Eterna will be what it was before Primero. Who knows? It might end up being much better.

"Sorry about your home," Jason tells the princes. "I mean, that Primero creature was mostly to blame, but I should've listened to Sevim earlier."

Aro and Feyn release each other.

"I'm sure you did what you thought was right," says Aro. "Thank you."

Jason bows. Then he stands perfectly still to stare at Feyn. "Is there anything we can do to help rebuild your homeland, Your Highness?"

"Oh, so now you address me properly? I was Feyn just a few moments ago."

"It was the adrenaline." Jason starts to smile, then turns serious. "Your *Highness*."

Feyn looks from him to me to Ryujin. I have no idea what's running through his mind, but he's not glaring coldly as usual. He's just pensive.

Ryujin stands closer to me. "Jason is right about listening to you earlier, Sevim. I'm sorry. And thank you for telling me about my mother."

"Of course. Do you remember it all?"

"Certain parts. Our last conversation isn't too clear. I don't know if everything will come back, but I know she did. I know she loved me."

I nod. "With all her heart."

Mami pulls Ryujin into a hug. "I'm sure she would've been so proud of you. I've never seen bravery like yours." She looks at me. "And yours."

"Gracias, Mami."

"Speaking of bravery," says Feyn, "what you did today . . . I have no words. Nevertheless, I do have something to say about what comes next. Each winner may keep our magical abilities as a token of our gratitude. You're also welcome to remain in Eterna as long as you wish. I know there are people waiting to see you back home, but the island will remain open to you forever."

Jason gasps. "So we can just visit whenever we want?"

"Yes."

"As many times as we want?"

"That's what visiting whenever you want means."

An open door policy is a kindness I didn't expect. So is allow-ing us to keep our powers. Life back on the mainland will be easier and harder at the same time. My world will be camera flashes, shouting spectators, critics. I still have to bring in the reb-els I left on the bridge, but there could be more lurking around the country—ready to avenge these newly imprisoned ones.

My world also includes Jason and Ryujin living in different countries. Keeping in touch won't be too hard. These are the first friends I've ever had, and I'm not going to let them go. Our friendship will reach beyond what we've survived here.

I have much to tell them about who I am. Including Mami and Aro.

But I question whether coming clean is best. If my mother discovers she never gave birth to me, raised me, helped me heal from her husband's murder—a man I've never met— will she love me any less? Would she resent me? Associate me with the beast that kidnapped her?

And Aro . . . I'm a torture device plucked from his subconscious. He could doubt my every word, my every action, as genuine. Even though Primero had been the one to accuse me of using him at the beach house, those feelings could become the real prince's, too.

Maybe one day they'll know the truth.

Maybe they never will.

Why should someone else dictate who I really am anyway?

"Sevim? May I speak with you for a moment?" Aro asks.

I look into his eyes—the ones that called my name while I pretended not to speak their language. A week ago, the sight of him infuriated me. Had I known he was about to die, I wouldn't have been compelled to protect him. To keep his entire species—his *home*—alive.

A week ago, I was a weapon.

Today I'm . . . something more. I'm some*one*. The details are still hazy, but they'll clear up in time. Or even better, I can create them.

Just like the rest of my life.

"Yes," I say.

We follow the golden dust behind us. We follow it until we're far enough from the crowd. The morning has finally arrived—the last sunrise I was supposed to experience in Eterna is over.

"I know you must be exhausted and I won't keep you long, but there's something I need to get off my chest." Aro stands directly in front of me, but he's three feet away. "I won't leave this Earth without paying you back for everything you've risked. And I'm definitely not going to let you face anything else alone . . . if you'll have me."

My smile comes easily. I could just give him a plain answer.

I lean in for a kiss instead.

He leans in, too, closing the gap between us.

Our mouths dance to musical notes only we hear; they sound like drums playing on arrival day, glass clinking after a rousing toast in our names, and fireworks crackling in the night sky. When we finally break apart, the heat from his lips still lingers on mine. We both breathe slowly, then he gives me a quick peck on the forehead, setting the rest of me on fire.

"I'm not writing five hundred and seventy-five love letters," I say.

"Oh, it's okay. *I'll* write them all. But you know what I actually need your help with?"

"What?"

Aro looks out to Vieques. "Rebuilding my real home and convincing Feyn we shouldn't keep all our attention focused here on Eterna." He looks back at me. "Want to join?"

There's an art to chasing an elf.

But the real adventure isn't catching one.

It's working together to find solutions that benefit all species. To know he'll care for the humans left behind on a land his family was forced to abandon. It's trusting that one mind, one spell, will never be enough. I'm sure we'll face difficulties trying to fulfill Aro's goals in Vieques. Challenges will always arise. He won't be alone, though, and that's the beauty of his plan—the past is a story we get to retell into a better future.

"I'd love to, Aro," I reply. "You're doing the right thing. I'm proud of you."

"Proud of *me*? May I remind you of everything you've accomplished in a week? You should be proud of *yourself*."

He's right. I've done things I never thought possible. And I'll keep doing them.

I might not know all about myself, but I know what I have. A mother who loves me. Friends who believe in me and will be there for me if asked. And from the loving smile he's offering this very moment, I possibly have a boyfriend, too, but we'll figure that out later.

"I am," I whisper. "I really am."

We hold each other close, enjoying the morning sun's warmth in silence.

ACKNOWLEDGMENTS

HANDS DOWN, THIS IS THE hardest book I've ever had to write. Most of it is because it lived in my head as *just vibes* for several years. I daydreamed of a goth girl and an elf . . .

And the elf was brown like me.

Specifically, he was Puerto Rican. I daydreamed of *more* Puerto Rican elves. Soon there was a hint of a story in my head . . . and no clear path forward. Why are there elves in Puerto Rico? What's their magic system like? What do they want? Are they hotter than Legolas? How does this goth girl fit into their world? Even though I thoroughly outlined my first draft, I didn't really have the answers I needed. I hoped that I was getting the right version of the story down.

I wasn't. Without the following brave souls, *Last Sunrise In Eterna* would've never gotten to where it is today. Special thanks and lots of hugs for the members of Team Eterna:

My outstanding editor and emotional support, Tamara Grasty. This book would literally not exist without you. I mean, it would, but not in its current state, which is miles beyond what my limited understanding of those initial vibes ever was. I'm eternally (get it?) grateful for your brainstorming chats/emails, vision, and above all, patience!

My rockstar agent, Linda Camacho. You once told me this was a very weird pitch for a book and that I should absolutely go for it. Thank you for always believing in my weirdness.

My Page Street & Macmillan family! You have all been so enthusiastic about this book long before it was ever written! To Lauren Knowles, Lizzy Mason, Lauren Cepero, and Kayla Tostevin for always hyping me up and making me feel at home. To my publisher, William Kiester, for rightfully suggesting we change the title to something that fit the story's tone. To Rosie Stewart for designing the book cover of my dreams for this story, and to Nicole Medina, for illustrating it. I can't tell you how hard I geeked out when I saw Sevim and Prince Aro with my name underneath their faces. Thank you for such a beautiful gift.

My dear friends and critique partners, the Iron Keys. Natasha and Kaye, there's a reason this book is dedicated to you. With hearts like yours, of course it's easy to believe in magic.

Circe Moskowitz, iconic author/editor/human. You were one of the very first people to read pages from this book. I can't believe you loved them as much as I did, but I'm so grateful for your feedback and spectacular moral support in the form of all caps.

Linda Raquel Nieves, for being an amazing friend, artist, and author. I adore seeing your illustrations and devouring your words. Keep them coming, please! This is only the beginning.

My Musas besties for life, Yamile Saied Méndez (a.k.a. Work Wife), Adrianna Cuevas, Mia García, Zoraida Córdova, Nikki Barthelmess, Francesca Flores, and fellow hardcore *Love Island* fan, Andrea Beatriz Arango. Your messages and hangouts have literally kept me afloat.

My group chats are on another level, okay? On. Another. *Level.* Specifically, the Pretty People Rights chat (Adriana, Marianne, Melanie, and Itzamar), the Fifteen Hundred Feelings chat (Jonny Garza Villa and Adri), and the Moridas chat (Sharline, Bea, and Yara). Thank you all for feeding my soul with love, chaos, and other stuff I can never publicly admit. <3

All my friends both in and out of publishing! You all know who you are, and thanking each one of you would take far too long. Still, let me shout-out a few people who've listened to me talk way too much/have read way too many texts and somehow haven't blocked me yet. Frances Zapata, Adriana De Persia, Paola Guerrero, Sydney Langford, Verónica Muñitz-Soto, Jean-Carlo Pérez, and Rafael Soto, you are all the sweetest. Thank you for helping me believe in myself.

My family, Mami, Papi, and Renis. Thank you for putting up with me! You deserve gold medals.

And to the readers, teachers, and librarians who've brought these brown elves to their shelves, I cannot thank you enough. I hope you find something in these pages that makes you remember just how magical you are, too.

ABOUT THE AUTHOR

AMPARO ORTIZ IS A YOUNG adult and middle grade author from Puerto Rico. She holds an MA in English and a BA in Psychology. Her speculative work includes the Blazewrath Games duology and the graphic novel *Saving Chupie*. She's published short story comics in *Marvel's Voices: Comunidades #1* and in the Eisner-award winning *Puerto Rico Strong*. She's also coeditor of *Our Shadows Have Claws*, a young adult horror anthology featuring monsters from Latin America. When she's not teaching ESL to her college students, she's streaming K-pop music videos and writing about Latinx characters in worlds both contemporary and fantastical. Follow her shenanigans online at www.amparoortiz.com.